Morocco

David Flusfeder is the author of *Man Kills Woman* (1993) and *Like Plastic* (1996). He lives in London.

Morocco

DAVID FLUSFEDER

FOURTH ESTATE • *London*

This paperback edition first published in 2001
First published in Great Britain in 2000 by
Fourth Estate
A Division of HarperCollins*Publishers*
77–85 Fulham Palace Road
London W6 8JB
www.4thestate.co.uk

3 5 7 9 10 8 6 4 2

A catalogue record for this book is available from the
British Library.

ISBN 1–85702–964–X

Typeset by Palimpsest Book Production Limited
Polmont, Stirlingshire
Printed in Great Britain by
Clays Ltd, St Ives plc

To Julius

Part One

CASE NOTES

I

The patient arrived in the city four years before. He suffers from vertigo and chronic, often acute digestive problems. When he first came to town all he had with him, he once uncharacteristically boasted, were the clothes on his back, a blueprint for making money and a bag filled with anti-dyspepsia pills. The blueprint has worked. The pills have not.

Solomon Heller is a slim blond balding man in his mid to late thirties. His most prominent features are his blue eyes, which protrude mildly in typical thyroidal fashion, and seem to convey gentleness and abstemiousness. One is also immediately struck by the succession of noises produced from his aberrant digestive system.

The tycoon runs his business empire from a grim office building in a poor part of town. He has no close confidants, no friends he thinks of as such—his societal world is divided into employees and rivals—and no contact with his family or indeed anyone from his home town.

Clearly, he left his home town in something of a hurry. Heller will not acknowledge this or even refer to it. Perhaps he was driven out or, more likely, he needed or felt he needed to get away from something or somebody. He does admit that the dyspepsia began shortly before his departure, and that is the extent of his reminiscences from his adult life. When pressed, he will talk about his early family memories but in a way that resists interpretation or even interest. Put simply: when I am with him I am bored. It is all too easy to say that he is boring me deliberately, a form of resistance to analysis, to hide the causes of his neurosis. Certainly the boredom is a weapon he brings to sabotage the therapeutic alliance. But one mustn't forget that the boredom could have almost nothing to do with Heller and all to do with something as yet unnamed inside me that resists *him*. (Why?)

Consequently, the analysis has not so far been a success. Heller has yet to realise this. Two factors are on my side. First, he is still impressed by the manner I displayed when I was first taken to see him. The initial interview took place at his headquarters (initiated by my brother in fact, who works for him). *I have a problematical digestion*, said Heller the mild-mannered, the notorious, not looking me in the eyes, looking far past me at the window which gives out on to the courtyard below. *No doctor or dietitian has been able to help. It is bad for business, embarrassing for me.* That short time ago, I was absolutely confident of my own powers. I forced the tycoon's gaze to meet my own. I held it, and said, softly, certainly, unprofessionally, I can fix that. Heller looked away from me again, lifted a hand to his mouth to stifle a burp, nodded, and waited for me to leave.

Second (and I write this modestly, this is nothing I am

4

proud of, I merely want to offer the clinical picture, entire)°, I do have a gift for listening or at least appearing to. No matter how bored I am I can still give the impression that I hear everything secret and shameful and marvellous that lies behind my patients' unrevelatory words. When actually of course I am often merely staving off sleep. So: twice a week Heller and I fail one another.

And then, things change. This is the magic and mystery of depth psychology. Analyst and analysed are alone in my consulting room. Heller is stretched out on the couch. I am in my too-comfortable leather chair. Eyes meet for the customary brief matching of selves. (What does he see? A young woman—too young—who gazes upon him eagerly—too eagerly—to stifle her ennui just as he stifles his belches and burps. Her looks, which are usually good enough, do not seem to be of interest except for her hair, deep red, which unsettles him.) I ask him a question about his father. He hiccoughs. His eyes close. His right hand, as usual, enters his shirt to lightly massage his treacherous belly. His left leg begins to twitch. *My father*, he says, *was a strong man who had been disappointed by things.*

And so it would go, nursery memories, nursery trials, the looming figure of the father, the soft aura of the mother, who was an invalid in exile in a dark forbidden room. And I nod every now and again even though Heller's eyes remain closed, and Heller's reminiscences are punctuated by burps and intestinal rumbles and the occasional fart.

Heller talks on and eructs on and I battle against an overwhelming exhaustion that pulls my eyes shut, which can only be defeated by pinching myself hard, which I do on the thigh, professional bruises to examine later when I bathe. I fight to listen to what he is saying. That being impossible, I try to work out what inside me is making this analysis such a failure, and I reach the inevitable conclusion that I am just too young and too inexperienced and too unalterably mediocre to cure the sickness in men's souls.

The tycoon's words stump meaninglessly by. What is he talking about now? A pet dog? An imaginary child-hood companion? A trusted family friend who had cruelly molested the infant Heller? *Then*, he says, in his light, not unpleasant voice, *I didn't see him again until the family went back to the lake that summer.*

Revelation. Where does it come from? Partly intuitive and partly through the counter-transference—again, I try again to examine my own reactions to the tycoon: why, lurking behind the boredom, is there such an element of distaste? When have I felt such distaste before? That's an easy one to answer: when having pressed upon me the unwelcome attentions of twitching inadequate men with dark circles under the eyes. (I offer no excuse for departing from the customary impersonality of case notes. There are two people in the consulting room. Every analysis is mutual.)

I make my intervention. Interrupting him I say, employ-ing my most bland clinical manner, Tell me, Mr Heller, how often do you masturbate?

The intervention startles me as much as him. Heller's eyes open. His hand pulls (guiltily?) away from his stom-ach. I think he realises as well as I that the insight, which had seemed to come almost from nowhere, is absolutely accurate and has attached to it, new-born and full-grown, a complete understanding of my patient's malady. This is where I should stop, let the silence spin out, wait for Heller to learn to reveal his own truth to himself. One of the skills I have yet to learn is how to withhold language from my patients.

Heller hiccoughs, looks angry. I press on.

You have told me before how you would like to have a family of your own. Find a wife, sire some children?

He, perhaps fearfully, nods.

But instead you are too busy making money. Tell me now, I think the time is right, why did you leave your home town?

Silence. And on I go, for this moment at least (at last) no longer intimidated by my patient's wealth and power and reputation.

Tell me about the woman you left behind.

Heller manages to say, *No no, there was no woman.* I carry on, merciless. I get to my feet. I stand over my patient who sits up in response. He and I glare at one another. I am breaking all the rules, facing him like this, psychic adversaries.

The woman. You know the one I mean.

The dyspepsia is only (as it could only be, a child would know that) a symptom of Heller's neurosis. In the beginning was a blockage of the libido and that was caused (I am sure of this, some things one knows) by the loss of a woman he had loved, to whom he had given himself or at least offered himself, fully, for probably the only time in his life; and maybe she had seemed at first to offer an equal love in return but then she had rejected him. Then came the libidinal blockage and because of the blockage there was the recourse to masturbation, which further dammed the blockage and strengthened the neurosis because on top of everything he now had the shame of a *disgraceful secret* to contend with. (A secret that the master of the discipline has written about so often I suspect it might be the great man's own.)

Your dyspepsia began shortly after she left you. And then you returned to the habit of your youth and became again a chronic masturbator and your dyspepsia got worse. This is so, isn't it? Why did she leave you?

Heller gazes furiously away from his accuser.

My hands move to hold my patient's arms. I grasp him in a way that suggests comradely understanding, maybe even forgiveness.

There is no shame to this. Forget the woman. Forget shame. Move on. And your digestion will return to normal. I guarantee it.

The chronic masturbator pulls himself away from my consoling touch.

And before you can forget, first you must properly remember.

Solomon Heller shakes his head like a boxer who has taken too many blows. He looks me in the eyes. He speaks,

If you talk about this to anyone I'll have you killed.

I smile. The warm clear smile of the confessor-healer.

A gurgle and a rumble issue from Heller's bowels. He climbs unsteadily to his feet and struggles with his overcoat. I help him force his left arm through a difficult sleeve as the sound gets louder of feet trudging up the staircase. Heller's driver, the hooligan Bernard, one of his bought protections from the world, has come to collect his master.

I meant what I said, says Heller. *Nonetheless. I'd like to see you more often. Can the sessions be four times a week now?*

Truth always finds a way to slip through the narrowest of holes. In Heller's proposal, readily agreed to, the answer to my intervention can be heard.

2

There is not just transference and counter-transference at work in the analytic alliance (or combat), there is also a kind of sideways t and c-t. Solomon Heller and I conduct business each time in the same room for the same duration and in a similar manner; he and I pretend that nothing is carried, or smuggled, into the session from elsewhere; and that when the session is over neither is taking anything of it away. Solomon Heller and I like to pretend that in this room there are only two people, that neither he nor I is liable to infect anyone else with the emotions that have transpired here and, conversely, that he is not infecting me, nor I him, with what has transpired elsewhere. [Possible discussion suitable for a future paper: Psychic disorder as a kind of contagion? The patients the victims, the analysts the carriers?]

In effect the pretence is that Heller is my only patient and I have no interior life independent of him. And certainly I try to pretend, at least to myself, that my feelings towards Heller do not suffer when I compare him, as I should not, to Igo Sym, who is, I would have to admit, my favourite.

Igo Sym is luminous. A movie star, with something

golden about him. His elegance is legendary, his courtesy a wonder. He is, though, even less forthcoming than Heller about the maladies that afflict him.

This is how it is at the first meeting. Patient takes the couch. Psychologist settles comfortably in her chair. Patient and psychologist light simultaneous cigarettes. The session begins.

I have to try to clear away what I think I know of the actor from seeing him perform in dozens of movies and cabaret shows. The characters he plays are dashing, urbane, witty, ironic. And he might be acting a part here, stretched out in western suit and shoes, left leg hooked gracefully over the right. The suave lover relaxing in a drawing room before dinner in a romantic comedy. He has a cigarette as prop, he only requires a cocktail glass. Soon the door should open and in run the gay little ingénue. Sym so gracefully to rise and the ingénue in her charming peasant's blouse and skirt, her hair coiled in naive little braids, flings her plump white arms around her seducer's neck; he smiles, the mask drops for a fraction of a moment, a flicker of lust; her sweet mouth opens, her adoring eyes blink up as she waits for his perfect kiss.

This is a pleasant room, the actor says. *Might I have some water?*

Of course. And what an attractive smile to go with the request. Oh Mr Sym (or should that be Dr? The 'Prince' had thought there might be a doctorate in economics in the actor's past), has anyone ever refused you anything?

I give him the water. Then I give him my usual introductory speech. It impresses patients with my educational accomplishments and professional training and an exaggerated sense (excuse me) of my standing at the Psychological Institute; it dismisses the notion that depth psychologists need to be medically qualified; it excites people looking for a cure with my just hinted-at powers and extraordinary success rate; it makes patients sure of my sympathy; and most of all it instils a fondness for my voice.

I pause. He waits. Clever Sym (he has undergone this process before, I think) knows that something else is about to be spoken. I speak it. It is my standard line.

You can now forget everything I've just said because the only important question is whether you and I can be good together in this room.

The sexual implication is obvious. It made Heller blush. Sym does not blush. He shifts in his position, his eyes candidly engage mine. What part is he playing now? His eyes (blue) declare curiosity and warmth. His lips (sensuous lower, austere upper) part. His brow (noble) wrinkles slightly. An eyebrow (cosmeticised?) lifts.

I am being inspected. I allow myself for a moment to be stripped bare. What does he see? Body that is too short and eats too much to qualify as beautiful. Facial features that men usually admire and which are—unlike my poor brother's—ambiguous of origin.

Does Sym have the power to peer through the ambiguity? I am not accustomed to being inspected quite so closely but this might just be one of the actor's repertoire of tricks. Not so dissimilar to the psychologist's. Do I want to be kissed by him? Or am I just habituated into thinking I do? I have no idea whether I pass in his eyes for an Other, undoubted, like him. Or if my racial origins glare out. Maybe it doesn't matter. It doesn't always.

Time to impress him. The way he lies on the couch, the comfortableness of his manner, the luxury of his pose, something can be deduced here. I ask him if I am right to suppose that this is not the first time he has sought out psychological treatment.

Sym doesn't bother asking the whys and hows of my coming to suppose this, nor do I need to explain; the good effect has been made.

It was a long time ago, he says, *after the war*.

I like to hear these words. Mr Mouse consented often in the early days to be persuaded to tell stories that began *It was a long time ago* . . .

How fascinating. Who was your analyst? And what led you into it?

Intellectual curiosity, says Sym, an obvious evasion. *The doctor was a rather grubby fellow called Tausk*.

Was that an emphasis on the word *doctor*? An implication that I although not grubby am somehow less than qualified?

And now? What brings you back to it? Your curiosity wasn't quite satisfied then?

Too sharp a remark. Sym looks up at me a little reprovingly. The actor removes a hair that clings to a pocket of his suit. He regards it for a moment as if trying to remember whose head it came from as he twines it around a finger, before carefully returning the hair to where he found it. He looks over at the three plaster busts that sit on the bookcase—the master of my discipline and his two most prominent disciples, eyeless and bearded—and away. His gaze prefers the paintings that hang over the couch.

Very attractive, he says.

(Heller has yet to notice these: a train station at dusk, a cornfield at daybreak.)

Useful objects of contemplation, I tell him.

For your patients or for you? he asks.

I nearly respond, then decide it better to answer with a chuckle. Sym joins in. His guard (and mine) drops or seems to.

I mention that after the war many people had certain *difficulties* making the transition from war to peace. The reaction I get from the actor surprises me. A flash of irritation, which he suppresses before replying.

I didn't find it that hard to give up my uniform, if that's what you mean.

That wasn't quite what I had meant. Interesting none-theless. Already a new place is being approached. Before it can be reached or the journey mapped Sym takes charge again, changes the rhythm.

I am in love, for perhaps the first time in my life. Her name happens to be Gloria as well. She is from the west, and astonishing. I have never felt this way before. Despite, many, erotic—no matter. It troubles me.

Tell me, I jealously say, about Gloria the Astonishing.

Sym is disappointed. *You're too eager. Tausk was always content to let me do all the work. He never interrupted, spent his time, I think, enjoying himself in his odd little mind.*

Let's go back to the beginning. Your name.

Igo? I was, I am sure, a horrible little boy, with kiss curls and speech impediments, which is why I probably talk too much now. I was christened Hugo. The name came out mangled in my mouth as Igo. It stuck. People declared it charming.

One becomes one's name, which is why I had to change mine.

And Sym. *Igo.* Pronounced almost identically to *Ego.* Once there was young Hugo, whose charming childhood tongue could only manage the sound Igo. Igo Sym he became and Ego Sym he remains.

Sym's ego is magnificent. An engine of intelligence and magnetism and charm. The man himself is a *star*, admired, loved, successful. So why then is he seeking my help? Ego Sym is being threatened by something nasty in his unconscious, revealing itself maybe in disquieting dreams and aberrant sexuality. Impotence?

If Sym were less accomplished a talker, and less adept at the therapeutic process I would already be enquiring into his dreams, his women, his war. But Sym, as he had warned he would do, talks on, in a compelling monologue that invites the psychologist to enjoy being his exclusive audience. A man and a woman sit companionably together in a closed room. Sym is telling anecdotes. I wait to hear the one about Gloria the Astonishing.

This must be the moment. Sym has started to talk about love and an actress.

I met her on a movie. Café Electrik. *Do you know it? Or before your time? That's all right, I'm not insulted, you didn't miss much, seedy little love triangle with a few neat futuristic touches. She was already a star—but extraordinary, an extraordinary kind of star. If you saw her on the street you'd walk right past. Maybe not even notice her. A chubby girl with a face that's interesting in an eastern peasant sort of way, but not at all pretty. In front of the camera something happens. An alchemical reaction, light, glass, skin, shadow. On the screen she becomes marvellous.*

Sym smiles. He lights another cigarette. I do not intervene. I like to hear erotic fairy tales. Maybe this is what I became a psychologist for.

She was having an affair with Willy Forst, who was the male lead in Electrik. *Forst is all right in his way but irritating, fleshy, there's too much of him.* (At this, the second quick reference to flesh and weight, I wince. Sym catches that.) *She might even have been engaged to him at the time. I don't actually remember. Jaray was the director. You'd like him. Very cultured.* (Trying to make up for it.) *She was having an affair with Jaray as well. So, she only needed me to complete the set. She came into my dressing room one evening. Forst and Jaray were at a local bar discussing some scene. She came in and assumed a pose and waited for me to make love to her, so I did, and it was all quite businesslike I suppose. I was expecting something phenomenal, but the point about sphinxes is that the promised secrets are never there, it's all for show.*

Sym appears lost for a moment, a mental stutter.

And then?

And then? I taught her to play the musical saw. It's my party piece. I'll teach you one day. You grip the saw between your knees, bend it as you bow—a cello bow with rosin smeared along it—the more you bend the higher the note. It makes a wonderful noise. The thing about Marlene, she's a believer in transactions. From every lover a souvenir. Not just a trinket, she wants a skill, a grace, an item of knowledge. She always takes away more than she gives.

Excuse me. Who's Marlene?

Marlene. The actress I'm talking about.

And what has this to do with Gloria?

With Gloria? Nothing. That shall came later. When I know you a little better. But the time must be over by now. Thank you. I should like to return next week.

The first session is over and I fetch the actor's cloak and hat and I am still waiting for Sym to explain why he has come, to name symptoms apart from love and a mild irascibility that are interfering with his life of ideal charm. Provisionally I might make a diagnosis of Sym as a narcissist terrified of getting old. But a narcissist's libidinal objects are in his own ego. Whereas Sym has hinted at certain erotic compulsions.

When he is gone I sit by the empty couch. I light a cigarette from the silver case that Sym has left behind—no accident, a sign of trust, a promise of return—and I try to name the emotions that have crossed over from Sym during the session. After my sessions with Heller I feel timid, half empty, under threat, dangerously grandiose. Now, smoking the star's cigarette and with some psychic souvenirs of Sym inside me, I am soothed, poised, touched with something mysterious, abundant with possibility.

3

Heller and I drive at night. The tycoon's Buick cruises slowly through the rain along Marshal Street.

Heller has decided it is convenient to hold night-time psychological sessions in his car. I have given my consent to this unorthodox practice. Two reasons: 1) artificial boundaries must be transcended: the psychologist's care must extend out of the consulting room. 2) I like to drive in Heller's car.

A thick soundproofed window has been installed behind the driver's seat. This is to protect Heller's secrets and, therefore, the safety and future of his driver. Sometimes my eyes will meet the hooligan's watching in the rear-view mirror. And sometimes I catch a glint of the steel razor that Bernard wears embedded in the front of his checked cloth cap. Why does Heller require this sort of physical protection? It's not my business. My job is to strip down his psychic defences.

The patient has been talking, fluently and mostly un-interrupted, for about twenty minutes in a kind of semi-hypnotic state. He refuses still to admit that there ever was a woman who had driven him from his home town, the woman he loved and lost and has dyspeptically mourned ever since, but he has consented to reminisce about his very first love. The psychologist listens and makes her old mistake of interrupting when she starts getting bored.

She was ten years older than me and to most people invisible. She had three children. A husband who was neither cruel to her nor kind. He was a merchant. I worked for him and learned very quickly from his example how not to succeed in business. Once, I remember, he was buying a shipment of horse grain from, from, I don't remember where from, there was an intermediary in the west but the shipment came from somewhere in the east—

Excuse me, says the foolish psychologist. Is it possible to return to the matter of the woman herself?

And the moment is lost. I realise straight away that I should have waited to see where the story was leading, should have considered the meaning of my patient's forgetfulness. Heller usually forgets nothing. What is the significance of east versus west? Or is the meaningful thing horse grain? The horse is an obvious erotic symbol, and in this anecdote the merchant is being cast as the inadequate feeder of Eros. The patient was telling me, in symbolic code, about the cuckold, about himself.

But now Heller wipes condensation away from the window and looks out at the shops (he likes to see which products are selling)—a department store, a bookshop, a milliner's, lingerie and ribbons, and cinemas, a mile of cinemas, the Elite, the Coliseum, Rialto, the Style, where *The Red Empress* is on, directed by my friend the 'Prince' and starring Sym's one-time protégée of the musical saw.

Heller lifts his hand away from his stomach to catch a
burp. Then the hand goes back inside his jacket.

My digestion is improving, he says. I tell him, That's
only the start.

Heller turns towards me. Marquee lights refracted through
rain glitter across his anxious mild face. I hold on to
Igo Sym's cigarette case, which I carry, talismanic, in
my coat pocket. Hard to imagine why this man is so
feared. Maybe when I am capable of imagining that the
analysis will move on to the next desired level. Could
I be afraid of him? Physically, no. Psychically, only a
little.

*If the point is that I should have a woman then I'll get
a woman.*

No, I tell him, that isn't quite the point.

Then, Gloria, what is?

(Be careful, Gloria.)

Sexual desire, I tell him, is not just an itch to be scratched,
a discharge into the momentary relief offered by a prostitute, a lover, or—excuse me—a hand. One must also
consider object-relations in the world.

*Too much jargon for a layman like me. What precisely
are you talking about?*

I am talking about, I suppose, the capacity for love.

Impossible to read Heller's response. Deadpan face,
glinting thyroidal eyes, the flash of some annoyance, but
something else too, deeper, an animal baited.

Then, unfortunately, I had to ask Heller to stop the car
so I could get out for a brief period to conduct a personal
matter.

Excuse me, I say. This is where I need to stop. Tell your man here. I won't be more than five minutes.

I'll come with you.

Through the voice trumpet fixed into the glass screen Heller instructs Bernard. The Buick pulls over and parks outside the Tip Top Club.

Gently, I say, I don't think this place would interest you much.

Gently, adamantly, he says, *I'm interested.*

I descend from the car into empty Willow Street. My patient follows me—not just patient any more, what is he then? boss? *friend?*—to the club. The rain has stopped. The city is silent. When, as slowly as I can, I pull open the door to the club waves of noise and heat crash up at us.

A few words of explanation are perhaps required here. The personal matter I refer to involves my brother and in some way impinges upon the cases both of Heller and Sym. I had recently visited my mother and stepfather's apartment on Valour Street, the place which had once been the site of the most dreary family romances and dramas. I was looking for my childhood collection of cigarette cards, donated by my absent father.

The movie star series. Number 13: Igo Sym. Wearing a fedora, Sym is almost full on to the camera but looking far past it—a passing girl has taken his fancy and he has been following her with his eyes while keeping his face still for the photographer and now she is about to disappear from view far off to the side. Sym's pale eyes watch her go with a mixture of admiration, anticipation and curious self-sufficient pleasure. Elfin ears. Fine nose. The sensuous mouth with just a hint of weakness about it. Sym's face, this card, had occupied a special place in my pubertal cosmology. For a start the cards came from father, so there was already glamour attached. And number 13 in the series had been my own private symbol of modernity and passion, never spoken of, carried everywhere.

I walked quickly through the apartment on tiptoes, careful to disturb nothing, not even dust. No one was here, just the maid, the house other, asleep in her kitchen cubbyhole, using her bible for a pillow. The dismal photograph of my stepfather stared at me from the living room, its face still white-scarred from the time it had to be cleaned after my brother and I defaced it with a moustache and horns. I went into the smaller bedroom that once was shared with my brother. He still sleeps here, and keeps his law books and papers here, in the space allowed by the junk that mother, with her more acute sense of taste, has forbidden her collector husband to display in the rest of the apartment. Somewhere here too, wrapped in oiled brown paper, was my old collection of movie star cigarette cards. I felt like a trespasser, opening stiff drawers of heavy ash furniture, peering into broken music boxes, moving aside rolls of paper tied with dark ribbon, searching for the cards in half-forgotten corners of times before.

What are you doing?

My brother, lawyer Daniel, standing by the doorway he'd silently entered through. I told him I was doing nothing.

Spying? What are you looking for?

His lower lip has always protruded, making him look permanently outraged and on the edge of tears. Now he added to the effect by jutting his chin forward. He brushed his wiry hair away from his brow. It sprung immediately back into its former position.

I couldn't resist teasing him a little. I asked him if he was worried that I might find his secret stash of money.

(The money that was received from father's estate—after the court fees were deducted for my brother's fruitless suit against the executors—I spent on the rental and furnishing of my consulting rooms. Daniel said he was saving his share, building up his capital. I suspect, though, that the money has already been lost in one of his get-rich-quick schemes, distilling gold from sea water, cornering the market in cut lilacs.)

Has he *sent you here?*

Lawyer Daniel was about to speak my old, forbidden name. I could see its initial letter take shape on his pouting lips. And then he thought better of it, the look of malice left his face, replaced by something sickly.

The situation had turned. He wanted something. Despite everything I've always liked my brother. I admire the transparency of his motives and the urgency of his drives. He, though, has never cared for me. On the day that I was born Daniel executed his favourite toy soldier and still blames me for its death. He holds me guilty of subsequent crimes nearly as bad as the original one of being born. My nose is good; his is ugly. Every time he sees me he convicts me again of dangerous philosophies and loose morals and worst of all an ability to pass where he cannot. I may walk through Saxon Gardens or Dolphin Park, dawdle by the statues of misty characters from lost wars, throw crusts to the swans, sit by the bandstand unmolested except by the occasional man with a wolfish face who fancies himself a gigolo. Daniel would not dare. He can't enter these places either alone or in a group. At night he will cross over to walk a road's width away from the lilac bushes and chestnut trees and copses and formal gardens in which lurk dimly moonlit hooligans and thugs, the others' youth militias, always on the lookout for examples of newcomers to punish for not knowing our place.

Newcomers, the traditional word for Us, first used when our merchants and refugees started to arrive five or six centuries ago, the latest stop of our ancient exile. Or maybe its origins are earlier, maybe there were always interlopers here, even before we came—it's a necessary category for the Others to feel like one nation: military threats from them and the Easterners are required as well as physiognomical difference to us. When the first foreign tribesmen came, it doesn't matter where from—north, south, east or west—bringing in spices, stained glass, printed books, or just fear and greed and hunger, the simple desire for pillows and feather beds, the others examined these first foreigners, noticed some differences, in the shape of the eyes perhaps or the length of the nose or in shade of hair colour or costume, found amusing too the thickness of a foreign tongue attempting to pronounce some very ordinary words, and these archetypal others wrinkled delicate archetypal noses, turned down mouths, pursed lips, and the disdainful word was pronounced, *Newcomers . . .*

And my particular family: the original ancestor came to the city a century or two ago, when things started to get bad living among them, and brought with him the too-fanciful name he had chosen. Streamwood must have sounded wonderfully authentic to him, he wouldn't have noticed how risible it was to their ears, a useless badge of failure to belong. I threw away the first half and changed my first name as well, left behind something ugly and chose to become Gloria, as soon as I was able.

Daniel Streamwood will try always to keep to our neighbourhoods, the places where newcomers belong. He has learned not to expose the crime of his difference to the others' fists and boots and crowbars and razors and knives. His ambition has been taught to restrict itself to the aim of climbing the ranks of Solomon Heller's organisation. Heller may be an unscrupulous tycoon, but he's *our* tycoon.

Perhaps you might do me a favour?

Of course.

I watched him struggle rather hopelessly and horribly with his face in an attempt to simulate fondness. The shaving rash over his throat looked redder and more diseased than ever, livid red dots customarily torturing his skin.

I don't see you often enough.

Nothing to say to that.

Zygelbojm asked me to put in a good word with you.

Zygelbojm is the superfluous man, the very least of my suitors.

Is that the favour?

Of course not. Hardly. I'm trying to get to see him. *But Mr Heller is always unavailable.*

Then the talk went this way and that about Heller's busyness and business. Daniel has a most secret scheme to put to him. It would make everyone's fortunes, he said. I let him talk, his dark eyes agleam as he devised scenarios for accidental meetings. He might be coming into my consulting room as Heller was leaving, or leaving it as Heller was coming in. He might be walking down the road as Heller's Buick suffered a pre-arranged flat tyre. Daniel would help, and in that moment could . . . Or perhaps I might take my patient for a walk, and Daniel, who could happen to be passing, might . . . In my face he read his own absurdity, even he recognised the transparency of his schemes. Finally he was spent. I didn't permit myself more than a few seconds of silence. I have better things to do with my time than to make my brother suffer. I asked him if he still goes to the Tip Top Club. I knew the answer. Of course he does. He goes there to ogle the dancing girls, graduates of Madame Tatiana's cruel Academy of Theatrical Dance. I told him that my routine with Mr Heller was changing, that some of the sessions were now being conducted in his car. (Daniel's eyes widened. Solomon Heller's Buick is an object of veneration to all his flunkeys and acolytes and supplicants.) I could say, I said, that I needed to stop inside the Tip Top. He hates those sorts of places. He'd wait outside. I could be absent for five minutes. And you could easily be going in or going out . . .

The rendezvous was fixed. Daniel was delighted. I felt a twinge of something, regret perhaps, no, worse than that, guilt, raw guilt, for allowing bad faith schemes into the therapeutic alliance. He and I left the apartment arm in arm, just like brother and sister. I hadn't found the cigarette cards.

[Note to self: some of this may be extraneous.]

The Tip Top Club is the sort of place where everyone seems to be waiting for something. It's also always crowded. Heller had not been expecting this. He does not like a crowd; he experiences it as pain. Pushing through the foyer into the bar area, Heller is nervous, I am flustered; my brother is probably out there now, waiting by the car. Heller burps. I am seeking, somewhat desperately, an excuse to be here. A cavalry officer with the look of a man about to vomit lurches past forcing shoulders, mine and Heller's, to touch. When the officer is gone the shoulders are still touching. I realise that what Heller is feeling above all is the desire for me to hold him by the hand.

On the narrow stage a poet of sorts is proclaiming, in surprisingly euphonious verse, the imminent arrival of the end of everything, in flames, because *They* are coming . . . I've heard this sort of prophecy before and never been moved by it before, just smoked and drank and talked over it as most of the crowd here tonight are doing, so why do I suddenly feel so chilled? Is it only the bridge of physical and psychical proximity to my patient that enables a small portion of the dread he always carries to pass into me?

Heller, buffeted, crying above the crowd, reminds me that I am meant to be here for a purpose. I look around and try to find one. Florid faces, cocaine art, silver-ringed dancers' arms. A waitress with bad hair and bad skin. Bored band members sitting in a puddle of liquor. The house comics, Rappaport and Rappaport, a sharper and his stooge, are bickering, waiting for the cue to go on. The manager, a spry lascivious little man who affects two monocles and a limp, is watching the singer who is also his wife conduct a whispery transaction with the pianist. Everyone else it seems is watching Heller and me. I am rather enjoying by now the looks I am getting. I've never felt so *noticed* before. Men and women gaze with respect, fear, distaste or brazen invitation. This is the benefit of appearing in public beside the tycoon Solomon Heller.

The manager's attention swoops away from his wife. His second-best monocle pops from his eye; he screws in his best, then rubs his hands together as if he needs to raise the temperature of his skin before he can presume to approach such honoured customers. Heller farts. He is shrinking.

And there, sitting against the far wall, is Igo Sym, and beside him the astonishing woman. Her mouth is wide, full lips painted scarlet. The dress she wears shimmers like lightning. Her eyes are blue and her long hair blonde. She looks like a lioness. Her body is voluptuous. She is astonishing.

Gloria! Heller has taken up hissing. He has seen enough, endured enough respect, awe, distaste, noise, contact. I have Sym's cigarette case in my pocket. I set off towards his table. Heller's left hand flails out. I reach back. I take it. He holds on.

I recognise that this is potentially damaging material I am working with here, allowing patients to meet. The outcome could be awful. The table has been reached. The star inclines his head in greeting. I realise I am staring too obviously at the astonishing woman. So I pretend briefly to be interested in the comics who are now on the stage. Fast-talking Rappaport is explaining the mysteries of finance to his stooge Rappaport. I bring out the cigarette case, my alibi prop, and by so doing create a conspiracy between myself and my patient Sym, which is a risky manoeuvre at the best of times of which this is not one. Somehow I manage to introduce the two men. Something passes between Sym and Heller but it is hard to say what; the beauty of Sym's mistress has scrambled all my powers.

Gloria the Astonishing favours Gloria the Astonished with her attention for the first time. The discovery of a flaw in her beauty perhaps might allow my legs to move, my tongue to unthicken. I discover no flaw. Heller tugs at my hand. Sym opens his cigarette case. The drummer executes a drum roll and everyone looks to the stage. Quick Rappaport is running off, hiding something precious in his hands. Slow Rappaport, abandoned, is looking for his wallet but failing to find it. Sudden clash of cymbals. The stooge falls over. The band strikes up. Gloria the Astonishing laughs. Her laughter enhances her beauty. I long to touch her hair with my fingertips. (Excuse me. But this is an exercise in laying bare.)

Lights glare on. Heller and I leave the Tip Top Club.

*   *   *

Patient and psychologist, both a little unsteady, return to the car. Bernard in the Buick is reading a newspaper and smoking a cigarette and ignoring the resentful sleet-soaked lawyer standing beside the car. Heller pushes past him with a brief, unanswerable *How are you, Daniel?* and climbs into the car and I follow after. The door slams shut. (My coat-tails get caught in the door but that is by the by.)

I release my coat. He chews on a bagel. (Heller is addicted to bagels.) Bernard drives the car through night-time streets towards my apartment. I wait for Heller to say something about what went on in the club, to enquire about Sym. Later in this session I will learn what I should have known—it is foolish ever to underestimate Solomon Heller.

Sienna Street is reached in silence. Just as I am gathering my coat and my thoughts Heller says, as if he is mentioning something of little interest, *I dreamed of my own death last night.*

I tell him that that is good. This is how the conversation then goes:

No. It was not good. It was fearsome. It still is. I haven't recovered from it since.

How did you die?

I threw myself out of a window. I was in my office and heard a noise at the window, then I was staring at the ground, which started pulling me towards it. I climbed over the window ledge and threw myself off and then I was falling. I hit the ground, my body broke, my head shattered. Shatters, keeps shattering, for ever. I woke up shouting.

Neurosis and pathology are very cunning. The closer you get to destroying disease the harder it fights to protect itself and destroy your will to change.

Heller says nothing but he obviously does not believe this to be an impressive line of interpretation.

You dreamed last night of transformation which as you say is fearsome. The neurosis advises you that the danger is too great to be risked. Destroy me, it whispers, and you destroy yourself. Resist change, protect me, and you protect the best part of you.

It is most persuasive.

And a damaged life is guaranteed. And what do you have to fight with? A desire—perhaps as yet still weak—for change, a tiredness of familiar unhappy patterns, and a depth psychologist.

Who might not have the energy for the battle.

I am surprised by this. The light in the car is far too dim to make out the expression on his face but his voice is kindly.

You look exhausted, Gloria.

My days are long.

And your nights? Do you have lovers?

Something lies behind this also surprising question but I can't decide what it is. I must be open up to a degree with my patients. Every analysis, acknowledged or not, is a mutual analysis. If I demand disquieting secrets from my patient then I have to give him some of mine in return. Am I to tell him then about my suitors? Each one, honestly? Mr Mouse, once my own psychologist and supervisor and lover, now gone? The unreliable 'Prince'? Werner at the

Institute who provides satisfactory libidinal services and, happily, nothing else? And what about the comic pursuit of me by a most superfluous man? My patients have to regard me as a loving woman who knows how to lead a psychically healthy life.

I have a lover.

You're happy with him?

Entirely.

Heller chuckles at a private joke or tragedy. His stomach rumbles.

I think you should stop working with the rest of your patients.

It is said so tentatively, as if Heller is timidly trying to share his thoughts for me to encourage, so together a decision might be reached. I am familiar enough with my patient to recognise an order when I hear one, regardless of tone.

All my patients?

All.

(Is this my punishment for insisting on telling uncomfortable truths? Or for knowing more than he cares to have me know? Or for having Igo Sym as a patient?)

This is not how it's done, there are procedures, that should be understood, one can't suddenly orphan one's patients, each must be looked after, made to feel indispensable; even if such a decision could be made, there has to be a working towards passing the patient over to someone else.

Solomon Heller shakes his head. *You're important to me. I do not wish to share your services.*

(No patient does. Few have the power or the certainty to insist that things must be different. His desire for me is flattering, with him at least I have been able to intuit all the way through to the heart—or bowel—of the neurosis. I am not so confident in my own powers to believe that an insight like this can occur with every case.)

And if I said I wanted to keep just one?

Even in this dim light I can see—with my eyes closed I'd still be able to see—the knowledge in his mild blue eyes of who the chosen one would be.

I'd say no. You're wasting your time on egomaniacs. Think about it.

When Heller says *Think about it*, he means that only one answer is possible. What would happen if I disobeyed? Is it so unthinkable?

There'll be a banker's draft for you at my cashier's office on the first of every month. For personal expenses. I know your landlord. The rent on these rooms will be paid for directly. Now you can concentrate on your real work. It will be good for me to know you're not frittering away your attentions on nonsense.

The subject is closed. The session is over.

4

How to tell a patient that the analysis, though hardly begun, is, through no fault of his own, over? This is abandonment, the great betrayal. One might send a note: *Due to circumstances beyond my control . . . sincere regrets . . . my very best wishes for you and your psyche . . .* It would be craven to send a note. The act must be done in person.

Sym lives on Willow Street, not far from the Tip Top Club. He lets me in himself, in an oriental robe, shows a brief surprise to see me, quickly replaced by hospitality, *Come up, come up, how nice to see you,* into the drawing room, impeccably modernist bachelor furnishings. I am looking out for signs of Gloria the Astonishing, that has to be her, the blue and gold Fracturist painting of a woman lying face down on marble with buttocks raised; and there, an echo of her there, a gilt vase of red tulips on a low glass table; and there, over there, the golden toe of a woman's silk shoe poking out from beneath a black leather chair. A naughty-looking cat idles around a cello bow angled against a bookcase. On the walls movie bills advertising Sym's starring roles are framed and mounted, an unsurprising vanity. And what about that door up there? along the gallery, closed, could be someone still sleeping off her pleasures behind it. Sym pulls open the curtains, bright morning sun.

The star offers me coffee, just made. I apologise for coming by unannounced. He assures me that it is a pleasure and asks how he can help.

By knowing what I'm here to say. Sym, so graceful, fetches the coffee pot and cups, which he places down beside the tulips. He generously asks me my opinion of the other Gloria. I tell him she is even more beautiful than he had said. He claims she had said complimentary things about me also, which I don't quite believe. *Though she didn't like the look of the fellow with you at the club. The gangster. Is he a patient?*

You know I can't answer that, I say.

Is Heller a gangster? I've heard the rumours.

You look nervous, Gloria. What actually are you here to say?

I hum and I haw and I cough and I say it. I am, I tell him, temporarily dropping all my patients to concentrate on my research project for the Institute. I apologise. I stutter. I mourn. I give a brief incoherent lecture on the fascinating phenomenon of psychic infection. Sym smiles throughout and fights down his irritation, which I wish I might have more opportunity to get to the bottom of, and allows the half-truths and evasions and lies to go past, unexamined, unexposed.

It's very decent of you to tell me in person, is all that he courteously remarks.

He refills my coffee cup, sits back again in his armchair.

The cat, a pale tom, sidles over to sit on Sym's lap. Father and son.

I'm a very skilful lover.

Oh my God. He didn't say that, did he? I smile at him. Maybe in his transference he requires to seduce his doctor before he can confess his disease. Maybe I completely misheard.

I employ tantric techniques, which I came across for the first time long ago in the war.

You did fight in the war then. What did you see? What happened to you?

I know how to do things that maybe only five men on this continent know how to do.

Has he researched this? Do the five men get together on a regular basis? Does each take it in turn to host the event and pass around cocktails and canapés while his guests compare techniques?

I can tell that you are a very passionate woman. I can give you many many orgasms.

I would like many many orgasms. I would like just one orgasm without having to do the bulk of the work myself. Nonetheless, it is time to put this coffee cup down and stub this cigarette out (it doesn't matter that the embers still burn, I'm in a hurry now), I do not like this Casanova-satyriac approach. The reassurance of Sym's poise was something to get used to living without. Why hadn't he just made a pleasantry about the weather instead?

The weather, I inform him, has turned glorious. Light on snow, beautiful. I have to go now.

Sym lays a starry hand on my shoulder. When he speaks his tone is unfamiliar.

If you ever need my help, Gloria, you can always call on it. They *might be coming soon. Everyone will have to be ready.*

Of course. Dashing Colonel Sym, the courageous war veteran, turning back their armies with his magnificent sabre.

Music appropriate for a war movie plays in my head as I wait for the streetcar. Once it arrives I manage to amuse myself by inspecting the passengers and jotting down the neuroses, obsessions, psychoses and vile practices each man and woman's face shows the suffering of as the tram rattles towards Heller's headquarters.

5

Under the new regime, the analysis itself has become utterly different. How could it not? I myself am often disgruntled, wishing back the old days, my consulting room, a variety of patients, liberty. I have to keep reminding myself that something very special is taking place. Already I had gone into the Case of Heller deeply. I am now being afforded the opportunity of going into it perhaps uniquely deeply, a new kind of analysis, a New Psychology. (Not to mention what the ensuing paper would do for my standing at the Institute.)

Nonetheless, at Heller's headquarters, where my work is now based, I practise sitting much more than I do any New Psychology. I sit in narrow, crowded corridors with clients and courtiers and petitioners and supplicants. (My own brother, Daniel, is often there. Because of certain misunderstandings that occurred some time ago, in addition to his own unworked-out childhood traumas, he never makes any attempt to speak to me, just gazes with an impatient, humbled fury.) I sit in the back of Heller's Buick, with Bernard silent in the front, the sky darkening in the wait for Heller to come, face always lowered, his right hand holding a briefcase, his left hand pressed tight to his guts, from out of the secret side door of the headquarters. I sit in Heller's office waiting for my master to be finished with telephone conversations, and sometimes I sit in the office alone, on the couch (my own precious couch, transported from my rooms on Sienna Street), reading books, surrounded and part-protected by Heller's aura of injured power.

Heller's footsteps leading to the office door are unmistakable, he takes light irregular steps, like a crippled dancer on uneven ground. I close my book, I go to stand by the window, symbolically guarding my master's fears. The door opens, Heller enters bestowing a quick smile, an acknowledging nod. And here comes the inevitable retinue. Eager young men with sharp suits and suspicious faces. A few ageing financiers and currency dealers. And today there is even a pietist, bearded, caftaned, hatted, stooped – whether he is adviser or petitioner it is impossible to guess.

Heller puts on his hat.

You all know Gloria, don't you? Meeting adjourned.

This is how I am introduced to members of his staff, no job title, no surname. On all sides I am regarded with suspicion and envy. (He knows this, this is how he wants it.) I hear myself being spoken of in corridors, ugly whispers designed to be heard by the unworthy courtier who has cast a spell to gain the ear of the master. I am his mistress, his country cousin, his witch, his evil familiar, his scheming counsellor. The retinue reluctantly departs. Heller opens the disguised library door and I follow the tycoon down his secret corridor.

Into the Buick, the mobile consulting room, which Bernard immediately hurls into gear. Heller speaks softly into the voice trumpet to instruct his driver where to go. The car speeds through twilight streets. Electric street lamps are flickering on. Heller begins to reminisce.

When I first came to town I was astonished by the street lamps. Electrified city.

He chuckles. Now that things have changed, Heller is more relaxed, more in control of himself, and more honest too. At least that's what he claims. And as his digestion improves, the absence of burps and farts and hiccoughs has created an aural void that is being filled by this new, not unpleasant, but somewhat humourless chuckle.

Your dream life. It is time to get back to it.

I sleep like a baby. Dreamless and peaceful. I expect that is because I am entirely guilt-free. Wouldn't you say, counsellor?

I say nothing. The purpose here is not the exchange of badinage.

Heller chuckles. He looks out of the window.

Excuse me a moment. Wait here. It'll be more comfortable in the car.

The Buick pulls over. My patient and I are on a slum street in the eastern part of town. No street lamps here, just a crowd angry in the darkness, which Heller, with Bernard hustling beside him, penetrates.

It is not comfortable in the car. Out of the darkness faces suddenly press to the window and just as quickly disappear, shoved away shouting by burly men who wear high boots and long coats and white hats with upturned brims.

Thuds on the car roof sound like small birds dropping dead from the sky.

This is how the New Psychology goes: The psychologist accompanies her patient everywhere. Together, patient and psychologist unlock the doors of the past and inspect the traumas that sit behind, shaking, and together the muddle of the present is experienced and disentangled. The adventure is a mutual one. Understanding is a machine built by two. Everything is case notes.

My eyes adjust to the darkness. The centre of the tumult is a narrow building. Women weep in front of it. Children are enjoying a licence to scream. Dirty-faced boys throw stones. Dogs bark. Men yell Judas-abuse at the hoodlums who carry out furniture to toss into the street. I see a young woman in a fox fur coat slip past Heller's bodyguard and approach the tycoon. She has the air of an assassin. Her hand touches his arm. He flinches. She whispers something in his ear. For a moment his self-possession, so painfully maintained in the violent hubbub, is lost. Quickly he turns away from the woman, says something to an older man standing nearby and returns to the car along a path efficiently beaten out by Bernard. Abuse chases tycoon and hooligan to the Buick. Chants, shouts, of *child-killer* and *parasite*.

When the car is safely away from the scene Heller looks at me for the first time.

Did you see that woman in furs? She offered herself to me.

Did you take her?

What do you think?

Solemn blue eyes regard me, waiting for me to probe, and then what?—fail?

I would think no.

And? I want more. More opinion, more psychic truth.

Did she offer herself out of desire or need?

Oh. Need, most definitely.

Then I would think you were disgusted by the situation.

The chuckle again.

Why did she have the need? I ask.

Because, says Heller, *she was losing her home. She thought I could prevent that happening.*

And could you?

Heller digs his index fingers into the corners of his eyes and executes several tired fingertip circles as if he is ministering to a sudden attack of headache or guilt.

I've been selling all my property, because—the because doesn't matter for the moment. I'm looking after myself. It was accidental that I happened to be driving past when the eviction was being done.

Happened to be? Accidental? Things never are.

Heller ignores the intervention, keeps talking.

The new owner was there, overseeing the bailiffs. The hired muscle was enjoying itself with too much gusto. These sorts of things are best done quietly. No fuss, as little damage as possible. Fortunately no blood was spilled. It seems that people recognise me. I am acquiring, I believe, a reputation.

Presumably these were all others who lived there?

Heller hiccoughs and nods.

Would it make any difference if it were us?

Of course not. I told you, I'm selling all my buildings.

Heller is shocked at my imputation of partiality. Business is business.

And were you tempted? By the woman?

She offered me her fur coat as well. It was sad. But what can you do?

As well as reputation you are acquiring a capacity for guilt. Or maybe reacquiring it.

You think so? Can you absolve me?

The question is said as if it were a joke. It is not to be treated as a joke.

Perhaps.

Heller starts to respond, then stops. He waits for me to say more. I have no more to say at this point. The illusion of psychological omniscience must endure. Without it I am powerless. Bernard takes the car down random streets, criss-crossing the city, statues, parks, outdoor cafés, lovers, the cathedral, violinists, street orators. When Heller does talk again the Buick is already on Sienna Street.

Did you sack all your patients?

All. As I said.

Even Sym.

Even Sym.

The sensation of feeling like a woman bribed away from her lover by a possessive husband is not one I enjoy. I do some gazing out of the window. Heller catches and holds my eyes in the reflection on the glass.

Stop sulking, Gloria.

I'm not sulking.

44

*Or disapproving. Whichever you're doing. By the way.
The woman is coming.*

Which woman? The one you say does not exist?

*That one. She arrives in town tomorrow. I should like
you to meet her.*

6

Heller sits at his desk, left hand to his stomach, the right holding on to the telephone receiver as if without this touch of permanence and possibility he will float away or sink. I sit facing my master. A vigil.

She should be here by now, the tycoon says.

Each whispered word emerges painful and dry.

Yes? More.

I'm like a schoolboy, this is intolerable. I don't know what to do.

More.

I'm terrified.

Thank you.

Waiting for the harpy to show. No one else is allowed into the tycoon's office. The tycoon makes telephone calls, issues orders, breaks men's lives. He does these things because he can. In business he finds consolation. He and I wait.

I wish she wasn't coming. She wants something from me, I don't know what. I'll give it, whatever it is, and then she'll go away again. She's got a husband somewhere. Say something.

Heller looks like a cadaver, his skin unnaturally pale, stretched over a dead man's bones, his blue eyes protruding, unblinking. Fireworks are ahead. A kiss from the harpy, the tycoon's libido reawakened—and the return of the repressed might set off explosions to illuminate or destroy. Meanwhile, I am learning the skill of withholding language from my patient.

He stares at me, keeps staring, mad blue tortoise eyes, as he walks over to the couch, lies upon it, and now he closes his eyes and brings his arms straight down by his sides like one of those corpses in the morgue that live in sliding drawers with a tag attached to a toe.

Heller wants to be liked, admired, adored, yet he does what he can to be rejected. I am required to reject him, at whatever cost to myself, just as his father rejected him and his mother and the horse grain dealer's wife and the harpy from his home town, because he is too contained, too pale, too ruthless, because he refuses to engage with the world except from positions of carefully arranged power. And I am required also to cherish him, to love him as his parents forgot to (as my father forgot to love me), and then to teach him how to go about winning a woman's heart. When what I should be doing is to lead him by the tongue to uncover his own life-denying truths.

And me. In the quiet he allows me I have peopled this office with phantoms. Just as the woman from Heller's home town has been present throughout the course of the analysis especially when the tycoon most strenuously denied her existence, so now are my suitors.

My suitors. One, Mr Mouse, gone but living in memory

stronger than he ever had in love. Two, the 'Prince', wearing so elegantly his inauthentic honour. Three, Werner from the Institute, untroublesome. Four, Zygelbojm, laughable, the superfluous man. Five, Igo Sym—or had his advance been only a Don Juan reflex, never to be repeated, the promised orgasms never to be granted? The suitors sit with Heller and me, phantoms in the consulting room, ghost riders in the car, watching over the analysis, silently taking part in it.

Zygelbojm exists as a single image. He is a long tall unnecessary man who boasts of a big-shot cousin in the west and has a trick that he joylessly taught himself to perform after seeing a dance film. He performs it, without affect, if ever my path crosses his in the street. What he does is jump into the air and click his heels together twice off to the side before lightly landing again. He performs the trick efficiently, without exuberance or any change in the doggish solemnity of his expression. That's Zygelbojm.

Mr Mouse. Once there had been Mr Mouse, first name Mickey, jaunty name, a more un-jaunty-like Mouse one could never hope to meet. He was, is, small and neat and brownish, with poetic features that never quite convinced. He had been my supervisor at the Institute and the analyst of my psyche, and he had become my most unsatisfactory lover and the 'Prince' had made atrocious fun of him, and now he was gone. The space he left behind was not very wide, a slight man could easily fill it, squeezing himself even, holding his breath, to fit into the gap. He was an oddly shaped man, Mr Mouse, and maybe I helped shape him that way and he was not strong enough to resist; but all the same I miss him.

I am not your natural erotic partner, nor you mine ... Mr Mouse announced some time before he fled for the west. He then initiated a series of what he called his 'open-ended libidinal tableaux', in which I, deciding not to question his naive use of the word 'natural', took full vigorous part.

Mr Mouse was, is, a practitioner, an adept, in the brown arts of depth psychology. (Previous terms are no longer applied, too redolent of the newcomer origins of the science.) He is not an erotic circus ringmaster. Nonetheless he tried. How he and I both tried. Taking parts, straining with sinews and vaginal muscles and fingertips and knuckles and mouths and unused corners of imaginations. And I—as lady boss to his oafish gardener, or as insolent chambermaid, or maybe a sister scintillating with forbidden love—found myself straining above all against the impulse to giggle which, Mr Mouse sternly informed me, was in this case a sign of repression not humour.

Outdoors he and I played strangers met by chance, at the cake stall on Church Street, or in the streetcar approaching the Institute, two morning commuters forced by the crush into intimate proximity. But the game was never played at the Institute, because of Mr Mouse's concern for reputations, his, and certainly not in Mr Mouse's own office hole on the leather couch that he claimed had once been reclined upon by the master himself. Some things were sacrosanct.

It ended on the night of the anniversary dinner, after a moonlight walk to the Hotel Bristol (glamour! high society!

so much glass and electricity and costume and swirl, the modern, transparent moment). Glorious futures were planned, the psychological field was open, the structures in flux, immense rewards awaited bold approaches, and the elevator—effulgent white iron and crystal—lifted and lowered while Mr Mouse and I drank cocktails in the lobby because the menus of the International Restaurant or even the Raspberry Room were out of reach for a psychologist who had no rich widows for clients and a trainee whose father was still alive. Then back to the apartment for supper. Mr Mouse did the cooking and I laid the table with the blue-painted ceramic that had been carted by sturdy Mr Mouse all the way back from a medieval hill town some months before. The food was very good.

That was the night it petered out. The timetable no longer to be followed. After dinner, the erotic ringmaster lost his thrilling moustache, his circus whip, even his inclination.

No, Gloria, he stretched, yawned, turned away, sighed, *I really am tired . . .*

A cheek-peck with chastely puckered lips and then he rolled away to the cold side of the bed, a betrayal which, even at this distance, seems greater than mine with the 'Prince' or Werner.

Werner. No, this one is not present. Every so often he and I met in a borrowed room, engaged with equal desire and lack of curiosity, and took nothing away upon departure. Institutional corridors do not echo when I see him if he ever happens to leave his obscure little laboratory; there's no image of him in my consulting room.

If one is to be honest about this, and one must be honest, that is the point—in the New Psychology, the psychologist is psychologised as robustly as the 'patient' (I am not here to disguise what I bring to the alliance behind a cloak of 'a friend of the psychologist had a typical absent-father-complex' or 'another patient of the author dreamed often of her father')—my father is twice in any room I share with a man.

The second part of my summer holidays I used to spend with father at the lakes. (My brother was there during the first part—father could not tolerate two children at a time.) The journey there ended with a sleepy ride up through the mountains, the world seen through untrustworthy eyes, dreading the glamorous summer to come, already wishing for September and the return to mother's and stepfather's more ordinary, less dreadful world. The first moment of the first morning would be gorgeous. Sunlight through gauze curtains. The taste of creased linen sheets. And then, awful, the memory, renewed, of where I was, the knowledge, foreordained, of what the days would hold.

Skip breakfast, don't want the first conversation to be him criticising my eating habits. Instead, I take the condemned prisoner's walk through the downstairs corridors of the summer house, out, blinking, into the sunshine of the jetty, the lake, to be dwarfed by gymnastic he-men and vivacious beauties in swimming costumes with mountains behind. I with my books trying to find a shady corner in which to read but yet drawn in, mesmerised, to sit on a sun-lounger on the edge of things, to admire and to scorn and to envy.

My father looks up from his documents. The chime of disappointment he cannot hide every time he sees me.

Here she is my daughter the bookworm. Gloria, I'd like you to meet . . .

. . . yes, yes, you too and you and you and you, yes, yes, no, my body is not like yours, you know how to stretch, so your breasts rise, muscles glide beneath sunned skin, hair trembles down to shoulders. A muscular man waves from a rowboat and I swear I can see his hairy belly still atwinkle with rainbow droplets from the lake. Father is controlling things, so very still even when he's gushing out the cocktails. Big-time guy, a hot shot. Watching all the time. Watching his guests, himself, seldom me.

Or not. This is hardly the truth of it. How many lakeside days were there like that one? A handful, yet the image shines brighter than the rest, dazzling. One would need dark glasses to resist the glare. And yet. Of my father this much I remember with warmth: there were times, sudden, surprising times, when the world outside was dark, and I was trying to sleep—or at least struggling not to be awake—in my alien summer room, and there father would be, at my bedside, silent apart from his cigar breathing, and his arms would come slowly around me, enfolding, enveloping. At first I would stiffen against it. This attention too would be perceived as threat. Then relax into it. The heat of his body, the beat of his heart, the tickle of his breath, a delicious holding and squeezing. The reassurance here of his love would soothe me towards sleep, fill—in that hot, tight moment—all the places labelled 'Father' that usually were left cold and empty. And I would be grateful for his touch, for his warmth, for his ability to silently reassure, for this unspoken, perhaps unspeakable, promise of his love; but sometimes, on these infrequent occasions, as I sped towards sleep, a doubt might pull me away back into wakefulness. It is only since his death that I have put words to the doubt: that perhaps this hug was not truly for me; perhaps the reassurance of touch, of skin and breath and squeeze and love and forgiveness did not have me for its object. Instead it was *I* who was reassuring *him*.

The 'Prince'. The hours I had before this vigil with Heller began I killed with the 'Prince'. I joined him at his customary restaurant table at the back of the wine shop on Bugle Street. Into the narrow room, the 'Prince' pushing away his emptied soup bowl and sipping from a glass of red wine as the waiter blocked my way delivering the next courses, pork stewed in cream, beef olives stuffed into a black bread crust and swimming in gruel.

The great sensualist will be fat one day. Eventually his body will bloat to approximate the size of his appetites. He is not yet fat. He looks austere, a priest or a revolutionary. He does not look like one of us and he does not look like a connoisseur of pleasures. (But already, one might note, perhaps even with a little satisfaction, the hint of jowliness where cheeks meet chin.)

The 'Prince' directs movies. He makes three or four movies a year, costume dramas and romantic comedies and apocalyptic prophecies and war stories and charming little forest fables. He has the egoless capacity to direct any film in any style and never leave a signature. Stefan (I don't know his 'real' name, just as he doesn't know mine) suffers from no aesthetic or philosophical ambitions. He has better things to do with himself, he says, melancholy-eyed, baritone-voiced, his elegant trousers belted in tight to his flat stomach; there is always eating and drinking and fucking and talking to be done. Some of it is done with me. Less though than in times before.

Stefan was pleased to see me. He invited me to eat. Unlike his, the shape my body intends to become does not permit me to indulge in all my appetites. A glass then, he said in mid-mouthful. He offered me burgundy or brandy. He ate, I drank brandy, both talked. Sometimes I watched the movements of his hands, which are very strong and very beautiful. Sometimes I glanced at the traces of food he was leaving in the narrow cracks at the corners of his mouth (which I like to see and also don't like to see, blemishes in the perfection of his surface).

How's Sym?

I'm not treating him any more.

Did he make a pass at you? Did you fuck him?

Yes to the first question. No to the second. But that's not why.

Your tycoon. He got jealous.

In a way. Yes. Maybe.

Or was it that you didn't like him coming to see you just because you share the name of his inamorata?

The tycoon's woman is arriving.

The legendary femme fatale. Your master's dominatrix.

It's not quite that simple.

It never is. What do you think she'll be like?

54

Not to your tastes.

A harpy?

Without doubt. Petite bourgeoise with impeccable provincial manners.

Platinum hair. Painted face. Trashy and prim. Not bad. I might be interested. And what about him? Do you think he's still masturbating furiously like a monkey as soon as everyone's back is turned?

I wish I hadn't told you about that.

And I do, strongly I wish I hadn't told him about that.

Of course you do. But you had to tell someone. And you can trust me.

I doubt it.

Here. Have a taste of this olive bread, it's sensational. I tell you what—I'm glad you didn't fuck Sym by the way— come with me to the heiress's house now. The bread's good, isn't it? Are you busy? Can you come? Come with me and your master's secret shame is safe.

Otherwise?

Otherwise . . . ? It'll be safe anyway. But come. I've worked out a strategy. I need you.

How flattering.

Gloria. Please. You know I love you. If I could afford to, if I was strong enough to endure your scrutiny, I'd be yours right now, forswear all others. One day I'll be strong enough for you and you'll have lost your tolerance of me and that'll be the tragedy of it and I'll feel it worse, of course, because it'll be my idiocy that'll have made it turn out the way it has, and you'll be beyond me, in the arms of your lover, or your husband, or a lesbian maybe, that's a nice one, I like it, should consider that, her arms around your legs, her naughty Sapphic tongue licking you to places no man has sent you to, and I'll be—

Fat. And bald. And you'll smell bad too.

That's right. And what'll be left for me? Suicide. Your name on my lips. A note left to you and you won't even care, my awful, pitiful death won't even disturb the rhythm of your lovemaking. Please come. I'm just going to order a jam omelette or maybe an apple charlotte, no, the omelette, and then I'll be stoked up for my greatest campaign. What's the matter anyway? What's on your mind?

Hunger. Dissatisfaction. Loneliness. It is true what the 'Prince' said, I need someone to tell things to and since Mr Mouse left for the west I had only him.

Come on. Let's go.

All right, 'Prince'. Let's go.

Out of the wine shop restaurant; along Bugle Street into Theatre Square; past the Hotel Angleterre where a great emperor had once spent a night on his retreat from the east back to the west. Did the humbled emperor sleep that night? Or did he pace his hotel room all night long, not so much furious as piqued that the world was refusing to bend to the shape that his will had determined? Or maybe it was all something of a relief. Reassured that he was a human being after all, secure in his own powerlessness, the emperor slept like a baby, thumbs clenched inside his fists.

On the journey the 'Prince' was strutting, whistling, the lover on his way to his grandest victory, confident absolutely, enjoying the sureness that unopposable, unambiguous appetite brings. At the top of the Town Hall tower, in his lonely wooden hutch above white plastered colonnades, a fire-watcher watched. There never are any fires in Theatre Square.

[Note to self: one day go through these case notes and remove anything extraneous.]

The next part of the story I tell to Heller to make the vigil more comfortable. Is Heller listening? I am sure he is. He gives no sign.

The Glade was reached. Long curving avenue through parkland that goes up to the house. The usual wait at the door. I felt as if the 'Prince' and I were characters in a myth with obstacles to overcome. At the top of the house, three flights of stairs away, were the attic rooms where virginal brother and sister slept and poeticised and played. Before these rooms could be reached—cut lilacs in blue glass vases, paintings of martyrs and poets on the walls, identical narrow beds in adjacent rooms covered with virginal white Persian cloths, bedroom windows showing the same view of the river, powdery silver, mermaids in the tide—the door was to open, the footman bested, a count and countess on separate floors endured.

Why are you on this expedition? Heller asks, despite everything, interested.

Why? A favour to a friend who thinks I'll be useful.

Why is he called the Prince?

It's 'Prince'. Always in inverted commas. A cameraman awarded him the nickname, in honour of his fine presumptuous ways.

What does he want you to do?

To keep the brother occupied while he tries to seduce the sister, the famously pious virgin.

To inflame the brother with desire, that's what he wants me to do.

The footman showed us his usual look of distaste. He was the only one in this house who recognised or showed that he recognised that we were not others. (His handsome nose stayed wrinkled against our goatish rankness.) The baronial hall was empty, the wide staircase was waiting. The love hero 'Prince' and I his sidekick walked up the first flight of stairs towards the glass skylight at the very top, where the virgin would be waiting.

The landing was achieved, now the turn towards the next flight of stairs. Maybe it was possible to keep walking, go up unmolested—of course not, the plot was preordained, the mythical structure held firm: Madame the Countess materialised. *Visitors!* she said. *How delightful! Tea?*

For just short of an eternity we interlopers sat in Madame's receiving room, surrounded by patriotic tracts. The Countess is obsessed with genealogy and apocalypse, her family's history of couplings, her country's destiny to redeem the world with suffering. Among the portraits of hideous ancestors on the walls there is one beautiful painting, hung above the fireplace, Zosia and Henry, sister and brother, repressed hysteric and introverted neurasthene in blue velvet suits, he sitting, she standing beside him with one arm over his shoulders, both gazing out with identical grey, clever, frightened eyes. The Countess lectured and I watched the painting and when she appeared to be boring even herself the 'Prince' would point to another deformed ogre on the wall and ask, *Was that the Thadeus who fought so bravely against them or the Jan who fought so bravely against the easterners?* and *Wasn't that the one who married Jadwiga the Bold?*

And then, just when it seemed that no life was possible ever again outside of this room, release. Back away, out through the door, up the next flight of stairs, past the bedroom of a never-seen aunt fallen on hard times, to the Count, a different kind of horror.

Heller is smiling. *You are exaggerating, Gloria.*

(Eliding, certainly. The visit I am describing occurred less recently than said—the visit this day concluded in bathos, disappointment, access refused by the footman, the heiress reported to be in the country, the door closed—but I don't see the value in telling my patient a story of unpassable barriers, hymenic or oak.)

Maybe a little. Maybe not at all.

The Count is deaf and has yellow lizard eyes and had been a hero of the victorious war against the easterners twenty years before, but he never talks of it. In fact, he never talks. Visitors are condemned to sit with him and talk at him and he gives no sign of understanding anything that is said. So the 'Prince' and I visited him in his usual place in the musicless music room. A brown leather chair, a wooden stool for his gouty feet, a table beside him for vodka bottle and glass, a pamphlet from the Society for Rational Game Hunting on his lap.

Stefan talked. It was his task. He filled the dusty room with monologue. Music and architecture and God and boxing and goats and patriotism—and Zosia, her beauty—

and poetry and cinema. The Count regarded him steadily through meaningless yellow eyes and regularly lifted his vodka glass to mouth and down again and sometimes coughed and finally, benevolently, winked: loose empty bags of skin rose slowly up one side of his face, balanced at a new precarious height, and then sank again, the signal that departure was now permitted.

And up now, the final staircase, towards coy Zosia, framing herself most becomingly in the skylight. The heiress was wearing a green silk dress with white lace brocaded around the waistband and short sleeves. The exposed flesh of her arms was freckled from too many horseback rides and picnic suns.

Zosia took the 'Prince's hand, she took mine, she led us into her own receiving room, miniaturised opposite of her mother's. Zosia sat on a low sofa. The 'Prince' sat beside her. I sat facing, on a Turkish divan. Light and air. Lovers. Youth. The scene looked very proper, most decorously romantic, adorable. Nothing bad can ever happen, to anybody.

For her birthday, the 'Prince' had given the heiress a crucifix to wear. It was supposedly a relic of the True Cross, dark Mediterranean wood ivied with silver. She wore it around her neck on a silver chain. The crucifix kept her virginity sacrosanct, it protected her from vampires and devils and us. The 'Prince' leaned towards Zosia, a hand glanced her breast as he whispered something gallant, and a clandestine thrill lifted blood to the heiress's cheeks, jerking her hands into nervous movements, fingering the dark wood of her cross.

A typical case, of religiosity defending repression, of unsatisfied libido steered into extravagant acts of piety and pity. Her brother, in he came, nervous, giggling, his pathology dependent on hers. Henry is the decadent twin of his sister, sickly rich, a tarnished boy beauty. All her attention is faced against the libidinous advances of the world, his is turned inward, a narcissist celebrating his own fragility of blood and body and spirit.

A series of looks was exchanged, between brother and sister, between virgin and pursuer, between suitor and ally. The choreography of romance, some more whispered words, hands to hands, ears to mouths, an excuse quickly given—and the 'Prince' and Zosia were gone, into her bedroom, leaving behind Henry and me yet to look one another in the eyes, sitting in river light.

So. Did you keep him occupied?

Hardly. It was like being with his father.

I tried several approaches. I made some provocative remarks about his parents, I encouraged him to imagine with me what was going on in the next room, to consider the character of Zosia's eventual surrender. Because she would surrender eventually, a sacramental rite, a virgin sacrifice. Unlikely, I said, that the deflowering would take place in there. Zosia would have decided on a place long ago, which her 'Prince' would have to prove himself by finding. Surely, I said to Henry, *you* know where it is? A tablecloth weighted down with stones at a picnic clearing in the forest? In the confessional at the Sisters of the Visitation Church, the bishop a breadth of wood and curtain away, his breathing responding to or maybe providing the rhythm

Morocco

of the coupling? Or out in the stables? Zosia does have a great love of horses. I even offered to listen to his poetry.

And I got nothing in return, no conversation, just a giggle or two—without his sister to protect him the boy was disabled in the company of women.

When suddenly he lunged at me. One moment he was sitting in a separate world on the opposite side of the room. The next I was being assaulted with bony arms and dry kisses, cold skin, fevered breathing.

What aroused him?

I don't think it actually had anything to do with me. And when I resisted he ran flustered out of the room.

So what did it have to do with?

It is tempting to interpret his attack as being a response to the moment of Zosia's surrender. The sister's rapture infected the brother with a brief fragile desire.

How do you know she surrendered?

I don't.

There was no triumph or disappointment on the suitor's face when the 'Prince' and Zosia returned. A look of alarm from Zosia when she saw her brother was missing. She tugged at her crucifix, she ran to Henry's room. On a floor below, the Count resumed coughing or perhaps he had been coughing all the way through. The river was silvery as before. The light was the same. Nothing had changed the afternoon.

What did your 'Prince' say?

Most unlike himself he said nothing.

That means he was unsuccessful.

I'm not so sure.

Silent the walk downstairs, silently received the footman's parting sneer, silent the walk away.

Heller. It is not part of the New Psychology to tell stories without knowing why. It can be risky for the therapeutic process to introduce stories that don't have a single obvious moral. Impossible to detect how Heller is responding to this one. Perhaps he is inspired or shrunk by this example of courtly seduction. Perhaps he is somehow reassured that I have told him something of my inner life, albeit in comic form. Perhaps not. Perhaps, in complicity with his silence, I was just filling the room with words.

Nonetheless, the wait continues. Any interest that I might have aroused in Heller dissipates. His body stiffens again. Everything about him screams one piece of information: he aspires to corpsehood. He wants to be suave and to be kissed and be dead. The only movement he makes is towards his death, which seems to be the only event that could interrupt this vigil.

When the knock does come on the door it comes as a surprise. Suffocated by Solomon Heller's mood, I had almost forgotten that there was an awaited visitor. A boy nervously opens the door and clears his throat, about to make an announcement.

Yes yes, says Heller. *Tell her please that I'm busy now. Ask her to wait.*

The boy withdraws. Heller's face cracks open at the mouth. This might be a smile. He looks like a hawk. Heller gets off the couch and walks to the window and rattles the security grille that has recently been installed.

I am going to be cruel to her, he says.
To what end?
Self-preservation.
He returns to the desk. We sit, sometimes looking at one another, usually not. Eventually he instructs me to fetch her in.

I go through the ante-room, which is always kept empty. Out into the corridor, which is more crowded than ever—petitioners, suppliants, hoodlums, more intellectuals than there used to be. I look for the harpy. The provincial wife who had won a victory over small-town boredom by toying with unworldly Heller.

The only woman waiting by herself in the maul outside the ante-room door is a serious-looking girl. Impressive appearance, admirable even. She is maybe twenty-five years old, slim and tall. Her skin is olive-coloured and doesn't need creams. Spectacles magnify dark brown eyes. Her hair is black but singed with a few flashes of early grey. Her clothes are dark and modest. Her nose is good. She is reading a book and that somehow is the greatest surprise. She looks up. Is this the small-town harpy? I wait for her to try a provincial coquette's smile. She waits to be invited into Heller's office. I yield first. I invite her in.

The woman who broke my patient's heart and ruined his digestion stands uncertainly in the room. Heller doesn't look up from paperwork on his desk. She approaches the desk. Heller does not stand to greet her or smile or even burp. I go towards the door. Heller, without looking up from the invoices on his desk, calls out to me to stay. The woman stops in the centre of the room, the kiss she might have been about to offer dies on her lips.

This won't take long, Heller says.

Nor does it. Heller adds up a few columns of numbers. Without looking up, he asks his visitor how long she intends to stay in town. He doesn't wait for her answer. He announces a rendezvous in two days' time, supper at the Café d'Europa, and then he pretends again she does not exist.

End of interview. The girl retreats. She ignores my conciliatory smile.

When she is gone Heller proudly removes his hand from his belly. Throughout the entire interview he has not burped or hiccoughed once.

How do you think I did?

Most impressively cruel.

I'm putting your advice into action. I hope you noticed.

I am not encouraged to answer. Heller makes two quick telephone calls. His pleasure at his own poise saves a business rival from bankruptcy and endows an orphanage on Starch Street.

7

Why had the woman come to the city? What had she left behind? Was she fleeing something or hoping to bring something back? Did she love Heller? Did she feel guilt over what had happened in the past? Did she want to renew the relationship? What did Heller represent for her? Was she looking for money or favour or the loan of his power? How far was she prepared to go to get it? Did she have a husband still? Did she want Heller to marry her? Did she desire him?

Did Heller ask any of these questions? No. Did he want to know the answers? Yes. Was he prepared to risk knowing the answers? No.

And so is determined Heller's strategy with the woman, who has at least a name, Sarah. He thinks that he is putting my advice into practice. He has set himself on a course of objectification leading to forgetting. He plans on carrying through with this plan absolutely. The ego-annihilation he fears will thus be avoided. For which he will have to pay a price.

Heller did not turn up for the supper date at the Café

d'Europa. He had never intended to. I went in his place. (Throughout the time I was with her, he stood, I would imagine, at the barred window in his office, looking out on to the moonlit yard below—that, anyway, was the position I found him in on my return, the room smelling quite powerfully of *boy*.)

Sarah had been seated at a table by a pillar in the centre of the room. Her dress, perfectly suitable for parochial intrigues and bridge games, was shabby against big-city marble and the silk gowns of generals' wives and high-class prostitutes. I brought out the small amount of cash that Heller had instructed me to give, with the stipulation that it must be passed over with some display.

He says sorry. He says you should treat yourself to a meal anyway. Here. His gift.

I fanned the notes, which I slapped down on the table so faces would turn to see the transaction.

How kind.

I recognised a functionary of Heller's at a neighbouring table, I stared long at him to try to give Sarah a clue as to what she was up against. Sarah hated to receive the money. She obviously needed it. She took the notes. She invited me to join her for supper. I turned her down. I had been instructed to turn her down. Sarah folded the money away, looked away, waiting for me to leave, daring me to depart from my script. I did not dare.

When I returned to Heller's headquarters he stayed looking out of the window. He made me go through every inch of the encounter, to describe the dress she wore, the way she flinched when I slapped the money down on the restaurant table, the expression in her eyes (*Was she scared, was she?*), the beauty of her arms. He pronounced himself satisfied.

Is that it? Satisfied?

Yes. Satisfied. Excuse me now. I have to order some bricks.

Bricks?

He stood at the window, waiting to be alone, his back to me, shoulders tense, lifted high like an asthmatic's.

Only sympathy heals.

8

The plan of cruelty is working most marvellously. (The New Psychology though, I admit, suffers.) Heller is coldly courteous to Sarah, never affectionate, shows no sign of human feeling. He meets her, briefly, at his headquarters, twice a week. Satisfied she has little money and no friends and few places to go, he abandons her to the cold courtesies of the city in the time between. It costs him negligible pain (none of it digestive) to wait for her to come begging to him, to plead. Sometimes it is arranged for me to spend time with her, and always he has his man, one of Bernard's innumerable cousins, to follow her and file bi-weekly reports.

The reports only interest Heller if Sarah's movements depart from what is expected, if there are any indications of her resistance: *The subject Miss S— left her hotel at 10.05, she walked along Marshal St, she visited Aster & Wolf bookseller's at 10.13, the Zodiac coffee shop at 11.29, returned to her room at 12.09, she did not re-emerge until her only visitor of the day, Miss G—* [that is myself, no physical description is included] *came to the hotel at 12.28. The two women left the hotel at 12.40. Subject and Miss*

*G— took the no. 9 streetcar to Castle Park. After sitting
for 11 minutes on a bench in the ornamental gardens, the
women met a man ('Mr X') at Lardelli's Restaurant at
13.37. Mr X ate some food. The women did not. The
man left at 14.23, subject and Miss G— took streetcar
back to subject's hotel, outside which Miss G— left and
where subject entered and remained. The following day
at 08.54 subject left hotel. She caught streetcar no. 14 to
western suburbs. At 10.48 subject met man Mr Y outside
a tea shop on March Street. Subject and Mr Y then walked
to a private house, entering at 11.02. The subject Miss S—
departed at 11.46, whereupon she returned to her hotel
from which she did not emerge for the rest of the day.*

So, says Solomon Heller. *Introducing her to men now?
Who was that? Mr X. Your brother? Or your friend with
the social pretensions?*

Yes. The 'Prince'.

*And she met a second man the following day. She's being
busy. I seem to have rivals.*

A terrifying jocularity on the part of Heller.

I had thought it a good idea to introduce Sarah to the
'Prince', but the meeting was not a success. Stefan had
turned lugubrious and even an encounter with the fabled
harpy from Heller's home town was not enough to lift his
spirits. He was still not being received at Zosia's house. The
congenial company of the Count was denied to him. The
Countess's interminable lecture had lost its most faithful
audience. His letters were returned. No heiress-blue flash
of silk under skylight, glimpsed at the bottom of the

stairs. No stairs, no entrance hall, no threshold. Just the customary footman, who now that the suitor had come unstuck, looked upon him quite favourably.

He's probably the only one, except for Gloria of course, and me, who understands the nuances of the situation, said the gloomy 'Prince'. *He winks at me now when he says, as he always says*—She's not at home . . .

The 'Prince' pushed aside his soup bowl. I envied him his loss of appetite.

I'm leaving town.

To go where? Not the west. Go south, I would.

(It is too late to go to the west: They are coming from the west. One would hope to go south. The south is for bright colours and pleasures. The southerners bake unleavened bread on hot stones in the sun.)

East. There's a place deep in the east where all the easterner film studios have gathered, it's called, in some arcane language that no one speaks any more, the Town of Love, that's where I'm going. Come with me.

And what would one do in the Town of Love? I asked.

What should one do? Don't be coy. One would make movies and drink and talk and fornicate with the nomad tribesmen riding into town. The local cuisine is, I am told, excellent.

I can't. I have to stay.

It's going to be dangerous here.

It's going to be dangerous everywhere.

He made a brief show of attempting to seduce Sarah into running away with him to the Town of Love, which she took in good part for the meaningless gallantry it was.

Sarah looked up only for a moment, solemn brown eyes. She smiled, a quite lovely smile, and retreated back into her own troubles. Then he gave me a goodbye kiss that he tried to make taste of freedom but neither of us was convinced by it and it tasted rather of the beetroot soup he had just been eating.

The 'Prince' now is gone, and Mr Mouse is gone, and I no longer see Werner at the Institute because the building has been closed 'for structural changes', and Heller remains, no thoughts of escape, he's more comfortable than he's ever been, a mood of city dread suits him as he goes on stockpiling bricks and gold and chicken wire. And Sarah and I stay with him.

9

Sarah visits Mr Y at least once a week. Sometimes, her pursuer reports, there is a Mrs Y as well.

Does she know she's being followed? Heller asks.

Of course she knows.

So she's not taking the trouble to hide her assignations. Whatever she's doing is out of a need that's stronger than her fear of being discovered. How does she know she's being followed?

I told her of course.

It seemed unfair not to. Heller gravely nods. Impossible to read if he is filing this information away to use against me later, or is accepting it as evidence of my unorthodox expertise.

Do you know yet why she's here? It can't just be the money.

I asked Sarah questions. I asked the questions that Heller would not. This is what she chose for me to uncover:

Her marriage had ended, loveless. There had been some adultery, on both sides, and one of Sarah's lovers had been a woman, which had scandalised the town and made it advisable for her to leave. She came to the city because

73

there was a man here called Heller whose love and kindness she had once been sure of and who had been—it is
surprising to hear this—the most ethical person she had
ever known.

I asked for more, the reasons she is not revealing. But
Sarah smiled and shook her head and said, *It's no good
you trying your mesmerism on me*. It's not mesmerism, I
told her, and why did you leave Heller in the first place?
Because, she said, there came someone else in whose need
for her she had fancied she'd glimpsed (here Sarah sighed,
laughed, lifted a hand to her throat) true love. Who is this
someone? I asked. It's more than scandal that drove you
here. She said nothing. There was something unapologetic
and defiant in her eyes.

No, I honestly tell Heller, I don't know why she's here.
She hasn't said.

The once-ethical Heller rubs his belly. He stands at the
window, he spreads his arms out wide as if hoping he might
have grown wings.

After the causes of trauma have been understood, these
must then be forgiven if healing is to occur. Heller, I think,
has buried his capacity for forgiveness. His digestion is
improved. The neurosis will now be cutting out another
avenue of exposure.

(I admit my doubts frankly—if this course of treatment
ends in failure, I am unstuck. There must be a successful
outcome for me to show and tell to the wise, disapproving
men at the Psychological Institute when the building is
opened again: look, here it is, a quite phenomenal paper
in the making, admit me please, I would like membership

of your august organisation, associate I would think at the very least.)

Now there is a secondary avenue of exposure to be searched for. I push Heller on the subject of his dreams, and he misunderstands the direction of my questions.

Don't worry, Gloria, I dream about you often. I don't usually tell you because the meanings of the dreams are obvious and I don't want you to get too full of yourself.

He wrongly thinks I am flattered by this. I am not enjoying this work. My ambitions used to demand more than being a cruel tycoon's witness. I do enjoy Sarah's distant company. How does she view me? As the wrong person? A flunkey of the heart? I know what the tycoon's employees call me; Daniel broke his silence to tell me. I am, the gossips say, Heller's tart's walker.

IO

The others have fallen into a hysteria of patriotism. We get on with the business of living. Heller and Sarah and I attend a revue, *The Cavalcade of Stars*, at the City Theatre. It was Heller's surprising suggestion. He claimed to think it a good idea to have an evening out all together.

Bernard drives the Buick through a carnival city protected by flags and rusty swords and guns. Uniforms from the war against the easterners and the war before that, when they last occupied the city, have been fetched out from wardrobes and museums, dusted down, crimson linings refitted (a boon for our tailors), brass buttons polished. The Buick passes patriots meeting in city squares and we catch sight of crowds through the chestnut trees marching towards park bandstands. Banners, trumpets, summer smiles. Old bald men make speeches and crowds cheer and fervent young men with sweat clinging to downy upper lips sing defiant songs, noble ancient faces, the mating calls of geese.

Rumours spread through the theatre lobby. *This is what is about to happen. This is your destiny, I have seen it . . .* Imminent catastrophe, imminent liberation.

They hate you, says the ancient music critic of the *Courier, with a violent passionate hate that fuels the ferocity of their armies: They will merely try to enslave the city but we are used to that, whereas you newcomers . . .*

No no. Remember how they were in the last occupation, says the equally ancient drama critic. *They were good to us, we are part of the same cultural tradition . . .*

His words trail off, he leaves unspoken the natural conclusion to his sentence, that they recognise our natural superiority over the others.

Heller leads on, towards the auditorium, marble pillars, red velvet, gossip all around of secret pacts, between them and the easterners, between the others and them, between the others and the easterners (no one, it seems, is looking to make a secret pact with us). Their armies are magnificent, but our allies in the west will save us.

None of this bothers Heller. Heller radiates intense good cheer. He doesn't seem to mind the bustle or regard of the theatre crowd. His skin is flushed. Sarah's nervous need for him, the city's emotions, have done marvellous things for his sense of self.

I don't know whether Heller knew the identity of the surprise mystery guest of *Cavalcade*; one must assume, I think, that he did, this expedition was his idea, a demonstration of his power and ease. The orchestra booms into a waltz, the house lights dim and there, spotlit on the apron of the stage, is Igo Sym, stage master. A flourish of his arms, a slash of his cane (and the ladies in the audience gasp and lift trembling handkerchiefs to parted lips), the curtains pull apart. Chorus girls and chorus boys in leafy pagan outfits dance with limbs at peculiar angles before a sylvan backcloth, and Heller jogs my arm—look, there's a second spotlight, follow the searching spotlight, up above, the spotlight holds and there is Gloria swinging gently on a trapeze, scarlet smile, golden hair, one high-heeled shoe already working its way off, legs straightening, translucent ball gown an aura of silk around her astonishing body. Dapper Sym slips off his cloak and his cruelty and lights a cigarette and—moon and stars twinkle on the vaulted ceiling—he sings in an airy tenor a love song to Gloria the Astonishing, and the rest of the world goes missing.

I forget the rest of the show, I probably never knew it. I only remember that Sym, without Gloria, reappeared once only, briefly crossing the stage in evening clothes on a bicycle. There would have been more songs, vaudeville routines and pratfalls, Madame Tatiana's dancing girls, satirical poems, jazz tunes. I saw none of it. Heard none of it. And I didn't notice when it was that Heller and Sarah left the theatre. I felt the absence before I realised the seats were empty. At the intermission I waited awhile in the crush bar, then looked outside but the Buick had gone leaving me alone.

I I

The psychologist feels conscious identity with her patient.
Yes. Me too. My father abandoned me too or *My mother
also showed no loyalty to me*. (Retreating into illness or
behind the shoulder of a weak second husband comes to
much the same thing.) Empathy can fail or overdetermine.
She looks longingly out of windows; perceives threat everywhere—nerves are jangling and candlelight throws shadows on to the door so the key appears to be slowly,
handlessly turning—she suffers all of a sudden from her
digestion. Or she is unaccountably, unusually melancholy
and needs to talk about what goes on in the sessions—but
Mr Mouse is gone and the 'Prince' is gone, to the Town
of Love, and there is no one left to trust.

Psychic infection is the penalty one pays for being with
people, the rent extracted for living in the world. Madness
is contagious. It spreads more virulently than kindness
or laughter. When I leave you I take away with me
briefly some of your emotions. When I read a book I
am psychically infected by its author. When a patient and
analyst are alone together in a room, she recognisably
feels what he cannot bear to: the violent conflicts of

79

the patient's psyche invade the analyst, and some of the analyst's seep back to the patient. When I was a child, seven years old, there was an incident in school assembly. A hot summery morning, the windows were closed, the headmistress droning on—a child lurched forward, vomited, fainted and fell. And then a second child, and then a third and soon a fourth and simultaneously a fifth and sixth and seventh, until nearly half of the children had swooned to the polished wooden, vomity floor. I did not faint or vomit. I was more resilient then. A psychologist from the department of education came to visit the next day. Excessive heat, he declared, insufficient fresh air. The diagnosis was accepted, the assembly hall floor was cleaned, windows were always kept open even in winter. Nothing to do with heat or air. One small child's hysteria spread through the assembly hall. Psychic infection.

I sit with Heller and nothing is said but I am overwhelmingly sad with inadequacy. That window, I want so to walk across to it, unlock the security grille, push open the window, gaze down at the inviting ground, throw myself out at it, voluptuous surrender. I have never felt this before. But it too will pass, ripples in the pond, this countertransfer of emotion to psychologist from psychologised. The dangerous ones cannot contain the madness inside. So the psychologist banks it by proxy in an internal armoured vault, guards it as the sufferer cannot: the rage, the fear, the hate, misery and lust, the will to self-annihilation, with experience and training and self-knowledge.

Go get her, said Heller. *Pick her up from the hotel. Bernard will take you.*

Yes. Thank you.

It was a relief to get out. I had not realised that Heller's situation was quite so precarious.

Mr Mouse warned me about all this. Mr Mouse was far better at protecting himself. In his consulting room he attacked shame and guilt, disabled the mechanisms, allowed his clients to go on sinning and causing suffering without self-reproach. Mr Mouse believed in *episode selves*: don't commit self-violence for the acts a past self has committed, that wasn't you who did it, that criminal is dead: now here is absolution, concentrate on living for now and, if you can, on making things good for future selves.

It was so plausible, and so very reassuring. Yes, Mr Mouse; thank you, Mr Mouse. One was encouraged to slough off past selves and invent new ones, to reject history; the procedure was exhilarating even if one felt that it was utterly wrong.

But then he decided to concentrate on making things good for his own self. He left for the west, to find a parish of rich widows. *I'll be the cat with the cream, Gloria, come along*—and then he said the unforgivable thing— *You can be my assistant, helper, answer the telephones, until* . . .

Until what? Until I have learned enough to treat the rich self-deluding patients as you do? Fake priest, fake confessor, fake friend, doling out handfuls of psychic pardons? This isn't what I became a psychologist for. Remember when you used to tell me stories about the pioneers? I intended then, still do, to heal.

Mr Mouse blushed. He wiped his delicate nose. He muttered something about marriage and children and busied himself with emigration documents.

So tempting it is to tell one's own details. Release them like a rush of inessential juices. (Even more so because I listen to someone else's for a living. Swallow back the opinions and memories, surrender my self to silence. This is not about me.)

12

At Sarah's hotel she and I sit on the balcony taking tea and watch the evening traffic along New World Street. Bernard waits below in the Buick. There is more grey in Sarah's hair than before, in her hair you can read the path of her defeat.

It's time to go.

She nods. She lifts a cup (delicate china, green and white pattern, the hotel's best) to her lips, blows on the hot tea. I take a third piece of sponge cake even though I had vowed not to.

It's time. Sarah. Go.

Heller has boasted to me of his tactics. He sends for her rarely now, at unpredictable intervals. Sometimes he will use her, without ceremony or tenderness (and these things Heller has reported with glee: each move of his hand, each flutter of his mistress's heart, the warmth of her body, the hurt in her eyes); but, more often, after she has answered his summons he claims he is too busy or fails to notice her and a flunkey sends her away again, with an insubstantial amount of money to make her feel worse.

She takes a long draught of tea, closes her eyes— emotional anguish? a sharp memory of humiliation? It might just be the pain of hot tea scalding her tongue.

He'll get angry.

The guns, *their* guns, are louder than before. They approach, they will soon be here. Another raggle-taggle militia of men and boys troops along New World Street, towards the northern outskirts of the city. Hopeful faces look up to the sky to find the airplanes that our allies in the west have promised will deliver us. The sky is cloudless and empty.

I'm not coming.

Not . . . ?

I'm not coming. Not today. I can't face it, him.

What's so special about today?

She doesn't answer. It's not the right question. She lowers her cup, looks at me, impenetrable brown eyes; she touches me briefly, meaninglessly on the arm.

What do you think he might do? I hope he doesn't blame you.

I'm touched by her consideration. Perturbed, I inadvertently take one more slice of sponge cake.

Boys too young to join up with the militias demonstrate patriotism by throwing stones at our famous Buick as Bernard and I return to Heller's headquarters. Their guns are tearing apart the city. Statues have fallen, apartment buildings broken, smashed, transformed. If I were not so preoccupied I might be able to admire the accidental beauty of the ruins that their guns have made. Coincidentally or

84

not, the most damaged parts of the city are the areas where we live.

Bernard, I discovered, has a mind of a surprisingly philosophical bent. At the corner of Mermaid and River streets he had to pull over to wait for a dead horse to be hoisted away. Bernard took a bottle of vodka from underneath the driver's seat of the Buick and gallantly showed it to me through the glass. I climbed out of the back, took the seat beside Bernard. While waiting for the road to open he and I drank vodka from the bottle and the street lights flickered on and off and sometimes the sky was illuminated by their big guns and Bernard talked of the way things are.

The hooligan has few beliefs. He doesn't believe in systems of government, neither of the right nor the left. He doesn't believe in the invincibility of their armies and nor does he believe that we are responsible for his own or the others' misfortunes. Bernard believes, theoretically, in God and the Devil. And he believes, practically, in forgetfulness. His own research has shown him that alcohol and women and violence are the means to acquiring forgetfulness.

This, he says, waving the vodka bottle about, *and this*, he says, clenching his free hand into a fist and putting a fearsome expression on his face, *and this*, he says, his expression softening into tender lust, his fist opening to stroke my unguarded breast, *this is what life is about*.

I push his hand away. The action does not offend him, he was merely making a point. He passes the vodka bottle back to me, nods as he looks at me taking a swig.

Beer and vodka and schnapps and ham and potatoes

and whores, he says. *That's my diet. The world of men is divided into two types. Muscle and brains. Each is useless on its own.*

The obstruction is cleared. The car is waved through by a policeman, his blue uniform ghostly under the flickering street lights. Bernard drives on, steering one-handed, drinking.

The Buick pulls into the courtyard of Heller's headquarters. An island of prosperity besieged by blank-faced petitioners drawn towards the possibility of a safety that will never be granted. Graffiti on the walls, which I'm trying to read while a squad of Bernard's cousins, caps pulled low over eyes, overcoat tails flapping, part the crowd to let the car through.

I pass unmolested. Metal doors. Long corridors. Stairs to climb. Along crowded corridors whispering conspirators fall silent, stare at me as I walk past. I go through the packed waiting room, the empty ante-room, into Solomon Heller's office. The tycoon is annoyed that I am late. He stands by the window. He makes me wait.

I thought, he finally says, *you were to pick up Sarah.*

She wouldn't come. I couldn't persuade her.

Heller ponders this. He turns to face me. He has a new smile that makes him wolflike.

Sit down. Have something to eat. Aren't you hungry?

The desk is too full of papers so he has used my couch to lay out the spread of delicacies. Smoked fish and caviar and soured cream and dark slices of lamb. One more delicatessen must have gone out of business.

Making some play of reluctance I pick at the food. It is very good.

Which one of your debtors provided this?

Don't worry about him. He received something more precious in return. Let's talk about Sarah.

The city is falling. His mistress already has.

Doesn't it trouble you that she's sitting there alone? Might she not find consolation somewhere else?

Don't try to taunt me. It won't work. She's making an attempt to demonstrate some sort of freedom from my control. I find it charming.

Am I to believe this? Certainly I have never known Heller so sure of himself. All the same, I imagine his penis stiff with an eroticised desire for revenge. My thoughts taste of vodka.

She's defying you. Trying to show she has no need for you. Doesn't that threaten? Doesn't that make you need to prove yourself, again, over her?

The greatest personal good is not the exertion of sexual power. Maybe for some men but not for me. As far as I'm concerned it all seems like a lot of work for poor reward.

But that's exactly what you're doing. It's an exertion of sexual power by withholding. What the libido demands is its satisfaction. What the rest of the body wants is pleasure and forgetfulness while satisfaction is being reached.

And this is what she came to the city for?

This has nothing to do with what she came to the city for. This has only to do with you exacting your revenge for her failing to love you in the past. And the way you're doing it is to humiliate her and to deny her. That's not what I advised. You may have beaten her, you haven't won her.

Be quiet now. You're annoying me.

That mild look from thyroidal eyes. *You too can be cast out. Without even snapping my fingers you are gone from this safe place, utterly into the pit. I don't need to bother with your truthing any more, psychic efficiency is the project now.*

I understand, Mr Heller. All business now, the brisk courtier who recognises her place and shivers to think that she might lose it: I'll pamper you, Mr Heller, I'll smear your bruised sense of self with salving creams, I'll massage you where you hurt and dress your ego with a crown and laurel wreaths, I'll send you all powdered into the world and celebrate each victory and then one day I won't be able to do a thing to help as I watch you go insane.

Or maybe not. A new order of things is being born, for which men like Heller might be ideally adapted.

13

I have to make my own way to Heller's headquarters. Bernard has left the city to join a militia forming by the River Bug. The Buick sits, driverless, gleaming, guarded, in the courtyard. I commute on foot and by streetcar.

I walk, as fast as I can, past shelled buildings on Forest Street, glimpses of refugees hiding in the ruins from the bombs—lightning doesn't strike twice, safety is to be found in here, shivering in mother's best furs, looking up at the sky through broken roofs, listening to the death-call of their guns.

Sudden terror. My walk becomes a run. Around a corner into Market Street, past apartment buildings painted yellow and pink, past the Persian Eye nightclub, which, I notice, has been renamed the Eye of the Sea, when behind me a bomb lands, a terrible percussion scattering an already shelled building into violent fragments.

I reach Heller's office. I do this blankly, without thought or volition, my momentum carries me there, or perhaps Heller's massive certainty pulls me, like gravity. My patient is all attentiveness. He sits me down on the couch, he wipes dust and blood away from my face, he makes me drink tea.

Fortunately none of this blood is yours. There are no cuts.

Heller's touch is reassuring, gentle, strong, like father's ought to be and seldom is.

You'll have to stay. It's getting too dangerous out there.

Perhaps I nod at this point.

Careful. It's hot. You're spilling.

Gently he relieves me of the burden of the tea cup, lifts it to my lips once, twice. Heller dabs at my lap, my hands, and then again at my face. As he bends down to lay the cup on the floor I see the woman for the first time. She is sitting behind him, in the red silk dress of a courtesan. Her skin is damp with cosmetics. Her hair is dyed platinum and stiffened into an elaborate shape like something a decadent artist has built out of metal.

I'll have your things sent for. There are rooms here, or perhaps the ante-room would be best, put a cot in there.

I need to use the lavatory.

Good. So you can still talk. I had been worried. After all, what use is a mute psychologist?

Perhaps that's the best sort.

Heller claps his hands together, the delight of a parent seeing his retarded child beat out something recognisable on the piano.

And you can still make jokes. Excellent. Go ahead. Go to the lavatory. You remember where it is?

I don't but I indicate that I do, trusting to familiarity to take me there. The woman pulls rustling silk around herself to protect everyone from the embarrassment of my treading on her dress. I leave the office, go into the ante-room. After a few false turns into monstrous corridors I find the lavatory. Lock the door. Sit above the bowl. Unwanted fluids leak out of me, tears, urine, menstrual blood.

At what point did I recognise the courtesan in red silk? Not when I returned to Heller's office, not when I falteringly whispered to ask her, when Heller's back was turned, if she happened to possess sanitary towels; perhaps it was after she reached surreptitiously into her bag and passed one over, sleight of her hand into mine, and her crimson mouth opened and she and I both uneasily smiled, awkward female complicity. Then she kissed her master and I knew her for sure as she was leaving. I recognised Sarah's walk.

Heller was watching me. He can read me so easily now.

What do you think?

A marvellous transformation.

Isn't she beautiful?

I didn't give him the moral disapproval he was expecting. Nor did I congratulate him on his success in making his mistress's appearance in the world correspond so precisely to the fearful image of her he had timidly carried around for so long.

I'm tired. I think I would like to sleep now.

Of course, of course. You've been through it today.

Solicitude returned to Solomon Heller. He took me to

his own rooms, laid me on his bed, removed my shoes, and covered me with blankets. The last thing I remember before sleep came to rescue me from the day was my hands being carefully tucked beneath the covers.

14

Wake surrounded by mementoes of home. The paintings from my consulting room are mounted on the wall; my best clothes, including an only once-used ball gown, are hanging on the outside of the wardrobe; psychological papers and books are neatly piled on the floor. All these are here, and photographs of family, and my favourite vase, toiletries, the plaster busts of the three masters of my discipline, whose irrelevance to this world I have found myself living in goes without saying; even the long-missing cigarette card of Igo Sym is propped, perhaps with ironical intent, against the dressing-table mirror.

Someone has removed my clothes in the night and dressed me in a nightshirt. When the door suddenly opens, Solomon Heller, bearing a tray, nearly catches me with my head beneath the covers inspecting the happily spotless, bloodless sheets.

I've brought you coffee and bread and jam. Breakfast.

That's kind of you.

No. Stay there. The tray hooks on to the bed over your legs, just sit up. There, it goes like that. How are you feeling?

The service is very good here.

Don't think it'll always be like this. How are you feeling?

I tell him I am feeling fine. And I am. I search for images and emotions of the previous day. These are very clear—bomb blast, transformed Sarah, fear, confusion, biological complicity, paternal care, peaceful sleep. No shadowy places where memory has chosen to hide. The image of Sarah is strongest. I hope that when I see her her appearance will have reverted to one she has chosen for herself. I suspect it will not have.

What time is it?

Late. Don't worry. Come when you're ready. I'll be in my office.

You are very . . .

Very what? Good?

No. Not good.

A wolfish smile from Heller before he departs.

I walk to Heller's office. Someone somewhere keeps playing a piano dance tune by the others' national composer, who died young of the usual diseases in the usual exile. I am beginning to envy that state. The ante-room is crowded. I push through into Solomon Heller's office. My master is on the telephone.

Heller lowers the receiver to the cradle. He clasps his hands together and pushes out the palms until his knuckles crack. His digestive problems are in remission; his body still insists on its right to make noises.

So. Let's get down to it. I'll lie on the couch. Would you like to hear my dreams?

You don't need me any more.

Oh but I do. More than you can possibly know.

Someone outside in the ante-room finally raises the courage to knock on the door. A little knock, so timid, and then, after a pause, comes the second knock, even quieter, as if it's trying to apologise for the first.

I had better get rid of the delegation. Open the door.

The men troop in, remove hats and stand docile like actors waiting for a missing director. I wave at my brother who drips out one ingratiating smile and from then on ignores me.

Sit down, Gloria. You fellows don't mind, do you?

There come some noises, abasement, demurral, respect, humility. Then silence, as the men wait in vain for the agreed spokesman to reveal himself. Heller is at his desk, I on the couch. Increasingly, I sense that what Heller wants me to be is not a psychologist but a witness.

A substitute spokesman finally emerges. (The first, by his clothes a judge or maybe a funeral director, had long ago made himself obvious, painfully so, by his attempts to acquire invisibility.) An elegant, flowery young man pays tribute to Solomon Heller. He praises Solomon Heller's economic power. Heller listens bored. It is time, says the elegant young man, to enter the public arena.

Political position is offered to Solomon Heller. Heller instantly turns it down. The elegant young man sighs. The original spokesman, with eyes downcast, finds bravery enough to take a step forward and suggest that our community is facing a common threat. They are occupying the city. They are already confiscating treasures, and forcing disinfection squads into homes where there is no disease simply because the requested bribe had not been paid. They might even be intending to concentrate all our households into our common quarter. It is a time for sticking together. Perhaps you're right, says Heller courteously. The delegation is dismissed.

After the men are gone I ask him if he feels flattered by the attention and the offer. Heller appears to be genuinely uninterested by the delegation or by my question. He wants to do more crowing over his success with the woman he has made his courtesan.

15

Sarah spends her entire energies alert to his slightest change of expression or caprice. Three lines crease her forehead in a permanent frown. She dresses with great care and vulgarity. Sometimes I help her prepare herself for him. I paint her face and nails. I chatter of this and that. She ignores me, as Heller customarily ignores her.

The electricity lines are down, and the gas supplies have stopped. I sit with Heller by candlelight. The telephone still works, our connecting cord to the world. Heller has been energised by war, he responds magnificently to cataclysm, it is wonderful to watch. All his property has been sold, alchemised into dollars and gold. He rents warehouses in obscure parts of the city, which he fills with canned delicacies and the materials for making bricks. I ask him why. He won't say why. He tells me that I am more necessary to him than before. *Don't leave me. You can't leave me.*

Solomon Heller wants to talk about luck. I walk with him, half a pace behind, out of the office and along an administrative corridor. Nervous young men work at typewriters behind half-opened doors. Solomon Heller says that he realised at an early age he was lucky, just as a different child would realise he's homosexual or an actor or born for the violin or boxing.

I was a timid child, but never any good at doing what people told me to do. You must do this, someone would say, or fear the consequences!—study hard at school, chew each mouthful of food thirty-two times, stand up when a lady enters the room, or suffer the consequences! I've always wanted to test the consequences. And somehow I'd always wriggle through. Before my confirmation ceremony I had to take the usual test. I was nervous. Twelve years old. Went by myself to the religious building. An old man who smelled of toilet odours and sour cream grabbed me hard by the wrist. It hurt. He took me to a room that smelled worse than he did. Shelves full of books. He dragged me down to sit next to him. Opened his biggest ugliest book. I didn't know any of the answers to his questions. I didn't even understand the questions. Couldn't understand the language he was speaking in. I kept looking at him instead of the book, long white-ginger beard, pale tongue. I didn't act my way out of the situation, it wasn't acting—and I might have been doing it for my father who was supposed to prepare me for this examination—I was already quick at sensing where luck was. Coldly, I sobbed my heart out. He was embarrassed and tried to console me, patted me very awkwardly on the back and told me not to worry. Then he signed the paper saying I'd passed the confirmation test.

A splitting of the self. At great cost to selves of the

future (as Mr Mouse would say). Which Solomon Heller calls lucky.

Fatherless children, me and Heller. My father failed with absence, Heller's despite being there, which might be worse.

You're lucky too, Gloria. I've always recognised that in you.

Is that why I have a job here?

Partly. Luck rubs off.

So it's a kind of infection then?

That's an odd way to look at it.

Even the most powerful infection can be cured. Heller collects papers from one of the nervous young men in one of the offices. On the way back I ask Solomon Heller about ethics. He stares at me for a moment, the return of his tortoise look of long ago. Then he shakes his head. *I tried doing the right thing once. Didn't get me anywhere.* He walks on. I follow. Back in his own office, I make my request.

My mother and stepfather. Family. My brother Daniel. I'm worried. Can you do something?

I thought you didn't like your family.

I don't.

It's partly a matter of face. I need to move Heller in directions not of his choosing. I need badly to be reassured that I still have an authority over him. And, too, there is some protective feeling. My family does not have my natural advantages for getting through dangerous events.

And what would you suggest your family can do for me?

My brother, for example. He can drive a car. He knows how to keep one clean and polished.

And in comes Sarah, dressed for seduction. Heller allows her one moment of his attention: he examines her from top to tail and then pretends again she doesn't exist.

You're very thoughtful. As it happens I don't require a driver. Why should I when there's nowhere worthwhile to go.

Please, I say.

I think I'm going to bed now. Don't worry, Gloria. I'll see what I can do.

He can be gracious when he wants to be. My favour is granted and I feel more uselessly in his power than ever.

Sarah sits behind Heller's desk. She picks at his papers.

You are safe here at least, she says, as if she knows what I'm thinking.

And if I wanted to leave?

You heard what he said. There's nowhere to go.

This, then, is the world. This grim complex. Perform my functions in Heller's psyche as he gets richer behind high brick walls decorated with graffiti I might not see again.

I'm going to sit in the car. Come sit with me.

She has no preferable invitations. Out through Heller's secret door we go, down his private corridor into the courtyard. The Buick has a fresh coating of dust. You can hear the streets from here, as well as the piano player who's somewhere in the building. Below the driver's seat is the bottle which thoughtful Bernard has left there. I open all the doors. Sarah and I huddle together under a tartan picnic blanket in the back; I have to adjust my position to the shape she creates beside her, in the space where her hips might touch be touching mine.

I take the first sip of vodka and after that the first gulp and pass her the bottle and listen out as I wait for it to return. Piano music coming from inside the headquarters. And, better, outside, a million furious city sounds. Hard to separate those from the sounds of the other side. I can just see the tips of the tallest chestnut trees in Dolphin Park. I stroke Sarah's forehead, try to smooth away some of the worry written there. Still there's an absence between. She hums a lullaby, which instead of lulling, awakens.

I don't like what he's doing to you.

Whatever he does to me I can put up with it.

Why? Because you think it's all your fault? The victim shouldn't blame herself.

When I knew him before he was very different.

Ethical, yes, you've claimed that already.

Not just ethical. Innocent.

(Hard to imagine him innocent, prudish yes, which maybe sometimes looks like the same thing. Whatever his original state it's become coarsened, perverted. He's subjugated his libido, he's pathologically bent on protecting the self from further injury.)

But it works, doesn't it? what he is now. You're in his power, so am I. And he's getting stronger, richer. He has a contract from them to build a wall around the residential district. He's going from strength to strength.

Is he? He has never seemed strong to me. Powerful yes, not strong. What he's doing to you isn't from strength, it's ugly, worse than ugly. A pornography of the soul.

He wasn't like that then. He used to be very good. It is my fault the way he is now.

Why then did you leave him? If it was going to make him suffer so much. If he was so good as you say.

Something came along, someone, who was more important.

Not your husband.

Not my husband.

Nor a lover.

She doesn't say anything. She doesn't need to.

Tell me about your child.

No response. The space between gets larger.

You're a mother, aren't you? That's the only explanation. You have a child somewhere. I'm sure you do.

Did.

Where is it?

He. He's a he. Not an it. A doctor and his wife have adopted him. Others. Who can't conceive, for medical reasons.

Mr Y.

Who?

Or rather Dr Y. It doesn't matter. Is he the father of your child? Heller?

Heller is not the father. The father is her estranged husband, to whom she returned after she discovered she had conceived. A boy was growing inside her. Her lover was no longer desired. She left her home town when the marriage ended, again, when her husband was trying to claim the child through the courts. Sarah came to the city because she could find a safe home here for the boy, away from his father, away from herself, away from any endangered *us*. Heller's spiteful gifts of money she sends on to the new parents, Dr and Mrs Dr Y, for the child's upkeep.

The day you wouldn't come to Heller's? At the hotel that time.

I signed the adoption papers. That was the last time I'll see him. It's better for him this way. He'll be safer with others than he could be with me.

And what about you?

I'm safe enough here. For the time being.

That wasn't what I was asking.

You're asking about feeling. It doesn't matter what I feel.

Does Heller know about the son?

Sarah says *No*, harshly, warning me to keep her secret safe from inquisitive masters.

She curls to me, I to her, the absence between temporarily diminishes. With each slug of vodka the world becomes a warmer place. A dance band. That's coming from the other side, not from ours. I wish the piano player would stop. Waltztime.

16

Startling, the first time a group of them comes to Heller's headquarters. Six of them—two officers, three soldiers, one doctor—walking so cocksure in their splendid black uniforms, looking at us with undisguisable loathing.

It was a treat to see Solomon Heller humble again. He stood up to greet them. He remained standing. Sarah and I were told to go and wait in the ante-room. When they left they walked quickly. The doctor looked at me, as if with some kind of reproach. The soldiers looked at Sarah unambiguously.

Guilt, the talk is of guilt. Or, rather, mine is. Heller stands by his open window. The bars have been removed, a testament to his buoyancy.

You are making money from the situation. A wall goes up around our residential quarter. You have been awarded the contract to build it. Our people suffer. You profit. Does this not make you feel guilty?

Heller turns to look at me coldly.

How do you know about the contract for the wall?

I shrug, try not to show embarrassment. He is silent,

something works within him that is revealed as anger—
he shouts, his face is red, his hands clenched into a double
fist, he rages against a collusion of women, against secrets
shared and passed (he makes this sound dirty) between
females.

Which I respond to as I used to with my father's
emotions: I take his anger, show no affect, refuse to let
any tears, in this supposedly adult moment, be revealed.
I concentrate instead on my doubt, that something in this
performance seems somewhat forced, as if a performance
is what it is. I look to find comfort in that.

*What else are you two lying about?! What more secrets
are you keeping!?*

Unerring, the ability of the besieged psyche to sniff out
real complicities among the imagined ones. I am moved
to tell him, to spill; but then, abruptly, his display of
mood changes from anger into softness, apology, perhaps
weakness.

I'm sorry, says Solomon Heller. *Please.*

He approaches me. His hand clumsily, it seems inno-
cently, strokes my hair. I receive a not unpleasant, slightly
shivery sensation of warmth. I bow towards the contact
and as his fingers, still tentative, begin to reach at my scalp,
the skin of my temples, I realise that what he is doing to
me—as his mouth opens and closes, as a strangled little
gulp comes from deep in his throat—is what he desperately
wants done to him, to make him feel like a child again, to
have mother caressing his unthinning hair, promising him
that nothing else really exists or can ever impinge. He is
giving me a cue for consolation, which for once I deny him,

because I can. And when it is over, and Heller's hands are at his sides again, and he has taken a final look down at the courtyard and is sitting at his desk, so perfectly still again, I return, as if unflustered, as if unashamed, to my earlier line of enquiry.

Our people suffer. You profit. Does this not make you feel guilty?

No, says Solomon Heller.

17

Take a day off, says Solomon Heller. *Go back to your rooms on Sienna Street, make sure there's nothing there you want.*

The surprising return, as he says this, of digestive noises. A hiccough, followed by two burps and a tummy rumble.

I don't think I need to. You've been most assiduous. I have everything I need right here.

Go anyway. My men may have missed something . . . See your friends. It'll be good for you.

The same is said to Sarah. *Take a day out of this routine, I know how hard it can get for you. Go to your old hotel room, some of your possessions might still be there.*

Both Sarah and I resist; one grows used to being here, the prospect of leaving, if only for a day, is fearful.

Go, says Heller.

Sarah needs to get changed for the expedition. When she returns her face is scrubbed clean of cosmetics. She wears the old modest clothes she came to the city in. Heller passes over two small piles of papers.

Identification documents. And money. Just in case.

The documents attest to unimpeachably other biology,

and very important jobs. (Mine, I am stupidly pleased to read—as if what I am being given here is an alternative, preferable truth—is at the Psychological Institute.) The money is five gold coins.

In case of what?

Bernard will accompany you out.

Heller farts, looks away, picks up the telephone. Time to go.

Bernard brings one of his cousins with him for the walk through the quarter. (The graffiti on the walls is disappointingly ordinary, the usual abuse.) The city is becoming something new. The quarter is full of crowds, with nothing better to do than to make loud noises and breathe shapes into the winter air. Some of their soldiers stroll through, night sticks and cameras at the ready. We pose for them like primitives hoping to please foreign anthropologists.

Bernard is chatty. He reminisces about his time at war. Army life had been a disappointment. On the march out of the city he had looked for a fellow volunteer with brains and failed to find him. The absence of a man with brains had made Bernard concerned for his own safety. So, somewhere in the countryside near the town of December, he had deserted. His unit had been wiped out by them several days later.

Bloody countryside. Full of animals. Took me weeks to find my own way back.

Sarah and Bernard's cousin go on to her hotel on New World Street. Our embrace goodbye is a casual one. If any more emotion were put into it things might become too frightening. Both of us are already anxious to get back to Heller's headquarters. Instead, Bernard and I move on to Sienna Street.

Nice neighbourhood, says Bernard.

As if nothing has happened. Fine ladies in furs walk poodles down to the corner and back. One thing has changed. We have policemen now. Handsome peaked caps, green military tunics, armband insignia. Our policemen smugly direct traffic and people with nothing better to do stand and watch and applaud. Something else has happened. Everyone wears armbands, identifying us as us.

I nod to the concierge of my building. The concierge does not nod back. He asks me where I think I am going. Home, I say. *Where's that?* he says. Up there, I say, under that archway, through the courtyard there, up the corner staircase to my rooms. *No*, he says. Bernard inflates himself to look more than tough. *What can I do?* says the concierge. His improved attitude gets me nowhere. My rooms have already been taken over by a new tenant. In return for my surrendered keys I receive three letters. Two are bills from the electricity company. The third is from the 'Prince'. None is from Mr Mouse.

Back to the headquarters, pushing through the crowds. The pietists have come in for special treatment. It is, we learn from our conquerors, hilarious to watch tired old men jumping up and down in underclothes. It is also most amusing to make the old men do push-ups; and when chicken-bone arms give way they grab the old men and scythe off pious beards with knives or bayonets. There's one, a most agreeable performer. I recognise him from

Valour Street: Zygelbojm senior, father to the superfluous man. They've got him dancing and sobbing in much-darned underclothes. Too big a crowd to push through. Watch the show.

He's singing and crying and dancing. His beard is half off, dead pelt chopped by their blades, fluffy white hairs stained red stuck to his face. He's crying from shame and pain, and for those who are dear to him who are watching this exhibition, but most of all he cries from joy, because God must love us so much, so heartbreakingly much, to favour us with this torment, this promise that the final days are at hand and soon the Messiah will be coming. Worship Him and He will come. Dance, sing, praise, cry and He will come.

Others in the crowd look sick and others have turned away and others are cheering in admiration for them who know how to treat us as we deserve, without qualms or pity, for sport. This is the new relationship, triangular in shape, between them, us, and the others.

And when they have become bored, and when his father is ready to drop from the pain and the shame and the exhaustion and the joy and the tears, and pity for those who have got off less lightly, the pietist's son Zygelbojm, who loves him, who honours him, who—a late, unasked for, most unexpected blessing—is his only child, removes his own coat and wraps it around his father's narrow shoulders and leads him, half carries him, home. Zygelbojm's eyes catch mine as he stumbles past with his load; there's a shadow of recognition on his face, he offers the slightest little hop and heel click to signify tribute.

*   *   *

I hold on to Bernard's arm on the walk back to Heller's headquarters. I could shut my eyes and be carried on by the crowd, which foolishly thinks I'm part of it.

The usual crowd of petitioners waits outside Heller's headquarters. No, the usual petitioners, but a different kind of crowd. Alarm on Bernard's face. I grab on to him, he grabs on to me, he fights a way through, through rubberneckers and ambulance chasers—something large has happened here—through the guarding squadron of hooligans, into the courtyard.

A respectful ring of men stands around the Buick with hats off, arms crossed. The car's roof has been crushed. Something lies on the ground, covered by a tartan blanket. I move towards it. Men in uniform hold me back. Something unmoving and man-shaped lies on the ground beneath the blanket. Look up, at the wide open unbarred window of Heller's office.

18

One last time in Heller's office. Questioned by policemen, a spectral hierarchy from green up to black with blue in the middle.

What was his state of mind?

Good. His state of mind was good.

Had he ever talked of suicide?

Yes. He had.

Had he ever talked about throwing himself out of the window?

Yes. He had.

He had warehouses. Do you know where the warehouses are?

That wasn't my job.

What was your job?

I was his, his psychologist.

Meaning, I was hired to save him and I failed. A blanket over crushed remains, the first kiss of impact.

Faces peer at me. None are benevolent. My brother, I notice, wears his green uniform so correctly.

I live here.

Do you? Does she?

Shaking of heads from Heller's dry-eyed employees. Nervous young men. The master has gone away.

Where's Sarah? I ask.

Who's Sarah?

The tart, someone says. *She's missing. Maybe she did it.*

No no no. Heller did it. The signs were all there and I was too stupid, too dependent to interpret the meanings. With a single blow the falling man strikes both at his own insupportable ego and at his loved and hated objects. Everyone is guilty. Everyone Heller let get close to him. I did it.

He told Sarah and me to go and so then he could be alone to stare at the courtyard and maybe recoil one time into the room clutching his head, imagining it shattered; and then he steels his nerve, he approaches the window again. This time he climbs on to the ledge, tests it with his weight, perches in the window frame, birdman. How long did he remain there? Not long. Did he just give himself up to gravity? let himself fall? Or did he jump? Was he shouting as he jumped? What was he shouting?

Just because he was stronger than me, I had supposed him safe.

See the way they look at me—without my protector I am nothing here. A courtier without a king is an embarrassing phenomenon, not even tragic. I rise up from the couch and someone in a uniform, green I think, pushes me back down, just to prove that he can.

Where are his warehouses?

I don't know about warehouses.

Sign this.

I sign this.

Here and here.

Here and here. The name that I chose, which corresponds to the name on the identification papers my late master gave me. Why did he need me gone? Did he think I might be able to prevent the act? A most generous judgement.

May I wait for Sarah?

Who's Sarah?

The tart, someone says.

No, someone else says.

I am allowed, under escort, to gather things from the bedroom that will stuff into one overnight bag. I am walked down corridors, past lines of watching people. I am pushed out of the headquarters. I am placed in the crowd on the pavement.

Fuck off now, someone says.

We had thought this the painful new reality, it was only the transition period.

19

Dear Gloria,

I write to you from the town of love. It's a dusty place. In the cafés everything is served covered by sheets of gauze. The easterners are building a modern studio in double quick time. I am at work on a scenario about a team of rock climbers that is to serve as an obvious allegory of the benefits of collective effort. I am writing it alone. The stories I could tell you of my journey. Campfires kicked over with earth, backpacks abandoned, carnage, soldiers in filthy uniforms with stories to tell, chancers who claim to have diamonds hidden in shoes and want you to join in with mad schemes.

All my money went on bribes. Each step of the way, bribes, for bandits, soldiers, customs men. As you approach the border you see signs that read 'In Times Of War Civilians Are Not Permitted To Approach The Frontier'. Only soldiers are allowed to run away.

I wish you would have come with me. You would probably hate it here but all the same. Maybe south was the place after all.

Will you see Zosia for me?
If ever things get too much, come to be with
Your Prince.
PS Opium is plentiful here. The food is awful.

I have a letter from Heller himself. I presume Sarah has the same one, or maybe she has the same instructions but written more intimately, because he loved her. I went to her hotel, I asked for her at the desk—my throat was raw from a sudden, unexpected jealousy—blankness from the night manager, a small amount of money passed over by me and, miraculous, the night manager became my very best friend. She had been and she had gone and a message from Heller was here for me and I expect to see her on the other side.

Heller's note is written in a dainty schoolgirlish hand:

Dear Gloria,
You won't see me again for reasons you should by now understand. Please go to this address on the other side: second floor back, 147 Long Avenue. Sarah will be there too. Things will be taken care of.
Think well of me,
Solomon.

I renounce psychology. Burn the books, smash the plaster idols. *Think well?* I might be thinking better of him if he hadn't proved with his death that my career is useless.

The Solomon is poignant. I have never thought of him as Solomon. That's probably what his mother used to call him.

Part Two

THE OTHER SIDE

How high is the wall that Heller made? The wall that Heller made already reaches up to your knees. Who builds it higher? Workmen selected by the guild, recruited from less important projects. What do you notice about the workmen? Dust and sweat, moisture on grimy skin, the physical arrogance of men who know how to lay the bricks just so, then step back, light cigarettes, remove damp shirts and flex shoulder muscles for any passing woman to adore.

To get beyond the wall what must she do? She must go through a gate, of which there are eighteen. Which gate does Gloria decide to go through? The gate at Vine Street. Why this one? Because it is close enough to the playground of Dolphin Park to hear ordinary sounds from the other side—children, scolding governesses, accordion music. What does the gate at Vine Street consist of? A hinged barrier striped red and white, a lonely coil of barbed wire to signify impassability, a sentry box off to the side, a docile queue. What is beyond the gate? A brief stretch of gravelly no-man's-land, another hinged barrier to the other side, freedom, the future. Is the gate on the other side guarded? It is not. Is the gate on this side guarded? It is, by three men. Is a hierarchy indicated? Of course: in diminishing order of power and increasing order of enthusiasm these men's uniforms are black, blue and green.

Does she have to wait to get across? She does. Is she alone? No: Gloria is one of many trying to get across to the other side. How would she describe the psychic mood of the crowd? As a mix of fearful and hopeful with fearful predominating. Is she infected by this general mood? She is not. To what does she ascribe her immunity? To the aura of grief that surrounds her; and to her faith in her future and her luck and the sustaining power of her late protector and benefactor, Solomon Heller.

Is she being observed as she waits? On the other side of the wall casual onlookers rest knees and umbrellas on the freshest bricks and gaze into the residential quarter, sometimes pointing. That might be the glint from a set of field glasses or the flashbulb of a camera. And on this side of the wall? Beggar children dart around, looking for likely marks. What do the children want? Money, bread, cigarettes and, if the shrill cries are to be believed, pity. Do the children go near the workmen or the guards? No. The children have learned by now not to bother the workmen or the guards. Do the children look well nourished? Hardly. The children have unnaturally yellow skin with thin bones poking through, and all move jerkily fast as if using energy stolen from future selves.

Behind her, what are the crowds doing? Walking interminably through the streets of the quarter. Do members of the crowds look at the queue waiting to get across? Sometimes, an occasional glance, when a crowd has to splinter to let the empty streetcar through or refugees with carts, but most often the people just pass by without malice or curiosity, expressionless damp eyes.

Has Gloria hidden her own eyes? She has. She wears dark glasses, as well as a beret pulled down over her hair. Why? She does not intend to be implicated by her presence in this queue. What are her hands doing? The right is gripping the handle of her overstuffed overnight bag, the left is lifted to cover her nose and mouth.

Is there a notice plastered to the bricks on this side of the wall? There is, repeatedly. If it were an animal what would this notice remind Gloria of? Of a nasty little dog, of an endless line of nasty little dogs yap-yap-barking at our ankles. What does it say? Is it an advertisement? It is not an advertisement. It is a promise. A jail sentence awaits any newcomer caught without a legitimate permit on the other side.

Has Gloria a permit? Gloria has. It is one of her legacies from Solomon Heller. Is it legitimate? It is not. Does she worry about the quality of the forgery? Hardly at all. How instead does she occupy her mind as she waits to get across? She devises analogies between notices and dogs and she wonders how Sarah will be dressed when the rendezvous on Long Avenue is made and she thinks of breakfast. What does she intend to eat for breakfast? An omelette with herbs and cheese and a fresh buttered roll for dunking in milky coffee. Where does she intend to eat this breakfast? At the café in Dolphin Park. What does she expect to be listening to while eating breakfast? A brass band? Too early for the band to be playing. Children and governesses and accordion music and birdsong. Does she look at her neighbours in the queue? She tries not to. She looks at the ground at her feet or at the workmen or to the chestnut trees of Dolphin Park. And, if still hungry, she plans on a piece of cinnamon pie with the second cup of coffee.

Lovely day.

Said to Gloria by the man just in front of her, part of a most ridiculous family group. His wife's dark hair is poorly hidden by a blonde wig worn atilt; his daughters—who sit hunched on cardboard suitcases, whispering, scarlet mouths close together, almost touching—have faces quite oddly painted with cosmetics. Father stands blinking like a mole, his chin and cheeks scabby with razor cuts from where his pietist's beard has been bluntly removed.

We're going to my wife's sister-in-law.

Does Gloria wish to hear this? She does not. She does not want to be contaminated by this family's incompetence, its hope, its insane trust in a sister-in-law, its delusion that provenance can be disguised by cosmetics and wig and beardlessness. Does she care about the family's predicament? She would be heartless not to care. Does she turn her head away? She does. Does this molish man continue to speak to her? He does not. He rubs his shin where his wife's foot has kicked him into silence. Then he rubs the darker band on his overcoat sleeve where his armband so obviously used to be.

Is the queue moving efficiently along? No. There is an

obstruction at the head, where an elderly man waits with a young boy for permission to cross. The elderly man wears a long brown coat and a grey snap-brimmed hat and a wise little beard trimmed to the chin. He carries a large medical bag. The boy beside him has his back to Gloria. All she sees of him are a black overcoat that's too big and a navy-blue cap that's too small on top of black curls. The green guard and blue guard are watching the event with the expression of connoisseurs enjoying good seats at the theatre. The black guard is shaking his head. *Your people are ugly. This boy is not ugly. This leads me to believe there is some deception practised.* The father smiles humbly. He softly replies. The guard insists he talk louder. The father is encouraged to shout. *I am a doctor! I am to treat an administrator! Each moment I am, excuse me! delayed! the administrator's sickness gets worse! This is my son! He helps me with examinations and procedures!*

Is the waiting queue as docile as before? It is not. Members of the queue are beginning, quietly, to grumble.

It's a question of logic, their guard amiably replies. *Dreks are ugly. He is not ugly. You say he is a drek. I have proved by logic that he is not. Therefore I know you are lying. Why are you lying?* The elderly doctor spreads his arms as if if he only can succeed in miming infinite patience then he will be rewarded.

Does their guard find a way through this situation without compromising his logic? He does. He lifts his black nightstick away from his belt and smashes it into the middle of the boy's face—a crack of bone, a spurt of blood (the green guard lays a warning hand on the elderly doctor)—

another blow, another crack of bone, blood gushes, boy and cap tumble separately to the ground.

Yes. He is one of your people after all. Pass through.

Does Gloria weep or vomit? She does neither; she merely catches her breath and holds it and watches the father wipe his eyes and awkwardly lift his son and walk him to the other side. And when the family ahead of her is tossed aside, when the man's papers and banknotes and the woman's jewellery and blonde wig are confiscated, when the younger prettier daughter is led into the sentry box for further questioning, what does Gloria do? She exhales; she walks slowly forward; she keeps her attention to the patch of ground between our side and the other; she finds a small navy-blue cap to stare at that lies abandoned on gravelly mud beside a splash of sunlight; she offers her papers for examination.

After her papers are barely scrutinised, after her heavy overnight bag is ignored, after she is permitted to pass between the sentry box and the barrier, when she is already halfway across to the other side, is Gloria relieved? She feels nothing but strain and hunger, not relief. Does she pick up the ownerless navy-blue cap? She does. Does she know why she picks up the cap? No. Some things are mysteries. Does she stop hunching her shoulders and remember to improve shallow breathing? Not yet. Does she catalogue or classify or in any way give a name to her symptoms? She subdivides her symptoms under category headings of panic, shock, incipient hysteria, sorrow, guilt and hunger. Is she reminded of any biblical parallels? She is reminded of the example of Lot's wife.

The Other Side

Does Gloria, like Lot's wife, look back? She does. Is she, like Lot's wife, turned into a pillar of salt? Not yet. What does she see? A large crowd parting to allow in a horseless cart tugged by refugees and then closing up again around it; a docile queue slowly moving to fill the space that she has left; three guards dressed in green, blue and black performing some business with cigarettes and matches; workmen stretching, glistening, smearing wet cement; a notice that is repeatedly plastered to this side of the wall. Is it a different notice? Does it refer to the residential quarter she has just left? It is. It does. What does it say? It says, *Forbidden District: Area Infected By Epidemic.*

2

Breakfast is a disappointment. The roll is stale, the coffee over-brewed and tepid. Gloria sits at a cracked café table trying to catch the waitress's eye. Omelettes are not available, nor eggs in any form. The waitress had said this haughtily and complainingly, the tone of a lady fallen on hard times, not used to this kind of life, these kinds of people. She is, Gloria suspects, keeping her eggs back for more important customers.

This does not feel like freedom. Gloria had been expecting freedom. Outside, a governess pulls a child off a merry-go-round. The child's wind-muffled screams and the waitress stacking cups and saucers into ungainly towers are the only sounds to hear. No accordion music. No birdsong. The branches of the chestnut trees are empty. The birds have probably all been killed by the waitress. Gloria imagines her first act after arriving at work, even before she removes her overcoat and pins her paper waitress hat to her dyed red hair, would be to lay down trails of bird poison in the enticing shapes of worms and bread crusts. And then, after the café had been opened and the tea urn heated and the first dissatisfied customer grumpily served,

128

the waitress, retrieving from a pocket of her apron the catapult confiscated from a nephew, picking up a stone, stands in the doorway, taking careful malicious aim at the top branches of a nearby tree where bird life still presumes to endure.

Do you have cinnamon pie?

The waitress shakes her head without looking at Gloria. A mutual dislike had quickly been established. The waitress is fleshily and sourly middle-aged. Her hair has been dyed to approximate the shade of red that Gloria's achieves naturally. This is being taken personally. The waitress suspects Gloria of having come here on purpose to flaunt her hair and youth at her. In turn, Gloria suspects the waitress of paranoiac tendencies, and alcoholism.

(This psychological habit can be hard to break. What are Gloria's legacies from Solomon Heller? A set of forged documents. Five gold coins. A rendezvous with Sarah. A new destiny that has yet to be revealed. A permanent mistrust of depth psychology. A refusal to be her own case study.)

She is not superfluous, this is what she tells herself, she has somewhere to go, an address; her new life waits for her, wearing its own clothes. Walk, keep walking. Make your manner appear confident, you're going somewhere, in not too much of a hurry—after all there's nothing you're frightened of, nothing you're running away from— but neither do you saunter too much because sauntering implies prosperity. She tries to look straight ahead, not to be caught staring at the sights, the ruined towers, the new electricity lines, the dead horses, the loudspeakers, the letter V that keeps recurring, on posters, on the windows of unpatriotic shops, because that would mark her out as refugee or a tourist, either way vulnerable. Nor does she dawdle because that declares superfluity and suddenly in this city of eyes all eyes are looking at her.

These are the people she sees examine her: A rouged man picking up a copy of the *Courier* at a newspaper-stand looks at her as he holds out a coin for the newspaper-seller's hand to claw. A neat little boy in grey shorts and shirt, toggled Boy Scout's tie, hands a package to a man in a dark lounge suit; the man slips the package inside his satchel and gives the boy a bar of chocolate in return; and at that moment both heads turn to inspect Gloria walking away more quickly now. A blue policeman's hand closes in an inferior's salute to the peak of his cap as a pair of their black policemen passes by while his eyes go at Gloria's sex like a reptile to a hole. An other man's attack is only at her face—he himself wears a hooligan outfit, white hat with a narrow brim, long dark coat, high boots. She sees him measuring her, quantifying her colouring, the angle of her cheekbones, the colour in her lips, the shape of her nose, that melancholy in her eyes—awfully reminiscent of a newcomer—the scarlet suit she wears beneath her overcoat, a little too flamboyant for perfect taste, the heavy bag she carries . . . is she . . . ? Gloria goes on, faster now, is jolted nearly into falling by the klaxon of one of their staff cars skidding around a bomb crater in the street.

Roads have been freshly tarmacked. New lamp-posts are everywhere. Coarse pools of light show up the worst blemishes of others' faces and, she supposes, her own. They stroll, mostly in black, usually in pairs, in the excited anticipatory way of students at the beginning of a new semester. Loudspeakers have been erected high on poles at street corners. On the corner of Long Avenue, through crackling interference, an actor's voice relishes the artistic challenge of reciting new ration regulations.

Long Avenue. Number 147. Gloria stands in front of a tall building painted yellow and pitted by war. Water seeps through the broken throats of corner gargoyles and drips down empty window frames. The sun slips past a castle of clouds, shines again; Gloria lays down her overnight bag, massages the red stripes that the handle has cut into her hand; the sun disappears again.

She walks over a courtyard rubbled with broken things, up a narrow staircase, and into a pleasant room. Second floor back. Wooden chairs rest against green walls. A central wooden table supports a statue of a mermaid built of alabaster and dust. Stepping into an office is a bureaucrat in crisp office clothes who reminds her of her brother.

I'm—

You'll have to wait, I'm afraid. Take a seat.

The bureaucrat closes his office door behind him. She sits down. The young man who was sitting opposite sidles over to sit beside her. He's sharp-snouted, hair greased back over a narrow skull, and he's offering her a cigarette from a pack of Junos. He looks like an otter.

Have you just come over?

He asks as if disinterested; he sits back on his chair, lifting the front legs into the air; he blows on the lighted end of his own cigarette. He's merely making conversation, two strangers waiting together in a waiting room.

How is it there? Pretty bad?

No no. You're under some mistake. I live locally.

His eyes and hers go to the overnight bag. Would you like to take a look inside, Mr Otter? see what's been packed for the journey? Superfluous textbooks from a former life. Two changes of clothing and, absurdly, a ball gown. A cigarette card of Igo Sym, matinée idol. A set of keys to the family apartment on Valour Street. A leather washbag containing toothbrush, cosmetics and a bottle of scent that mostly holds air. A snapshot of father at the wheel of a sports boat on the lake, bare-chested, sun-visored, leaning the opposite direction from white-capped waves behind; another of the 'Prince' on set, in riding trousers and high shiny boots, drunkenly pretending for the studio photographer to be bellowing instructions through a megaphone. Two items of correspondence from Mr Mouse which might be called love letters. A child's navy-blue cap. And the Case Notes, pressed inside brown cardboard covers, tied with a ribbon the colour of rust, her discontinued pathbreaking study of Solomon Heller, deceased.

No thank you. I don't want a cigarette.

She doesn't want to be beholden to him, to be in his debt for something even so cheap and temporary as a cigarette. Yet somehow she finds herself holding her hair away from the flame that he is offering as she leans forward sucking the cigarette that has found its way into her mouth.

You're not from here. You're from the other side, aren't you?

What do you mean? This is the other side, is what she wants to say. But instead she responds with a silent indulgent smile, so patient with her misguided new friend. The cigarette tastes stale. A stomach rumbles. She can't tell whose. Where are you, Sarah? You should be here now, wearing your own clothes again; come in now, saunter in like a fashion mannequin, or even bashfully, it doesn't matter how you enter, how you walk is hardly the point, just don't be too late, our new lives are due to start.

If I may offer my services I would be so very glad, people like you often need help settling in, I have quite a wide circle of influential friends . . .

How very impressive. I still don't trust you. Excuse me.

She wonders how Sarah will be mourning the death of the tycoon. With tears? Laughter? *Relief?* Gloria expects Sarah's reaction to Heller's end will in part determine her own. Gloria hauls up her bag. She knocks on the office door, which, after some persistence on her part, opens. The bureaucrat glares at her as if she has already disappointed him utterly. He returns to his desk, looks at the telephone receiver that her interruption has forced him to abandon, picks it up again, murmurs an apology and nods and makes notes as he listens or (and this might be fanciful on Gloria's part, but she hears no dictating voice) pretends to listen. Either he is a very busy man who lives importantly in the world or the illusion of activity is what he builds to make his life seem endurable. He shakes his head. He calls out a hearty farewell to his maybe imaginary conversation partner. He lowers the receiver. Reluctantly, he looks at Gloria.

My name is Gloria Wood. Solomon Heller—

Impatiently, the bureaucrat waves at her to be quiet. He opens a large ledger book, and, licking his page-turning finger every second page, finds the item he was looking for.

You have the wrong date. Look, I have it here, written here. You're two weeks early.

Can't we maybe start now?

Mr Heller's instructions were very clear.

But you don't understand. There must be some mistake.

There can be no mistake.

What about Sarah? I am meant to be meeting someone here. My friend.

I wouldn't know about that.

Gloria's overnight bag threatens to pull out of her straining reddened fingers and settle on the floor. She worries that if she were to let it fall now she might never find the strength to pick it up again. The telephone rings. Bureaucrat lifts documents in the air. *You see*, says his expression, *how busy I am?*

Come back when you're meant to. Maybe your friend will be here.

Maybe.

He looks anxiously about. Women make him nervous.

That man, in the waiting room . . . ?

Did he ask you questions?

He wanted to know where I was from.

You weren't, I hope, candid with him?

Candid? No. I wasn't candid. I was evasive.

Good. Beware of him, of men like him. Men like him turn in people like you. There are rewards, or . . .

Or?

Or there is the opportunity of blackmail. Men like him are called, excuse me, rat-catchers.

She had never seen a bureaucrat blush before. It is an awful sight. He manages to hand her a business card.

I am most terribly busy. If you have no friends to go to then you might consider this charity house. Here is the address. Come back in two weeks.

Wordlessly she goes through the waiting room, out, and down the stairs; Mr Otter might be following, or it might be the belated echo of her own footsteps. Perhaps she is wrong to start running. Perhaps she is wrong to assume that because his face corresponds to that of an animal then as a man he can't be any good.

She had not considered the possibility that Sarah might not be there to meet her. Gloria goes as fast as she can down Long Avenue. She holds her overnight case with weak hands. Her knees kick it forward with every uncomfortable step. Passers-by stare lubriciously at her. *People like you.* Foolishly Gloria had thought herself unique.

Gloria waits at a streetcar stop, eyes downcast, hoping for invisibility—then she carries on walking when the streetcar arrives. From the loudspeakers at every corner, voices bellow out hygiene regulations, water distribution rules, curfew hours. Everywhere she goes, she sees, in parks and plazas, on billboards behind glass, the letter V, usually in black. It stands for Victory, theirs.

Outside the train station, which she has uselessly passed

for a second time, there is a display of posters for productions at the City Theatre. *Drunk Walter* is reaching the end of its run. (A comic's eyes are crossed, his hat askew, his jacket buttons are all in the wrong holes, he raises an unmarked bottle to his wet lips.) *The 40 Husbands of Madame Ilona* will soon start. (Forty men— she counts each one—in top hats and tails holding dance cards like anxious suitors surround a woman; she is naked, voluptuous.) The managers of the City Theatre are named at the bottom of each poster, in a clean, modern type. The names are E. Claudius and I. Sym.

Perhaps it is sufficient to say that the former psychologist identifies within herself the infections of fear, despair, guilt, grief, hopefulness.

3

On her second day, when Gloria visits the bureaucrat again, he allows her less time than before. And the third day, even less again. She hasn't even stepped into the waiting room (which is full; she is reminded of Heller's own courtiers by the faces of these bureaucratic petitioners, most of whom carry folios of papers like treasures) before he has emerged flapping out of the office.

I'm sorry. Your friend has not come. Why don't you return when I told you to?

I would like, Gloria says, to—

Excuse me. Look around you. Some of us have jobs to do. Really I think if you have friends to go to you might want to. Really, I think that. Come back when you're meant to.

The bureaucrat inspects her state with some evident satisfaction, and, with a turn to—Gloria is sure—a random petitioner, he summons him into the office before turning on Gloria a look of quite unwholesome power, as if to say, *This man is lucky, blessed, do not think this can happen to you!*

The bureaucrat appears triumphant: it is as if he and

Gloria have been fighting a secret war, which he has quite magnificently won.

Afterwards, Gloria washes herself in the bathroom next to the bureaucrat's waiting room. No matter how hard she scrubs at the sink with the heel of her hand she is unable entirely to eradicate the tracks of river dirt left behind on the porcelain.

The first two nights of her freedom, the refugee spent at a hotel. The third night she slept by the river. She didn't have the heart or the stomach for cordial desk staff with insinuating manners, for the handing over of identification documents and the moment while the papers were being inspected of feeling entirely bereft. Some hotels were *restricted* to them (*Sorry, Madam, now excuse me, if you please . . . ?*), which meant that the ones that accepted bogus others put up rates accordingly, and Gloria's cache of coins was shrinking.

So she went on a long oblivious walk, ending up across the river, over the bridge, and down stairs made of cement and mud and murk, expecting to find cities hidden there in the aqueducts and walkways. Her mother had always enjoyed frightening child Gloria with threats of the renegades who lived by the river. Convicts and lunatics and perverted lovers, and desperadoes who had started off as ordinary men but then discovered a taste for blood. Gloria walked along the upper slope of a quiet bank, trying to keep mud off her shoes, her coat lifted high, alert for monsters in the shadows.

The population she found there was a shanty town of

drinkers arranged around a fire, none of whom even bothered to leer at her as she passed by. A little further on one solitary drinker had built a palace for himself from boxes and planks and blankets. He neither threatened nor welcomed her so she presumed he didn't care either way if she chose him for a neighbour. And the very practical, almost mechanical way that he lifted his vodka bottle to his mouth with no waste of effort reminded her of Bernard, so she settled in near him. Under the sheltering shadow of his cardboard minarets she made a sort of bed for herself on top of wet wood, with her coat for cover, her overnight bag for a pillow.

She felt extraordinarily alone. Gloria fell asleep looking sideways at the water, which was dark and sullen, refusing to reflect the stars.

In the mornings, muscles aching, hair dirtier, eyes and throat choked with self-pity, Gloria breakfasted again in the park café, where the waitress was always as sour and eggless and unfriendly as before. Before setting out for Long Avenue for the third time, as Gloria drank insultingly weak coffee, watching a table of skittish scented old ladies who were dressed like young girls, with white flowers embroidered on to transparent red blouses, she condemned herself for this pathetic attempt to establish some kind of routine to her days.

4

The 'Prince' had asked her in his letter to see Zosia for him. After her third rejection at the bureaucrat's office Gloria decides to visit the virgin. The road to the Glade is bounded by trees and dangers. The ex-psychologist walks silently, eyes down, looking neither left nor right, keeping her attention on the road just ahead. Attempts to accost her are made, by suave men in fox fur coats, by rat-catchers, by soldiers, she can feel their eyes upon her, hear too the sexual suggestions that they make, the creak and chafe of metal and leather on their thighs. She walks on, footsteps stuttering. Like a child, if she doesn't see them then they aren't real and can't harm her. If you don't show fear then there is nothing to be frightened of. She would reach the virgin's house.

She is at the beginning of the final stretch, the lane that curls up through parkland to the Glade. She had not expected this—their soldiers are everywhere, relaxing by the side of the path, playing cards, smoking cigarettes, riding horses across the park. No matter how tightly she clenches her eyes shut she cannot escape being seen. Comments come at her, she can understand the slangy tone but not the words. Gloria's knowledge of their language is mostly limited to the vocabulary of depth psychology. She knows the names for neuroses and psychoses and manias, the correct words for anal erotism and coprophilia and brooding mania, but whatever propositions are being made, whatever crude conjugations are being suggested, Gloria can only guess at their meaning. All she can do is to press on, hope that one there, with the piggy eyes and the bristly hair, does not stop her, swing her around, demonstrate his own psychopathology on the instrument of her body; or that one, sallow, disappointed, what gruesome devices does he keep in his kitbag? or that one, the boy sports champion, sunny open face, farm-boy ease of limbs; when these types go wrong, they're by far the worst . . . no one would miss her here.

It is wrong, all wrong, she wants to stop now, just stand here with open arms, wait for her final disaster to show itself. The nearer she gets to the Glade, the more of them there are, not fewer. She turns the final corner. There's the house itself, recognisable at least, intact, but she can't go on, too many staff cars and motorcycles and sidecars. Too many elegant young men in black uniforms leaning or walking busy with document cases underneath arms. Too many black gloves on dangerous fingers. She is grubby, dank, exposed. Perhaps too grubby to rise to the focus of their attention. (Maybe she has discovered the secret of invisibility. How can she apply this? It would be useful for observing timid patients in the bedroom and bathroom. Why is she still thinking therapeutically? Her patient is dead.) She is beneath reproach.

Excuse me!?

Even the lonely triumph of invisibility is denied her. A civilian stands before her, blinking behind round spectacles.

May I take the liberty of introducing myself? My name is Oscar W. Stone.

Oscar W. Stone carries a brown briefcase. All of his clothing, too, is brown. He is a pale young man, ardent.

I wonder, forgive me, but I noticed you approach the house, I am guessing you have been here before, in former times, would you know some of its history?

Too much of it.

Everything has changed. Zosia's family cannot be inside. The house is too full of them. A black hive, briskly buzzing. What's happened to the Count? (Did he meet his end in silence?) Madame the Countess, Zosia, neurasthenic Henry?

Oh that's wonderful. From his pocket Oscar removes a notebook, yellow covers with a golden pencil that fits snugly into its binding.

No one here seems to care that much about local history.

The house has been taken?

Requisitioned, yes. The military governor has his head-quarters here. I am told a most illustrious family used to live here.

Do you know what happened to the illustrious family?

No. Alas. No. (Oscar W. Stone wears his look of sorrow longer than a less sensitive man would have.) *But may I ask you please—I have some questions, but first—let me explain first who I am.*

From out of his briefcase he produces a little book with soft red covers and gold letters for the title.

I'm researching a guidebook. Oscar W. Stone coughs. *It will look like this. You see, how strong the binding is? And the pages too, made from the finest pulp.* He strokes the covers, lifts the red ribbon bookmark and runs his fingers along its length as if it is the tail of a cat he is adoring. Oscar then laughs, as if he has performed a joke.

He takes his professional duties very seriously, he tells her (nervously, shyly, proud to be an author), a job is for doing well. *In my little notebook I try to write down all information I learn whether I think it's valuable or not. One never knows. Our company has a hard-won reputation for accuracy. Tell me some of the history of this house, the windows, aren't those windows magnificent? I'm assuming the additions were made in the last century? The style looks easterner.*

He puts his face too close to hers when he talks. His breath tastes of cough lozenges and milk. She has always been a magnet for unsuitable men.

I don't know anything about windows, or additions. Excuse me.

This obviously was a most beautiful city before, before the, intervention. Tell me: where would I find the best collection of old masters here? and how about the moderns? Did you know your country is referred to as the Wild East back home, most undeserved. I hope my little book will do something to redress the balance. The hot springs are the

*most beautiful I've ever bathed in. Are you familiar with
many of the mountain resorts?*

She cannot bear him. She goes. She retreats from Oscar
W. Stone, retreats from the Glade—on the way back she
receives again their attentions and suggestions, which are
worse this time for being endured twice.

Gloria goes to the train station. She goes to the train station
because she has to go somewhere. (One walks as if one has
a right to a destination. One walks as if ruins are no longer
surprising.) She goes to the train station because she can't
keep on walking for ever. She sits on a bench. She may do
this for a time without suspicion. Sometimes she looks up
to the departures board as if she had somewhere to go.

Pairs of eyes are watching her. Her anonymity is increasingly questionable the longer she stays. She pulls her
bag around the station concourse; she reads timetables;
she smiles in a superior fashion at advertisements. She
has to do something. Or she can just wait, for someone
else's will or more brutish appetite to announce itself
and prevail. The next intercessor will be worse, she is
sure, than Oscar W. Stone. She reads hygiene regulations,
train timetables, curfew hours, coming attractions at the
City Theatre (Managing Director, I. Sym), where she is
already impatient for *The 40 Husbands of Madame Ilona*
to begin its run. She stays looking at his name because it
is comforting to her, even though she feels ashamed, that
at any moment she might be caught out enjoying a secret
pleasure. A restricted intimacy she is not eligible for.

Gloria washes herself again, this time in the station

lavatory. (She will soon be, if this is to go on, a connoisseur of toilets and ruins, her own.) She tries to compose some thoughts. Sarah. Maybe Sarah didn't ever get across. Unlikely: Heller's forgeries are, of course, good. So, out there, somewhere, Sarah is looking for Gloria. Bureaucrats are not above dishonesty and deceit—Gloria's path may have crossed Sarah's several times already, the women may have sat in the same chair at different moments both waiting to be quickly rebuffed. If Sarah were looking for her, where would she look? (Or maybe the bureaucrat is on the right side after all—the business card he gave her, maybe Sarah carries the same one, has already gone to the charity house, is waiting for her there, patiently.) Gloria's documents declare her to be a psychologist who works at the Institute. That means the Institute is open again. Sarah would at least have left a message for her there. It is also the only place Gloria can remember where she had ever chosen to belong.

She applies make-up, trying to remember whether, when she and Werner used to meet, she wore lipstick, and how. She tweezers away three new hairs that are spoiling the perfect arch of her eyebrows. Werner used to take her to the cinema; he liked her to wear a cashmere jumper, beneath which he would stroke her breasts. Afterwards it was a short walk to a borrowed room, where she arranged to have an orgasm at much the same time as him.

Gaily, with a handful of copper coins, she tips the crone whose towels she has soiled with mascara. Gloria goes quickly back upstairs and leaves the train station and carries her load towards the Psychological Institute.

5

The Psychological Institute has, had, high glass windows. The only previous time Gloria had gone to the Institute without knowing what to expect had been when she had taken her brother there one night. The building had intimidated Daniel, as it had been designed to do—it was as solid and respectable as a bank or grand hotel, except for its windows, which promised mystery.

Gloria had walked Daniel down the long corridors overlit by strips of neon on the white ceilings. The windows attracted sunlight during the day and cold at night. She hadn't been able to resist boasting as she walked him through: This is the depth psychology area, the largest part of the building, both in terms of floor space and personnel. *Where you fiddle about with people's souls.* Daniel was nervous. His scepticism about anything unfamiliar was always easily unmasked. Precisely, Gloria had said, relishing his clearing of his throat, the anxious way he tapped the walls going past.

She had led him quickly past Werner's unfashionable domain, two small rooms where lights still burned. *What goes on in there?* She had told him: It's the experimental psychology room, the men in there like to use electricity and chemicals instead of sympathy. *Sounds interesting*, her brother had remarked, to annoy her. No, not interesting, deluded, and, fortunately, out of favour. One or two zealots only.

Gloria took Daniel into Mr Mouse's office, sat him down on the couch, picked up the apparatus Mr Mouse had left out for her to use. *If I'm impressed I'll introduce you to men of influence*, Daniel said. No, said Gloria, the point isn't to impress. It purports to be an instrument to dig out the truth. Now sit still. *What's that?* Don't worry. Only a stopwatch.

She was fighting for Mr Mouse. Gloria was helping her supervisor compile data for his battle with the Assistant Director, who was an adherent of beards and word association tests and quotas for newcomers. (A quota which, with Mr Mouse's complicity, Gloria had evaded by passing as an other.) *We have to strike back*, Mr Mouse had said. *Hit the enemy where it hurts most, in theory.*

The blinds were up, the night looked liquid, and brother and sister enacted a dramatic dialogue. He was inhibited at first, scowling, slow, but even a malcontent likes to have attention paid to the bruises on his psyche. Gloria read words to her brother from the Assistant Director's favourite trigger list, and Daniel replied with increasingly passionate one-word speeches that she transcribed along with the reaction time.

G: Dance.
D: Not.

G: Threaten.
D: Bad.
G: Blue.
D: Lake.
G: Bake.
D: Pie!
G: White.
D: Snow.
G: Doctor.
D: Quack.
G: Brother.
D: Sister.
G: Dead.
D: Dog.

After the hundredth trigger word (Insult) had been answered (*Us*, 1 second) Gloria clicked the stopwatch button for the final time. Daniel sat back on the master's couch and wiped his forehead.

Nothing here, she had written, except for, maybe, the length of time the subject took to answer 'white' with 'snow' (1.9 seconds) seems to indicate that the subconscious has been plumbed. This psychologist is not convinced of the test's value as a diagnostic or therapeutic tool. The same material could be gathered more quickly and in more sympathetic fashion. One is tempted to say that the primary use of the test is to implant a (delusional?) belief in the subject that the practitioner is possessed of a scientific method.

The subject though was of a different mind. *That was quite gruelling. Interesting though. I said dog, didn't I?*

when you said dead. Obvious what that means. What's your diagnosis?

An emotional character type. The presence of a recent trauma as well as more from childhood. It might be useful to talk further about snow. But I have to finish writing my conclusions.

Perhaps, she wrote, the test might be performed again, with the same subject, when the initial emotion aroused by the death of the subject's father might have faded.

Father's funeral had taken place the previous day, on the other side of the world. He had died a week before in his swimming pool in the west, possibly alone, probably not.

Gloria and Daniel had received the same letter about father's death from the same lawyer. *He'll charge twice for this*, said Daniel, infuriated, impressed. Gloria had also received two cards of commiseration without return addresses from women friends of her father who each made the unlikely claim to have fond memories of Gloria as a child.

The cause of death was a blocked valve of the heart. In Daniel's version, narcotics had been involved, and alcohol, and starlets, two. *Sisters I bet. Twins. And outside interests, accountants who know all the tricks.*

Maybe his heart just gave out. He wasn't in the habit of using it very often. Maybe he had a fond thought and died from the effort.

Ha! her brother said. (It was his customary way of announcing the defeat of his opponent when something had been said that was too absurd, self-defeating or specious to argue against.) He had then looked challengingly at her as he reached for the final piece of cinnamon pie.

Daniel began his lawsuit against the estate and its executor a few days later. (*Don't worry, I'm looking after your interests too, we're in this together. You'll get what's coming to you.*) He responded to his father's death with a quickening of libido. Gloria's response was sentimental. She reread her childhood diaries. She wanted quite badly to be hugged, and held.

It was towards the end of the evening of father's funeral. Mother was clearing away the supper things (and keeping secret whatever emotions had been aroused in her); stepfather was sitting proud in his armchair, silently smug that he had outlasted husband number one—whatever people might say, he was alive and the supposed better man was dead in the ground, Mr Glamour covered by earth; and brother and sister were both eyeing up the last piece of pie.

Daniel took the piece for himself. He chewed off the first mouthfuls, waited, with crumbs on his parted lips, for Gloria to demand her share. Gloria didn't. She found it reassuring that at least Daniel was getting what he thought he wanted.

It was then that she bribed him with a girlfriend's telephone number to come to the Institute the following night. And now the test was over, Gloria's conclusions summarised, Poldie's number passed over, the rest of the Institute was silent, brother and sister were still in one another's company and Gloria stuttered as she tried to make a request.

What?

It was very hard to say; to make the speech was almost as uncomfortable for Gloria as the emotion that lay behind it.

Hug me.

Which was how Mr Mouse found the pair when he arrived in the room. Sister being awkwardly held by older brother, Daniel patting Gloria insistently on the back, as if she had choked something.

Mr Mouse showed himself at his best in moments of extreme emotion. His personality grew. It was only in everyday life that he proved himself to be something of a disappointment. He relieved relieved Daniel, and the rest of the night was spent at Mr Mouse's apartment, Gloria and Mr Mouse awake in the bedroom, sometimes hugging, sometimes taking it in turns to remember childhood moments that had once demanded to be treated as significant.

The date with Poldie was a failure, doomed, like Daniel's suit against father's estate: Gloria lost a friend and Daniel didn't gain a lover. And Mr Mouse's campaign against the Assistant Director had ended when the Assistant Director became Acting Director and Mr Mouse fled the Institute and the city. There was one unforeseen consequence of the psychological exercise: some months later, Daniel introduced his sister to his boss, the tycoon Solomon Heller, now dead.

Gloria approaches the Institute, broken window glass crunches beneath her shoes.

6

Says Werner:

Fear, we discover, is the therapy. Not the shock, but the anticipation of shock. Not the insulin coma itself but fear of it. Not the metrazol but the fear of metrazol, the awful moment before syringe pierces flesh. The swinging bed, the surprise iced bath. The electric-shock machine, the patient screams, the psychiatrist winces, and hope is on the way.

Why then go through with it? says Gloria. If it's just fear, why not cultivate the emotion without its consummation? Why the coma or the metrazol or the electric shock?

Because then, says sensible Werner, *the patient wouldn't be truly frightened. We tried pretending—the emotion without the consummation, as you put it—apparatus, nasty lights, rough handling, but that didn't work. Somehow the patients manage to communicate experience to one another without language or even contact. Somehow it became known that nothing bad happened, was only theatre.*

It's called psychic infection, Gloria does not say. That's how your patients communicate. I'm trying to use it right now. Can't you hear me? My psyche is yelling to yours right now. It's shrieking.

The theory began, of course, I'm sure you're aware, in the observation that epilepsy and schizophrenia won't coexist in the same psyche . . . ?

Of course, says Gloria, hoping in her tone she has expressed boredom, impatience, the complacency of old knowledge.

Perhaps overdone: Werner looks at her sharply and oddly, then resumes:

But we are moving beyond that. The beauty of research. Empirical knowledge supersedes theory. If you could see the eyes, Gloria, something magical takes place. An astonishing experience, almost erotic, the sure anticipation of shock and terror and oblivion, the fear and the cure all bound up together. Excuse me. I can become quite evangelical on the subject.

Werner smiles. His eyes gleam beneath finger-smeared spectacles. He had once been her least regarded lover. Everything had been simple then, a libidinal transaction that had created no dependency, on either side.

How I wish you could see . . .

And now he is a scientist out of the movies, white lab coat, strand of sandy hair drooping. The magnified look in his eyes of conviction and excitement and certainty. In a moment, he will mention the times lived in, the irony that the conditions that have brought so much harm to so many are at least helping the mad into lucidity.

The ironical thing, of course, is that—

May I see the lab? I should like to.

She really should not like to. She can think of few things that she would less prefer to do. Except, now, to leave. The Institute is a safe place. Despite its battered exterior, its missing windows, the cold corridors. Here in Werner's office everything is reassuring. The white wooden desk piled with papers, ampoules, coffee cups, measuring jugs, books. Wire trays containing scholarly papers, correspondence from overseas. High wooden stools, one comfortable chair, in which Werner now sits, rocking gently to and fro. Here in this dusty office Gloria can breathe.

Werner's hand lifts to stroke his freshly shaved chin. His skin had always been delightfully soft, perfectly pale, unblemished, no fat on him anywhere, the body of a schoolboy athlete.

I don't know. It's not really . . .

I am alone! I don't know where else to go! Heller is dead! is what Gloria wants to scream. Do you know what it is like? To help bring about a man's extinction? Just because the event is all too common does not make my own part in this one any easier to bear. He trusted me. He thought I might save him. I could not, and neither could my psychology, which I have rejected, but which, nonetheless, I prefer to yours.

Please. I should love to.

Show him the flicker of something nostalgic. It would be wrong, tactically, to try to seduce this man, but show him the memory of seduction, a ghost of pleasure, and . . . ?

I don't know.

He strokes his pen. One almost expects a little drip of pale ink to seep out, like the precursor of seminal fluid.

(I'm hungry! I feel like a wounded beast in the jungle. Or like a gangster in one of those movies we used to enjoy seeing together, when desire was being stimulated. Or simulated.)

It sounds as if you are on the verge of doing some remarkable things—

Verge?! I am already there. Come with me. Would you like to leave your bag here?

No. I should like to carry it with me.

Another strange look from Werner—she has become eccentric, but she probably always seemed so to him. Her bag is getting heavier. Whenever she puts it down anywhere damp it takes in water. She hasn't detected where the hole is yet. Her ball gown smells of the river. The Case Notes of Solomon Heller are becoming sodden and dark at the edges. Perhaps she should show the document now to Werner. Look! This is what I have been doing, I know it's a very different avenue to your research, but all the same there are points along the way to interest everyone. Aren't there? No, probably not. The subject's self-annihilation is probably the most effective refutation of the treatment.

As you like. Wear this.

A little green clip. The word *Authorised* printed on it in our conquerors' language.

The colour changes every day. Security purposes. Hold on. Maybe you should wear this too.

White lab coat. She slips it on over her clothes; Werner helps her pin the green clip to the left breast pocket and, she is pleased to hear, something changes in his breathing.

He leads her along hard corridors, she too is a scientist or at least can walk like one. Footsteps echo. Identical doors are passed, one after another, painted blue with little square windows covered by security grilles. This is where she had done her training. Every door is labelled *Experimental Psychology* now. In one of these rooms she had met her supervisor, at first only once a week. Mr Mouse and she sat closer together as the weeks went by; a mutual fascination for the occult workings of the mind climaxed with her body finding his.

It's all very different. The last time I was here depth psychology was still the vogue.

That was a decadent instrument for decadent times. The newcomer science. Renounced long ago. Where have you been?

She quite wants to tell him. Inside her is an urge to talk, to confess, to grab a witness by the arm and not let him go. But maybe Werner is going to offer her a place here, in this haven, asylum in the asylum.

Where is everyone? There used to be more psychologists than neuroses here.

For a moment Werner looks almost embarrassed.

Certain people have been relocated. Quite useful really. You'll be surprised by the tranquillity of the place.

Werner opens a number of locks and bolts. He steps aside for Gloria to enter the lab ahead of him. This unconsidered courtesy makes her feel like weeping.

First is a kind of dormitory. Tranquil is not the word she would have chosen. Patients are exhausted, lying at mad angles, muscular rictus, teeth exposed. Some are asleep or pretending to be. Nurses stand at beds, jotting notes down on clipboards.

You see? It's not really like a hospital ward at all.

You mean it's not decorated like one.

Plants are dying in earthenware pots. The lilac-blue walls are decorated with film posters. In this difficult city one is rewarded for being mad by the sight of Igo Sym's face. Amazing the therapeutic value of the glamour of his face, for her anyway. On a poster behind the door Sym's face is set into martial mode, stern, unforgiving, magnificent. He watches Gloria and eventually her eyes reluctantly withdraw, can't quite bear to—another look back at him and then away.

Where do you get your subjects from?

A mixture. Rather good cross-section as it happens. Civil prisoners. Soldiers who have been through it. Prisoners of war. A few administrators even. And a number of long-term lunatics of course.

Newcomers?

Well, no, I wouldn't have thought so, perhaps though. You can never rule it out. Some might be on forged papers. Why do you ask?

To attract suspicion to myself of course. To make you puzzled by my question and then you will have to think harder and further about it and then you will examine my features more closely than you were ever tempted to before and maybe you will ask me some cunning questions that drive me towards confession until finally I fall upon your chest spilling secrets and tears and in that still moment before police and cataclysm I might feel purged.

But Werner has the happy quality of being able to ignore everything that he does not immediately understand or find relevant.

Let me show you the insulin shock therapy room. The patient is medicated with sufficient insulin to shock his body into a coma. Fifteen or so minutes later a sugar solution is intravenously applied, with subsequent startling therapeutic results. But as I say, I'm not convinced that the physical shock is of much greater value than the psychic fear of coma.

He leads Gloria towards the insulin shock therapy room. She touches each table she goes past. She can't get rid of the fear that if she goes into the insulin shock therapy room she will never be allowed out again.

I don't know if you're familiar with the latest statistics? The suicide rate has gone quite dramatically down. Particularly in the forbidden zone. That's in line with my theories, further research is needed of course, but what I think we're seeing is the therapeutic value of fear on the biggest possible scale. The healing, brutal shock of occupation. Although, also, I have to be fair on this, it might also have something to do with the shortage of bullets and cyanide pills.

People can always jump out of windows.

I suppose so.

Even though this supports his argument it is not the response he wanted. He wants admiration, applause.

It seems an eminently sensible thing to do.

She could plead with him: Let me in here. I need help. If you won't let me keep this lab coat, and this clip badge that magically changes colour every day—if you won't let me be a practitioner here, then let me volunteer. I don't need insulin shock therapy. My body doesn't have to be medicated into a coma, then wrenched out with sugar, intravenously applied. Look: my body can go into awful paralysis all by itself; my eyes too can look mad and empty. To sleep and recuperate in one of these army beds, to have only dying flowers to look at and Igo Sym's face and doctors and nurses to report my symptoms to, heavenly. Please, Werner.

I'd like to go now. Thank you for your time. It's been fascinating.

His hand rests on the door to the insulin treatment room. He is puzzled, even a little hurt. He hasn't yet shown her his proudest accomplishment and already she is making to leave.

She can't ask him for anything. Not only is she unsure what effect the clinical application of fear would have on her, either as agent or subject—she rather fears, as it were, that it might have the opposite effect to the one desired and predicted, a counter-force that will push her out of this hopeful hysteria into madness, foam-flecked, delusional— but also she cannot bear to ask Werner for a favour. Once, he and she had a relationship. It was based on equal or equivalent need and it left no surplus. Nothing exists of it any longer. Gloria can better imagine her brother granting her a favour than this smooth diligent young man.

7

Are you a charity case?

No.

Are you a charity case?

I'm just hungry.

You are welcome to come in for supper but after that you'll have to leave.

I have nowhere else to go.

You must be a charity case then.

No.

(Why doesn't she just swallow her pride and admit it?— Yes yes, I'm a charity case, I surrender, give me a bed, look after me please.)

The doorkeeper is a long narrow individual under a long dark overcoat and a fur aviator's hat with earflaps hanging loosely down. He hops quite high from foot to foot, earflaps flapping, in order to warm or to amuse himself. She is losing his attention. The dilemma she presents is not an interesting one.

Supper in the refectory. Followed by prayers. After that you'll have to leave.

That puts me on the streets after curfew.

We only take charity cases.

He waves Gloria into a raggedy troop of other indigents and penitents that is marched over a wet yellow-
cobblestoned courtyard into the refectory. Gloria picks
up a bowl from a pile, joins a queue for food. And is
barked-shoved into a second queue. Men and women have
to line up separately. Modesty passes for virtue here.

It has come to this. Under a high ceiling, cracked plaster,
the rustle of pigeons and vice in the rafters, surrounded by
lunatics and prostitutes in donated overcoats over glamorous remnants, waiting to be fed by piety. Because Sarah
has not kept the rendezvous Gloria is here, because the
bureaucrat will not allow Gloria entrance to her own
destiny Gloria is here, because she does not have the taste
for another night on the river bank (she assumes something
dreadful will happen to her there, violent, unrecuperable)
Gloria is here, because Sarah might be here Gloria is here,
because Werner is mad for science she is here, because
they are there she is here; because everyone she loves
is unattainably elsewhere she has walked to the western
suburbs to an address printed on a business card, she has
waited in cold and wet outside a charity house for the
door to open, and now she is waiting in line for food with
another woman's breath spicy-hot on her neck.

One is meant to receive food with a simper. The man
whose wooden spoon is poised dripping over Gloria's
waiting bowl doesn't continue with his movement. His
eyes flash a warning through thick spectacles. There is
something nastier about this one, apart from which he
looks exactly the same as the rest. Smug angular angels in

sombre clothing and round-framed spectacles and greasy dark hair, like holy librarians whose piety of purpose somehow doesn't preclude the erotic. Gloria is hungry. Gloria wants food. Something oaty drips in front of her on to a muddy wet floor.

Gloria does not feel gratitude nor does she wish to express it. The woman with alcoholic breath is growing impatient. Phlegm passes from one internal channel to another and is grumpily swallowed.

Say please.

Gloria smiles stonily. She does not choose to say please.

Say please.

The spoon threatens to withdraw. She receives an elbow in the ribs from the woman behind.

I can't hear you.

Please.

That wasn't so hard, was it?

He slops her an extra spoonful as reward. She can't remember ever hating anyone quite so much. The emotion pierces her.

Gloria manages to squeeze on to the end of a bench in time for grace to be performed. She watches the holy librarians at the top table bless the food with eyes cast down, slender uncalloused hands tilting in at the fingertips like sails, thin lips silently moving. Then a sudden exhalation of praise, spoons are allowed away from tables into bowls.

The food is chillingly bad. Around her people complain, about the food, about the weather, about them, about the newcomers, about luck. Gloria stares at the dirt around her fingernails which is so unlikely, crusted, impossible to remove. The grumbling diminishes; a mood catches her, it's spreading through the room, an anticipation, as if a seance is about to take place.

A door opens, mouths and eyes widen, hearts lift, holy librarians sigh, adore, Gloria hears whispered all around the sainted word, *Madame*. Gloria stretches her neck to see, she half stands, her own spoon falls to the table— in, holding by the hand a small boy, the woman comes. *Madame*.

It is Zosia, the 'Prince's virgin, changed.

She wears a black headscarf and a long black dress made of some rough mortifying fabric that doesn't quite hide her body. No trace of baby fat on her any more. Her skin and hair seem paler than before, almost translucent. Dressing for sorrow suits her very well. Zosia would, Gloria is sure, inflame the 'Prince' more than ever.

The boy beside her is dressed all in black also. He acts very proud, proprietorial, he stands very straight. Barely more than a toddler, he has copper-coloured hair, a solemn wide face, enormous blue eyes.

Gloria's line of vision to the virgin is blocked. She stands up, someone roughly shoves her down again, she stands up again, takes a step, sees Zosia sitting surrounded by librarians—male or female, it's impossible sometimes to distinguish—sipping soup, nodding at something just said. Gloria tries to approach, the way is denied her. A holy librarian sends her back to her table. He is implacable. *No.* Gloria spends the rest of the meal failing to catch Madame's eye.

Zosia and the boy simultaneously dab identical pretty mouths. A fat woman comes in to take the boy away. He puts up some kind of struggle that he obviously knows to be doomed, but bravely he fights on to the end. His lower lip protrudes, trembles. Madame grants him the concession of a kiss. He stands on tiptoes to receive it, fighting with his own smile now. Gloria stands along with him. She feels her own lips mimicking a kiss. And she is then caught up in a sudden mass choreography.

A screech of chairs, bowls go to one table, spoons to another, librarians cluster in scholarly circles, charity cases troop into two lines—Gloria is helpless, the boy departs with his nurse, Madame Zosia is gone, and Gloria is across the courtyard, damp dangerous cobblestones, into a chapel, mass worship with the dispossessed.

Once, long before, when Gloria—or a girl precursor with an earlier, more obvious name—was young, there was a windy Sunday, no one else in the house (father already gone, stepfather yet to arrive, mother elsewhere, brother busy with some doomed scheme) and the new maid, dressed in the clothes she wore for dancing and family visits in the country, left the kitchen, took Gloria's hand, led her away from the apartment in a manner that couldn't be refused or questioned. A long walk along unfamiliar streets, the doubt rising, the discomfort in her legs increasing, the complaints beginning to be voiced and then abruptly silenced when she realised she was being led towards the heart of the great forbidden, a church. Tugged along now, up the aisle, Gloria's head bloody with images, gory schoolyard gossip, the promises of torture that her brother had made her, *That is what the Others do to Us in there . . . if you get caught . . . secret rites . . .*

The maid's rough hand gripped Gloria's neck, made her kneel in front of a huge Messiah on a desolate cross. *This*, said the maid, *is God and He loves you even though your forefathers killed Him and you mustn't tell your mother.* He dripped gilt and blood and pain; if the maid had not been watching her Gloria would have wept, at the shame and pity of Him. *Now stay here.* Gloria stayed. She apologised, she grieved, she waited for the maid to be finished kneeling in a wooden cabinet, confessing behind dark velvet.

Nausea and terror. Gloria refused to hold the maid's hand on the way home. When she got to the apartment, Gloria immediately went to her bed and sobbed for the rest of the day and night and refused all food and was indifferent even to brother Daniel's taunts. Gloria dates her rescue fantasies from this point. Other girls applied bandages to dolls and painted on tomato juice. Gloria searched for broken birds to mend and illnesses to cure. (If Mr Mouse were here she would demolish his notion of episode selves with this one anecdote: in that church, misnamed, was Gloria, unalterably. She wishes Mr Mouse were here, and not just for purposes of refutation.)

It's a libidinal group ecstasy of the soul that excludes Gloria's. She moves her lips to approximate the words of unknown prayers and hymns; she inspects every woman's face for signs of Sarah; she pretends there is a view out of the bricked-up window but can't think of what it might be; and whenever Zosia—who is at the front of the chapel, with her spiritual bodyguard of librarians proudly surrounding—might be looking in her direction Gloria the hypocrite stands a little straighter, tries to feign the enthusiasm of the divine spark in her countenance and bearing, makes her mouth appear to bellow grateful pieties. Zosia gives no sign of seeing her; and anyway Gloria's head is now filling with sense-pictures of the chapel and all its occupants consumed by fire—except, miraculously, herself: only Gloria is untouched by conflagration—the screams hurt her ears, the stench of burning flesh is surprisingly invigorating; she carries Zosia out to a garden safety, she runs in again, leaving the holy librarians to last.

A holy librarian is delivering a sermon. In a dull pleased voice he or she informs the congregation that everyone is low. Everyone is filthy. Everyone is degraded. (Except, it seems, Zosia.) Some of the charity cases are drowsing, but most sway in accord, amen every line, give thanks to a merciful God for being generously allowed the spiritual distinction of sinking so very low.

When the sermon is over, holy librarians cluster around Zosia, not daring quite to touch, but standing close as if saintliness is communicable merely by proximity, like disease. A librarian inclines his head towards his mistress, whispers; Zosia rewards him with a faint touch on his shoulder. Gloria makes towards her. The way is blocked. She tries a different way. She is blocked again. Has Zosia even noticed her? Gloria tries dancing. She hops up and down, hoping in this way to attract Madame. She tries shouting. *Madame! Zosia!* Too much noise, too many people in the way. Zosia is leaving the chapel and Gloria has inspected every face and none belongs to Sarah and she is being approached by the doorkeeper. He at least has not forgotten her.

I would like to speak to Madame. It's a personal matter.

I'll show you the way out.

I would like to stay.

You want a bed for the night.

I have nowhere else to go.

Do you want a bed for the night?

Yes. I am a charity case.

Gloria is bathed, disinfected, towelled, sneered at, collectivised, humbled. She is marched twice over mossy cobblestones, she ends up kneeling beside an iron bed in Dormitory 3, which is hardly preferable to the dormitory room at the Psychological Institute.

More prayers before the charity machine can be switched off for the night. Gloria kneels, presses her forehead to cold bedstead metal. A bucket beside her holds a residue of murky water.

And then the candles are extinguished, the charity cases are permitted to climb into bed, the dormitory door is locked. The outline of army beds fades into blackness; the snores and moans get louder. She tries to summon up the image of her and Mr Mouse together in his kitchen, he preparing the stew, she sitting on the wooden laboratory stool or laying out the crockery, but it doesn't work, the image doesn't hold, and she tries to fill in the details but she is already so tired or so removed from her own past that she keeps forgetting the name of kitchen implements. She is in a room suitable only for prayer and sleep and masturbation, which reminds her of Heller and makes her weep.

8

She is woken by sobbing. At first she thinks it's her own crying that has woken her, and she lies there, eyes closed; the sadness she's listening to accords in some way with the dream that she's just had and which she's trying to retrieve but it's receding so fast that she has already lost all sight of it. She thinks dead birds might have been involved in some way, but it's gone.

Gloria touches her face. No tears. Her skin is dry. The sobbing continues. Shrill gulping sounds of desolation. For want of anything better to do, she opens her eyes. The room slowly rebuilds itself into Dormitory 3. The sound could be coming out of any one of these beds. She goes back to sleep. She dreams of dead birds.

And is woken a second time by her bedcover being pulled harshly away, a bright light, hands clapping. Two librarians work along the line of beds, wrenching charity cases back muttering into the dry-mouthed world of piety and praise.

Gloria stares at the ceiling, manages to pull herself out of bed. She pursues the nearest holy librarian.

Excuse me. Excuse me. I wish to see Madame, Zosia—*Madame.*

She is scorned, laughed at. *Of course you would.*

It's a personal matter.

Breakfast. Then prayers.

Gloria looks around for the single friendly face that will alleviate this situation. There is no friendly face. So she looks for someone worse off than her, a timid spirit, more easily bruised. The women of Dormitory 3 rouse, stretch, belch, rub fingers inside mouths, finger-comb hair and inspect the results on the bedsheets. Woollen cardigans and skirts are pulled over satin undergarments. Everyone is more malicious and resourceful than Gloria. Golden hair, beautiful in the silvery light, is pulled back, dressed high. Shivery hands apply cosmetics to unwashed faces. Gloria returns to where she slept. She wishes her nearest neighbour a good morning and asks about how she might check if a message has been left for her, and who sleeps in dormitories 1 and 2 and how many more dormitories there are. All she gets in response is an incredulous stare from the woman, who then looks away, hitches up her stockings and secures the tops with string.

Gloria sits on the bed. The women of Dormitory 3 march towards breakfast. Gloria's stomach rumbles, her body announcing its first needs of the day. Gloria gets out her own make-up and starts to apply it to what no longer feels like her own face. Then she will attend to her hair and then she will lie back on the bed, where she will remain until someone comes to rescue her.

Or she will eat first. Resistance is easier on a full stomach.

*   *   *

The refectory is full. Holy librarians ladle out the same kind of food as before. Yesterday's dinner is today's breakfast. Gloria goes to the correct queue, picks up a bowl from the appropriate place, and looks to the top table, where Madame sits, unapproachable. A portrait of Henry shines in this room, she hadn't noticed it the night before: he wears medieval armour, a halo around his head; a shaft of light pierces the armour to his frail aesthetic heart.

Gloria looks at Zosia and Zosia looks straight back at Gloria, the slightest movement of her head is Gloria's rejection. A holy librarian whispers. Zosia nods and touches the scarf that's knotted at her throat. Another librarian blocks Gloria's view.

Gloria leaves the charity house when the charity house is still at prayers. A pair of librarians watch her go. She walks, because that is what she has become accustomed to do, until she reaches the City Theatre.

Theatre Square has been bombed. The Town Hall is in ruins, there's an immense absence where its middle used to be. The arcade of shops is still open for business, selling jewellery and fancy hats. And the theatre is still grand; the damage it has suffered makes it grander, ancient, monumental. Scaffolding obscures the turrets, the balcony. Gymnasts balance, hammering, on the roof. Gloria affects to be a connoisseur of restoration work, her look appraises the different colour plasters being applied to the colonnades, the not quite perfect brickwork of reconstruction.

The poster outside the entrance is different to the one at the train station. The forty suitors of Madame Ilona quail

in comical poses in the face of her again naked beauty.
Gloria is here with no plan beyond coincidence. Igo Sym
might be passing, even stars have to get to work, use doors
like people do, and he might see her and then . . . ? She
doesn't know. He once said she could count on him, he
might even have been telling the truth.

She goes into the theatre. It is too cold to do one's
pretending outdoors. A young man with floppy hair sits
in the box office. He condescends to speak to her.

The première for Madame Ilona *is sold out.*

I'd like to make an appointment to meet Mr Sym.

Insane that she thinks she can just put herself forward
like that.

Oh yes?

It's a personal matter.

Really.

Tell him that it's Gloria who wants to see him.

He shrugs his shoulders.

Gloria. Not the astonishing one.

Gloria who's not the astonishing one wants to see him.
An alopecic usher carries the message slowly past a
velvet rope, through a curtain in the wall, she hears him
walk up hidden stairs. Around are the usual preparations
for a new show—technicians carrying lights, a mother
comforting her daughter, chorus girls with cigarettes and
broken heels, lesbians and corsets. And a bald usher in red
corduroy uniform who returns, pushes aside a curtain and
a rope, and announces:

He says he can see you.

Now?

172

It can't be now. She hadn't been ready for now. This isn't what she expected. She is accustomed to failure, to resistance, to being rebuffed. She isn't prepared.

Now. I'll take you through to him.

On he goes and she follows after, velvet rope unhitched, curtain pushed aside, up a curved staircase into where the crush bar used to be and has now been made into dressing rooms, she glimpses pots of cosmetics under harsh round lights; the usher pulls her away from a broom cupboard, he makes another turn, up more stairs, portraits of tragedians glower, along a corridor, and to a handsome door on which the usher knocks twice.

Just here. Wait till he calls.

The Managing Director deserves no less a door. Dark wood, it permits her to touch it. A man's voice, not Sym's, is talking fast behind it. She imagines Igo Sym listening, the shape of his mouth, the cut of his clothes, his smile, his voice, his warmth. She is more nervous than she has ever been.

Fantasy: Gloria and her ideal father are about to be reunited. The door will open, he will envelop her, his arms surround her, a kiss that tastes of cologne and lake air, and nothing bad can ever happen to her ever again.

Fear: Her hair is too wild, her face looks ludicrous, painted. He will notice her fingernails, be disgusted, fastidious Sym, by the cracks in her skin filled for ever with river dirt.

Fear: Igo Sym is not the same man as before. War has done terrible things to the city, to buildings, to people, think what it will have done to him. Consider all the parts he might have lost. He was never young; he might have failed to remain beautiful.

Fear: The lack is all with her—Sym will be as perfect as ever, and she is the failure, who has not matched up to the image that sustains in his too courteous memory. Gloria pictures his expression, the awful moment before disappointment is expertly concealed, a horrifying look of pity.

Fantasy: She has just walked her circuitous path to true love. Forget Mr Mouse, forget the 'Prince'. Forget Heller, Sarah. Forget us, them, the others. The door opens, miraculously the city dissolves, the space between Gloria and Igo disappears, she is in his arms.

Suddenly the door does open, a man rushes out. He stands in the corridor, a forlorn whimper leaves him. He wears an outsized hat, an angry little brush of a moustache—the face belongs to one of the posters from outside, this is the actor who plays Drunk Walter. She recognises him from somewhere else too but she's not sure where, a movie maybe, she can imagine him as a drunken guest at a rural comedy wedding. And she is sure—with a thrill of a more elemental recognition—that he is a newcomer too, passing, like her. He stands in the corridor, holding on to his hat; he looks desolate. But then he sees Gloria and she can be an audience so he immediately becomes a performer again. He crosses his eyes madly. He pushes his head at her. His disturbing face fills her view.

Do you believe I can wiggle my ears at will?

Laughter in the corridor. Admirers from nowhere gather. Chorus girls and dapper gents ready to express delight.

The comic grabs his own ears with his large hands and pulls each this way and that. Laughter from the retinue. Applause.

See? I can wiggle my ears at will. My name is Damecki. I can also simulate the noise a telephone makes.

Why does he pick on her? Because he can. Because something had made him sad and self-piteous and this is the way he returns himself to himself. Damecki proves his boast, his lips thrum together, several important types glance anxiously around before remembering that there is no telephone in this corridor, and there's the comic's retinue laughing and oh look, should've known, it's Damecki up to his tricks again.

Excuse me. I have an appointment.

Damecki, with a flourish, wipes something away from his eye and knocks on Sym's door. Sym calls to enter—that voice anyway is unchanged in its power over her. Damecki and his retinue wander away, chuckling. Gloria dares to push open the door and step inside.

Sym is behind a desk, beneath a window. He is smoking a cigar. His hair is greyer than before. His face is, if anything, more handsome. He looks up.

His eyes open wider, his mouth (thin upper lip, sensuous lower) pulls into the familiar gorgeous smile. The cigar is dropped into a crystal ashtray, he stands, leaves the desk, approaches her—she hasn't yet moved away or towards—the black tunic he wears is cinched in at the waist, the black trousers billow out above the knees, the black boots are high up his calves. This uniform he wears is utterly dismaying.

Reunion, a kiss—his lips glide against her cheeks; hers, in turn, in consternation, pucker against his nose. He holds her arms, he takes a step back to smile fondly and inspect. She had thought him a patriot, on horseback, ready with cutlass and charisma to push back their armies. And after the defeat? Lounge suit. Heavy overcoat and wide-brimmed hat. Conspiratorial twilight meetings by the linden trees. In the strange magic of this time he is transformed. Virgins are accompanied by children. Neurasthenes are pictured as medieval war heroes. These are miracles she can swallow whole but she cannot accept this. Apart from the cap, which sits atop a marble bust on the mantelpiece, Sym is impeccably dressed in their uniform. He kisses her again just as she makes another attempt to speak. His lips are salty.

How pleased I am to see you!

Major Sym?

Colonel.

Despite himself, despite all his self-control and self-possession and tantric skills, he preens, just a little.

Excuse me. Colonel.

Come with me. Let me show you around my theatre.

He puts on his cap. Their eagle insignia reflects in the shiny black visor. His mouth smiles because it has to, his grey eyes are alert for admiration and desire.

And he steers her, Sym's strong hand on the nape of Gloria's neck, into a tour of his theatre.

9

Workers are everywhere, most not quite working. Everyone stops when Sym goes by and he has a word for everybody. Programme sellers and commissionaires and flower girls and lighting men and scene shifters and juvenile leads and character actors carrying ivory-tipped canes and lavatory cleaners with buckets. Each one smiles to be greeted by him. Wherever he goes the star bestows improved sense of self. And all the while he is keeping a conversation alive with Gloria: he describes the restoration of the theatre; she is encouraged to praise the splendour of the auditorium; he points out the brocaded cloth in the presidential box; she asks a question about the actors on the stage below, waits for the confusing emotions to lava away.

He tells her again at least twice how good it is to see her. She tells him he looks very fine in his uniform. He looks sharply at her. He never could detect when she was making fun of him; narcissists seldom have much of a sense of humour, even those as ungrandiose as Sym.

One makes accommodations. Things aren't as straightforward as might appear. I could get you a job here, if you needed one.

It already seems somewhat overpopulated.

One does what one can.

This might be his way of apology. If it were not him in this job, he is saying, it would be someone less scrupulous, who would take his duty less seriously, who would elicit far fewer smiles, who would be far less kind. Or he might just be warning her not to refuse his patronage.

A lighting man is suddenly winched up the curtain high above. Gloria shivers.

Are you still psychologising?

No.

Might you start again? One patient perhaps? From the old days . . . ?

She doesn't want her surprise to show. Is this a joke? Maybe he can do self-mockery after all. (That could be a glint of it he's making shine in his eyes—or he's just acting.) *You see*, he pretends to be saying, *I don't take myself so seriously as all that!*

She can't psychologise him. He must realise this. He wears their uniform. Can't you see my dismay? taste it? The counter-transference would kill us both.

It's all charlatanry and chicanery. I have retired. I don't do it any more.

Down on the stage, a boyish girl in a man's suit strolls briskly on to the stage. She sits on a chair, lights a cigarette, inhales, blows a smoke ring. She pushes aside the field glasses hanging around her neck and releases the top five buttons on her white shirt. Dreamily she inserts a hand, pulls apart the shirt-front to expose her breasts, and

smokes. Her hair has been roughly cropped, tufts stick up
at the crown of her head.

Is this Madame Ilona?

Her daughter.

A huntsman, accompanied by a huge staghound, bounds
on to the stage. He strikes a pose, lifting a monocle to
inspect the ingénue. She notices him, is abashed, apologetic,
perhaps pleased—she moves away from the chair, he sits
upon it, she is too modest to order her clothing. She offers
a cigar to the huntsman. *Master*, she sighs, and bows. He
takes the cigar, puts it into his mouth, evinces a pleasant
surprise at the taste, waits to be offered a flame—and the
director claps his hands. A stage manager comes on and
draws white chalk crosses at the actors' feet. A clarinet in
the orchestra pit plays a quick hunting air. The ingénue
hugs her jacket tightly around herself and sneezes.

The lighting man winches himself down from the ceiling.
The huntsman strokes the belly of his dog. The dog's eyes
are the same pink colour as the girl's nipples.

What are the field glasses for?

*Ah, you'll have to see the whole show for that. What do
you think?*

A little unsubtle in its effects.

One does what one can.

You said that before.

Did I? You see? You see? I need you.

(Is this seduction or just extended courtesy?)

The huntsman is suddenly startled. The ingénue smiles.
Sym looks irritated. Now, entering stage right, it's Damecki
bare-legged, tottering on to the stage as if drunk, wearing

his outsized hat and baby moustache, carrying a pair of trousers and a cocktail glass. And from this distance she recognises him now, from long ago, he used to perform with his quicker namesake, it's the stooge Rappaport.

Buffoon.

Damecki-Rappaport performs a lavish bow to Sym in the presidential box, nearly spills his drink; champagne arcs into the air, the ex-stooge catches it in his mouth, bows again. Laughter from the stage crew, a sniff from Sym. The stage manager tries to shepherd the comic off the stage. Does Sym recognise Damecki too? Doubtful: the stooge Rappaport never performed with this exuberance. And Sym doesn't usually waste attention on the supporting cast. He chooses to mirror his self with only the most pleasing objects.

Two men with large muscles and tight black uniforms arrive in the doorway of the presidential box. They look hapless and violent. Their heads are very small, out of proportion to the rest of their bulk. Their rough chins bristle. They probably have to shave several times a day to keep their faces approximately human. Sym makes a strange noise in his throat. He waves them away. They apologetically step back, discreetly almost out of earshot. Gloria feels an at first inexplicable irritation against them and then realises she is feeling a fraction of Sym's.

Who are they?

Sent to protect me.

Protect? From what?

From powerless people who make threats after dark.

His response could be deemed inappropriate. The gorillas annoy him. Whatever threats have been made seem not to bother him at all. Punishment might be what he thinks he deserves, or else it is entirely irrelevant to his plans.

I had better show you out.

Sym tells them to wait for him in his office. Perfectly calm again, he steers her leisurely out of the theatre on to the steps. An ordinary crowd passes by.

Will you think about resuming psychology?

Why is he so insistent? Don Juan Sym, with his uniform and charm. Classical narcissism does not quite describe. There is nothing inflated or imagined about him. He is no less delightful than his own opinion of himself. What troubles him? He brought his secret to her in that beginning, daring her to uncover and expose. She failed. Heller stole her away and died, unhealed. It is not just charity Sym is proposing. He suffers. Was he always this irascible? She doesn't remember.

Do you still perform?

I've done a couple of films. That's all. Too busy with management these days.

Maybe all he wants is an audience. A witness. Even housemaids need the confessional.

Come to dinner with me soon. Do you have a ball gown?

Yes. Yes. I do.

Yes yes. I do.

The ideal parting embrace is broken, perhaps on purpose, by Damecki jostling past. Trousered now, he walks whistling, with a peroxide blonde hanging on to each arm.

He has a reputation for being an orgiast.

Sym reports this without rancour, but with some wonder. He glances his lips across her face, invites her to dinner at the Hotel Bristol, looks anxiously up at the sky, and retreats inside his theatre.

Gloria feels impregnable. The only looks she receives are of admiration. The city wears its benevolent aspects. Only occasionally does she sense that she is being observed or followed. She straightens her stockings by the empty windows of a department store, looks around, no pursuer announces himself, she's standing on an innocent boulevard. The loudspeakers are barking at everyone.

She is tiring. She delays returning to the charity house. She waits in line for a streetcar. When she starts to climb on, a passenger climbing down wordlessly presses a ticket into her hand. Most of the passengers around her have been slipped a ticket (that man there in the tatty overcoat has not, he's shivering, attempting, despite his bad looks, to pass), a secret complicity—*they* at least shall not profit from *us* . . .

Gloria avoids looking at other people, she avoids making the discovery that other people are looking at her. She stands at the rear of the streetcar looking out. The wall surrounding the district has grown much taller. No sign of workmen. It might be finished. The streetcar is going too fast for her to read the notices plastered to the wall. She can make out the words *Warning* and *Prohibition* and

Epidemic and that's all. If she were going in the opposite direction, this streetcar would pass her through the forbidden district and out again, ending in the industrial district, the glass factories. An enormous black wooden V has been erected in Saxon Square, where the winter ice rink used to be.

Someone is standing too close to her. She looks at him, the expression of innocence on his face is so strong that it hits her like aggression. And she feels, too, now his hand, gliding through her overcoat pocket like a fish in water sliding for food. Gloria wriggles away. Twice she bats at the pickpocket's arm before his hand consents to withdraw. He displays no shame, no alarm, the expression on his face is more aggressively innocent than before.

She gets off the streetcar at a random street, the sky is already dark. Gloria has to race the curfew back to the charity house. A couple of their soldiers raise rifles to shoulders and solemnly inspect her through the sights as she runs through shadows and ruins.

10

A librarian with a malicious set to his face stops her in the courtyard on her way to the chapel where she can hear the dirge of evening prayers rising. He leads her into the main building, reluctantly shows her a door that is almost hidden, allows her into a bedroom.

This is unmistakably a boy's room. A small bed, a scattering of play-hats, brightly coloured walls. *Madame* leans against a wardrobe, its doors behind her painted with pirate ships. Zosia doesn't wear a scarf tonight. On her throat, just off centre, is the largest pimple Gloria has ever seen. It's like a parody of a man's Adam's apple. Gloria wants to praise it or stroke it, she can't remember ever seeing such a phenomenon. Its immense yellow head is supported by a sturdy, round, scarlet body. Gloria vaguely remembers a code of etiquette by which one is meant to wait for the wearer to draw attention to extraordinary growths or blemishes. She tries to find some competing interest in the deep window ledge which is filled with books and toy soldiers from all kinds of different wars.

I tried to see you yesterday. I don't know if you saw me?

Madame shrugs.

I'm a recipient of your charity. I live in Dormitory Three now.

Gloria is about to pick up one of the soldiers when Zosia stops her.

You mustn't. Even I am not, says Zosia, as she retrieves a book of cowboy stories that has found its way under the bed, *permitted to touch his soldiers, nobody is, that's one of only two things that will ever drive him into a tantrum.*

What's the second?

Zosia shakes her head. She is not going to say anything more, nor—and it produces an odd kind of fury in Gloria—is she going to ask anything about Gloria. And yet, she is finally being attended to. With Sym's kiss of benediction the city has stopped resisting her. She should leave this room, go to see the bureaucrat now, he would smile to greet her, bring her into his office, fill her with tea and cakes, give her the choice of any kind of destinies, produce Sarah from a secret compartment like the climax to a magic act.

She imagines she would have to sign for the destiny she selected (or would she be allowed more than one? a trial offer? Here's your future, if you don't like it come back to the office, we'll give you a different one, no questions asked . . .); the bureaucrat would enjoy watching her write her name in an immense ledger book.

I saw—

Who? Who did you see?

Nobody. I was just walking—How is your family? I tried to visit you at the Glade.

Gloria is initiated into the tragedies of Zosia's family.

Father was arrested: they took the Count away, a silent adversary of past wars, supposedly still dangerous; they returned a medical certificate in his place a few weeks later, attesting to his death by typhus. Mother died shortly after. She swallowed poison.

All the equivalent poison in Zosia has collected at the front of her throat into that enormous pimple. Someone with a more materialist turn of mind than Gloria might see it as the fruit of constant chafing from the silver chain she still wears around her neck.

They requisitioned the Glade then disinfected it, filled it with their soldiers.

Yes I saw.

A flurry of activity. The door swings open, in rushes the copper-haired boy, his large nurse puffing after. The boy comes running to Zosia, bellowing *I want, she won't, I want*—and then sees the stranger in his room, looks alarmed, grabs hold of Zosia's hand, pulls her towards the safety of the fortified window ledge. Zosia dismisses the nurse.

This is Uri.

Hello, Uri.

Say how do you do.

How do you do.

The boy's hair is tinged somehow with pink as if the colours that compose it have not quite blended. The woman and the boy both inspect Gloria with the same unwavering look, the same mixture of disinterested curiosity and solemn self-regard. What is she to him? His mother? His aunt? *Both?*

What were we talking about?
Your brother.
Another portrait of Henry shines in this room, halo around his head, a divine shaft of light illuminating his frail heart. He died, Gloria is told, a martyr's death in one of the first battles against them, leaving behind a slim manuscript of poems and his eternal glory.
Only the good die young.
Poor Uri then, who sits on the bed, amiably waiting, playing with two of his lead soldiers. Zosia's own demeanour suggests her stoical acceptance of God's extreme judgement upon her. What crimes has she committed that are so monstrous she has been condemned to go on living? Lurid thoughts of incest continue to excite Gloria. Or could the boy's father be someone else, more scandalous even, racial impurity?
The 'Prince' sends his regards. I got a letter from him. He's safe in the east.
Zosia shakes her head as if something disagreeable inside it needs to be dislodged.
Come to the light. Let me look at you.
Gloria allows herself to be inspected. Zosia clicks her tongue.
This won't quite do.
A handkerchief (with the family crest embroidered in gold thread in one corner) is produced, twisted at one end, moistened with Zosia's own saliva, briskly applied to Gloria's face. Gloria looks at Uri and he looks at her as Zosia rubs at her face.
You're wearing far too much make-up. (Zosia herself

wears nothing to interfere with her own ethereal pallor.) *The lipstick is dangerous. I'd even consider bleaching your hair if I were you, and certainly*—a comb is produced, drawn roughly through Gloria's hair—*Ssh, don't be a baby, this doesn't hurt*—*you have to wear your hair away from your eyes and brow. Untamed hair gives a bad impression.*

A bad impression to whom?

Don't raise your voice. And don't use your hands when you're speaking. Your nose is good. That's something. That's probably what's got you through so far. Don't wear loud colours. Avoid red, yellow, green.

What about black?

Don't make fun. Even black can be a bad colour. The best is grey, that's what I'd recommend.

Recommend? For what? What are you talking about?

And Gloria sees it, even before Zosia mouths the incriminating word with her face averted from Uri so the boy won't know what the grown-ups are talking about.

(Whisper) *They're shooting* (the next word is signified just by the shapes it makes on Zosia's lips, grotesquely transforming her for that moment into a caricature of one herself, like in their propaganda) *Newcomers* (whisper) *now*.

On the boy's bedside table is the family insignia in steel, it looks like a badge that's been separated from a flunkey's hat—ornate martial crest, the bullock and the sword. Gloria reaches for it, palms it, an open pin pricks her hand, she holds on to it more tightly. There is something reassuring about the pain.

Why are you doing this? You never liked us.

Zosia scowls. Uri looks up interestedly.

My religion tells me to help the weakest. And not least, it's a way of spiting them. If they hate you so much, there must be some good in helping you. And you are, aren't you? very weak. Goodbye now, Gloria. Do you remember the way back to the chapel? It's not just a humiliation making you pray. You'll find it useful for getting through the city. Not everyone shares our attitude. Their demagogue is mad. They'll stop at nothing.

Is this charity Zosia's revenge as well as her duty? Gloria does not wish to pay, with humility, with life, for whatever impieties the 'Prince' seduced Zosia into. (The 'Prince's tongue tapered at the tip almost to a point.)

Wait. I have something.

Her hand feels it in her overcoat pocket, a kind of talisman.

I have a hat, for the boy.

Out comes the navy-blue hat that she picked up on the first day of this anti-freedom. Gloria smoothes some of the creases away with a fist, hands it to Uri. Uri receives the hat, looks it all over, shakes his head.

Thank you, he says.

He is a good-mannered boy, gentle. Nonetheless, his disappointment shows. It will not do. She wonders if Sarah's child is the same age, the same type. She hopes so. He blinks his eyes; Gloria blinks hers, feels the quick stab of infection.

Wait a moment.

She takes the hat back, twists the soft cloth until it has

stiffened into an approximation of something military. With a dexterity that impresses herself she fixes the family badge to the front. Uri's smile grows. He too is impressed. When she releases the cap, he puts it on his head, rushes to the looking-glass and crisply salutes his stern proud self.

Put it aside now, says his mother. Uri shakes his head while keeping his hands tight to the cap so it can't fall off.

May I show Malka? he respectfully asks.

Zosia nods. Uri rushes to the door, turns, performs a marvellous smile, bows to Gloria and clicks his heels at the same time and is gone.

He is very beautiful, says Gloria.

How did you know? asks Zosia.

Know what? asks Gloria.

I I

We should have got married, that might have staved it all off, you and I, Mr and Mrs Mouse; we had our moments and places of unquestioned accord—cinema seats, park picnics, at home with the latest issue of the *Psychological Bulletin*, arguing, dissenting, occasionally concurring— and, natural erotic partners or not, shared libidinal release, comparable satisfactions; I remember the feel of your tough little body, of stroking your shoulder with its fine beginning tufts of mousy brown hair. If my prideful ambition, and yours, hadn't got in the way I could have gone with you.

I should have gone with you. I could have given up then all these useless ambitions of curing the sickness in men's souls, sharpened your pencils, polished your couch, taken your messages and written every appointment down in a ledger book the size of something holy. Clattered around with pots and pans in the kitchen, busy bustling house-proud Mrs Mouse. Welcome you home with a kiss that tastes of soup, wipe my forehead with the back of a floury hand, smile, as if posing for a photograph, or not, just smile, unguarded moment, and nothing bad would have happened, to these streets, these buildings, these children, those soldiers, those trees, our lives. In the east and in the west the emperors die and in their final agonies curse our untroubled lives.

And where are you now, Mr Mouse? You sent me your final proposal from a station, waiting for a train to the dockside. I wish you'd stayed. Did you get away? Did you get across? Did all your clever plans turn out the way you'd imagined? Are you spooning rich widows the cream of self-validation? Everything about you announces your ardent relationship with truth, so why are you leaning forward, Mr Mouse, why are your fingers still resting on that silky widow's breast and why do I feel so jealous?

Oh, Mr Mouse, do you thrive? Do you live even? Did you find a rodenty trail through all of this? You should have stayed, trusted me better, I would have looked after you. Better I think you with the pots and the pans and the appointments ledger. You with the apron preparing the soup and talking on the telephone with the travel agents planning our vacation to the mountains.

And around us our little mouselings and little mousettes, squeaking for cheese.

I2

Gloria is glad to discover she is not at all superfluous. This industrial relief house, the pious eroticism of the holy librarians, is unsustainable without people like her. The charity machine cannot work without its basic element, the coarse raw material of indigents.

And Igo Sym. Gloria is sure it is an old wound of his that requires psychological treatment. He was first analysed at the end of the previous war. He never would tell her why. Shell-shock? The handsome young lieutenant rides away from the battlefield, he has been through too much, those grey eyes have seen too many awful events, been frightened too many times, too many men close to him have been violently made soft and empty, even his own shapely fingers are bloody with shame, cowardice, assassination.

Carnage on the battlefield had polluted his psyche. Some things had died, and in recompense new things, his satyriasis, his need for admiration and the giving of pleasure, had grown, to monstrous proportions, not even a new war and a magnificent black uniform and colonel's insignia could begin to make him well.

Or maybe it was just peace that had done the damage. Modern life is the original cataclysm that impelled him to play out the same unconfessible drama on a succession of willing women's bodies. (But not, alas, hers.)

What is his guilty secret? The friends he betrayed, the puppies he drowned, the babies he left to die on mountain tops, the women he drove mad? She is sure that a few sessions would uncover answers that would be at the least plausible questions to begin further investigations. But Gloria has given up depth psychology. That is the extent of her inheritance from Solomon Heller.

She gets up and washes her face with stale water. Everyone else in Dormitory 3 is already sleeping. One is sent to bed early in the charity house. And one takes refuge quickly in sleep.

Her neighbour's mouth is open, words are being shovelled out of it like earth from a grave. Eyes agitate beneath closed lids. Gloria briefly attempts to brush her hair, tame it away from her brow, then she makes the walk downstairs, her overcoat held tight over her ball gown.

Gloria approaches the Hotel Bristol. Like the theatre, this is a building the occupiers must consider worthy of them. Liveried doormen stand between white-stuccoed pillars. The window glass is intact, the mirrored corners are still dizzying. The round belvedere at the top is untouched except by birds. Gloria has to apologise her way through a rush of diners and residents, most in heavy fur coats, to reach Igo Sym waiting by the side of the main door.

I have to escort you in. This place is, I'm sorry, restricted.

The discreet sign by the door is engraved in brass, already it looks established, shortly it will look as if it has always been here, older even than the brick it is bolted into: *For Nationals Only*, the way they designate themselves in their own language. Igo Sym half conceals the sign with his body, as if to say, I'm hiding nothing from you, but all the same there are some things you might prefer not to see . . .

Sym without flinching touches her threadbare arm (does his nose wrinkle? the coat is appalling, and river rankness might still be detectable beneath affronting waves of perfume; she has doused the gown with the last of her scent, and stolen some more from her sleeping neighbour, perhaps too much). He walks her into the lobby, which is still magnificent, white iron, electricity and glass. Their officers and administrators stroll around, dressed in military uniforms that the angels would wear in Uri's notion of heaven. Sym guides-protects her towards the hat-check girl.

The woman ahead shakes off her furs, reveals the oyster satin gown and her body beneath, perfect pale shoulder blades. She adjusts a shoe while holding on to her companion's arm, her tongue dips out between her teeth in concentration. The hat-check girl doesn't sneer at Gloria's overcoat. This is a good place.

Gloria had hoped for the International Restaurant but Sym takes her, between potted palm trees, through a red velvet curtain, into the Raspberry Room. The air is different here, the light is richer, like blood. The maître d' advances, performs an elegant curtsey and leads Sym and Gloria to a table, which is, Sym confides (as neighbouring diners freeze, forks are suspended between plates and mouths, whisper, *Isn't that Igo Sym . . . ?*), the second-best in the joint.

Sym and the maître d' are waiting for her to sit down, so she does; she receives a flourish of something in her lap that turns from a swan into a napkin, she smiles, tries to act grand, tries to seem not unused to grandeur and their uniforms. Cocktails arrive, courtesy of an administrator at a nearby table. The administrator raises his glass. Sym lifts his in return, adding the legendary Sym smile. Gloria stares at her menu. (She might be meant to lift her glass also. She decides to do nothing. Better to be unmasked by an act omitted than committed.) At the far end of the room a quartet of soldierly men in green velvet hunting lodge suits carve out a melody. Didn't, once upon a time, Sym promise he would teach her to play the musical saw? Or had she just hoped he would?

What would you like? Should I order for you as well?
Yes. Please. Do.

She is giddy here, in their victorious world, faced by Igo Sym's smile, surrounded by them and their trophies and their utter confidence that the world is being twisted into their preferred shape, wine bottles, roasted duck, pork dumplings, olive bread, red wine, crystal glasses, silver trays, spinning chandeliers, red faces flickering in the raspberry light.

This is a room full of men who like cigars and food and throwing their heads back at jokes, it's an arena for profiteers and women the texture of cream and anyone, like Igo Sym, who knows how to make a rich life in this city. Gloria is sure that she is the only newcomer who has ever sat here or who ever shall, demure, sipping, nodding, unexamined.

The food arrives on silver trays carried by tired waiters in white uniforms like sailors, who all become prouder in proximity to Igo Sym. Waiters' backs straighten, creased faces turn amiable, smiling. Waitresses' mouths open, sincere invitations are issued with eyes and lips, that unmistakable look of frankness—*you and I, maybe could . . . ?*

Tell me. What happened to your gangster? Does he flourish?

Dead. He killed himself.

Oh, I'm sorry.

Sympathetic Sym. He reaches across, his hands clasp hers. He understands, or seems to, her failure and her solitude and her heart.

Gloria.

His hands on her and it is true, he does have a gift like electricity. Her skin receives it, something blue and invisible sparks up her arms, her shoulders.

His hands refuse to stop clasping hers. She manages to free her left and work knife and fork alternately one-handed, cumbersome yet effective. Gloria had forgotten just how good food can be.

Will you come and visit me at my apartment? It's the same place as before. Remember? Near the Tip Top Club. I won't take no for an answer.

She wasn't going to give it.

197

A narcissist requires his audience. He will seduce her into wanting him more than anything and then he will relax and tell her some story, he and some starlet, Madame Ilona's daughter she supposes, the libidinal adventures, the Dameckian orgies, every erotic gesture.

I've given up psychology. It's only fair to tell you.

Yes. Yes of course. Will you come?

She doesn't say anything, just looks down at her imprisoned hand, flutters it a little to indicate that it might be about to perish through lack of blood supply.

Do you remember why I came to you in the first place?

You never revealed why.

I don't think I was allowed much of a chance.

He is reminding her that she dropped him, that he came to her because he was unhappy and needed her help, and she refused to help.

I'm sorry, I didn't mean to embarrass you. I needed help. I'm sure I said that. And now I need it more than before, more than ever.

He is very good at flirting with her, pretending to expose his psyche for her—the chase after secrets and shames, she likes few activities better. She is not yet entirely convinced that there is anything wrong with Sym. Who is he trying to protect? Himself? Her? He might be just doing what he can, offering her his protection in a way he knows will be acceptable to her. Everything Sym does he does with kindness so maybe there is nothing he needs to confess to, it's all, like the uniform, play-acting.

I'm sorry, he says, releasing her hand, wiping his mouth

with his napkin. *I didn't mean to put you under any pressure. Forgive me.*

Gloria manages not to respond with an Of course, or There's nothing to forgive—she won't be tricked into that one: she concentrates on taking small measures of food and in between mouthfuls showing him a half-smile that she hopes is wise and enigmatic.

She experiences no further hormonal excitations in the course of the dinner and he displays no libidinal compulsions. Sym doesn't mention any starlets, so Gloria does. She asks after Madame Ilona's daughter and Sym examines Gloria's face for a moment before he tells her that a few days earlier the ingénue's hair was shorn on a street corner by members of the underground.

One patriot held her by the mouth. The second kept lookout. The third patriot chopped away her hair with a butcher's knife. It was her punishment for a liaison with one of the occupiers. Or at least for there being a rumour of it.

Are you a target? Are you scared?

I get anonymous letters sometimes, but then I always did. Equally passionate, just offering different scenarios. And fewer spelling mistakes now.

Which means?

I suppose members of the underground are better educated than movie fans.

Some dishes have been cleared away and some more have arrived. Her plates of pig and cabbage have gone, now there is apple tart and cheese to consume.

What's your mistress like? I assume you have one.

She has very wide apart eyes. You wouldn't like her.

Why does she like you? Because you are a movie star or because you wear that uniform?

Both, I suppose. Or maybe she likes me for myself.

I'm sorry. I didn't mean to be insulting.

I'm sure.

She is flustered. He is amused. Maybe that's why he invites her in, she is his jester. She plunges on.

You have justifications.

Justifications imply guilt. So no, I have no justifications.

A rationale.

You want me to rehearse it? For whose benefit?

He waits for her to answer his questions. She says nothing.

You're still using the old tricks. I thought you'd given up psychology? The theatre is overstaffed. If my people didn't have work then who knows? I'm doing my best, giving everyone I can paid labour. One does—I think I've said this before—what one can. Of course political opposition isn't allowed in the theatre, so it's foolish to attempt it. The censor hears the offending words, immediately ten people, twenty, a hundred, are arrested, imprisoned, shot. They have made it very clear where they stand on collective responsibility. If one person commits a crime, then the city is guilty. So meanwhile the theatre must put on revues celebrating drunkenness and eroticism—if meaning can be smuggled in then it's all the more powerful. I try not to worry about politics. Well? (Igo Sym draws a breath. He sits back in his chair, quite pleased with himself.) *What do you think?*

She is allowed to ask it now. What Sym has been keeping back. What he wishes no one to know and yet needs above all to confess.

When you came to me in the first place, it was because of a woman.

Your namesake.

The Astonishing.

She left me, Gloria. She was in love with me and then she fell out of love because of something she saw. It—I— scared her away.

What did she see?

I don't know. It might happen again.

It is said so plaintively. His bewilderment is, Gloria feels, honest. And then he remembers who he is, he's Igo Sym, he can't be plaintive or confused for long, his role doesn't allow it, so he lifts his glass in a meaningful way and offers a toast, *To our continuing association*, which Gloria echoes (Association!), as glasses clink, as burgundy wine slips down her throat, as the world becomes almost likeable.

The urge to punish herself stabs at her. Heller is dead, Sarah is lost, and she is enjoying a pleasant meaningful meal in the least dangerous place in the city. She feels exposed. She feels ashamed. She should at least enjoy herself. Or purge herself. Or pursue whatever it is Sym is trying to show her.

I saw some graffiti outside a cinema. It said, Only pigs go to the cinema. And someone had added, And rich pigs go to the theatre. What I mean to say is, the theatre must be finished as long as they're in town. An impossible glamour.

People seem to either wear opposing uniforms or else want to dress like them, play general with toy armies.

Really? says Sym politely, refusing entirely to follow where Gloria wants to lead. She might even be boring him.

I know a boy who does. He's mad for toy soldiers that no one else is allowed to touch.

Lead soldiers?

Yes I suppose so, lead.

Hard to get nowadays.

Burgundy and vodka are making her reckless. Gloria plugs her words with mouthfuls of tart and sips of the sweet wine that's arrived, when something happens. Sym lays his fork carefully down on his plate, he dabs his lips with a movement that's so quiet and correct and dramatic that it is obviously the result of absolute concentration of will and perhaps pathology. Gloria's chair squeaks as she has to turn to find the focus of his attention. His two gorillas in black stand at the door of the Raspberry Room. The maître d' bars their way.

They're lowering the tone of the place, whatever uniform they're wearing they still won't belong here and the sight of them is a vulgarity that spoils Sym's view and reflects badly on him and he is for a moment completely disabled.

Excuse me.

He manages to get up as if untroubled. The sound Gloria made with her chair alarmed the nearby diners, it was a vulgarity itself that doesn't belong here either; disapproving faces turn swiftly admiring as they watch Igo Sym walking to the door. Whatever he chooses to show on his face dismisses his bodyguard instantly. He says something to the maître d' that makes the maître d' preen. When he has returned he is himself again.

The only time I can get rid of those two is when a woman is with me.

He isn't trying for effect, he is merely stating the facts as if to a doctor. Gloria is sure that in that disabling moment something had been revealed of his secret weight, his secret battleground, the repelling thing that Gloria the Astonishing saw, and she would like, despite his uniform, to make him well.

Your boy, the general, with his soldiers. Do you think you might be able to borrow one? Send it to the theatre and I know you'll be at my apartment the next morning and I can arrange that those two will be off-duty.

Gloria busies herself with a napkin that bears no sign of ever being swanlike. She feels a terrible guilt for implicating Uri, who has done nothing wrong to deserve to be in this conversation. Sym then says something she doesn't understand about a ceremony and he takes her hand.

It's nearly curfew now. You had better be careful. Will you come? You will come. I do need you.

She doesn't remind him that she's given up psychology. Sym and Gloria, naturally entwined, go into the lobby. His arm is around her waist, the world is amiable again; it smells of brandy and cigar smoke and its good opinion of Igo Sym, whose hand is stroking her hair.

Gloria doesn't want to be remembered by Sym for the misery of her coat so she makes him leave her there in the lobby, she claims her coat from the hat-check girl and gives in exchange a tip she can't afford, she walks quickly between palm trees, a doorman opens a door for her, the laughter around her is louder than before—and she is outside, suddenly terrified.

The way back is treacherous. It is after curfew. She hears footsteps always behind her. She goes faster. Gloria skirts around checkpoints where their soldiers and blue police stand, faces hidden under helmets, breath ghosts puffing into the blue lantern air, rifles moving as if by instinct looking for someone to shoot at. Guns, like charity, are useless without a target.

She's at the scrub of bombsite that marks the final corner before Zosia's street—and out of the bushes a short, dark thing is grabbing at her. Sinewy arms. Hard breathing. She assumes rape and murder. So this is how it is to end, in violent forgetting. The moon is merciless. Something busy wriggles under her assailant's nose. She must scream, that's what she has to do, but a hand smashes against her mouth, his force against her is too strong, hard breathing, alcohol breath. She is pushed through leaves and branches, into the woods, forced to keep moving, never allowed her own balance. He has taken her into a clearing now. Pine cones, frozen leaves underfoot. She hears a whimper. Unavoidably her own. So this is where it all ends, in a clearing in the woods.

This was, says Damecki-Rappaport, letting go, revealing himself, releasing her, letting her fall against a tree, letting her have, needing himself, some restorative breathing, *This*

*was my seduction chamber in warmer weather. I used to
come here, on picnics.*

He waves a pile of papers at her, edges cracked from
too much fingertipping.

*Look. Excuse me. I'm sorry for all this. This isn't me.
I'm a desperate man, circumstances have driven me to
this. Look. I have these to show you. I must show you
these. This one, this one is by the dramatic critic of the
Courier—and here's a personal letter from him, you feel
the weight of that notepaper? but that's on another matter
so you needn't read it, I just wanted you to—Read what
it says, I'll read it to you, it starts here. You'd think it
was a one-man show the way he goes on. Forgive me. I'm
suddenly bashful. Here: 'In the eponymous role of Drunk
Walter, the actor Damecki—' Note that. Damecki. 'The
actor Damecki displays comic variety and ingenuity.' He
goes on. What do you think of that? Variety! Ingenuity!
Eponymous!*

Gloria is beginning to realise that Damecki does not
intend rape for her or death or injury, just boredom.

I don't really see et cetera what this has to do with me.

*He listens to you. I've seen his face when you're speak-
ing. An actor observes. Please. I beg you. You might be able
to sway him. Here, more notices, here, this one is, you'll
like this, I know you will—letters from audiences—grateful
audiences one might say. Listen—'Thank you'—and—
'Having seen your show for the tenth time', hear that?
'tenth'! and—oh, this, by a small girl with an illness of the
lungs. See her handwriting? Doesn't that break your heart?
'Never before,' she says, 'have I,' she says—My personal*

feeling is, this might be controversial, my personal feeling is that one letter like this is worth a thousand reviews— And here's another, from a national publication. Again singling out for special praise—Forgive me again if I quote directly. I'm not so good at paraphrasing, and here too, not just comedy you'll see—'the actor Damecki'—I began my career in the classics. Even in my former life I wasn't always a stooge.

It's a beautiful night. The tree is warm against her hand. Something moves in the leaves above her head, broken rectangles of night sky through the branches. Stars. He probably doesn't know either which constellation that is. The former Rappaport's moustache wiggles as he talks. His eyes are not crossed. His ears tremble.

I am Drunk Walter! He beats a fist into his open hand for unnecessary emphasis. *Talk to him. Please. Talk to him. Tell him, tell him that I desire to be—No! I demand! I demand to be reinstated! I AM DRUNK WALTER!*

Damecki subsides. He wipes his forehead with an out-sized grey handkerchief.

You're very kind. No one can know what I've been through. Surrounded. Vipers, parasites, yes-men, gold-diggers, coquettes, teases. Surrounding you. Feeding you strawberries. And then, in a moment, some has-been administrator, and it's gone, like that, puff!—All gone.

He looks suspiciously around, inspects the trees.

Will you talk to him?

I will talk to him.

You mean it? Truly? You do, I can see that you do, may I kiss you?

She allows it. It is very timidly, sweetly done, quite contrary to his reputation as an orgiast. He approaches, his lips pucker, his moustache shivers; she lowers her head; he kisses her brow, as if he were her pardoner.

On her return to the charity house Gloria looks for Zosia; she can't find her. The machine has slowed down for the night. The refectory is nearly empty, a man mops the floor, a woman carries a tray of plates into the kitchen. In the chapel a pair of librarians are locking candles and censers away in a cupboard behind the altar. Zosia is not to be found. Gloria looks for dormitories 1 and 2.

In an alcove near Uri's room a librarian stops her by insolently touching her breast. He introduces himself with the unlikely name of Hindrance.

And this is my friend Little, he says, indicating a man of indistinction whom Gloria had taken for shadows. *Let's have a chat.*

No thank you.

Gloria returns to the putative safety of Dormitory 3.

13

Uri wears shiny black boots. His black miniature riding trousers puff out at the thighs like a cavalry officer's. His shirt is black, with breast pockets and epaulettes. The only clothing he wears that isn't black is the navy-blue cap that Gloria gave to him, with the family crest of the bullock and the sword pinned militarily above the peak. He polished the boots himself, he is proud to tell her.

The day is like early spring. She experiences sun warmth, as if for the first time. It makes her limbs tremble. Uri pulls her through the city towards the playground in Dolphin Park.

After breakfast prayers, a holy librarian—who is neither Hindrance nor, she can be relatively sure, Little—had disapprovingly told her that there had been a request from the boy to be taken to the park by her, a request that had been surprisingly granted. Gloria had intended to visit the bureaucrat's office again. But instead of going to Long Avenue Gloria walked with Uri out through the courtyard while holy librarians stood at windows to watch with sharp magnified eyes, disappointed lips pressed close to the glass. She is too new, too suspicious to be entrusted with a holy boy, no matter how eccentric he is in matters of dress.

Uri wants to peer over the wall. Gloria has to lift him, he is heavier than he looks, she warns him to keep his fingers clear of the green and white splinters of glass cemented to the top. She can't decipher his description of what he sees. (Even if she wanted to hear, she wouldn't be able to; Uri's speech disintegrates when he gets excited.) Eventually, just when she is about to give way beneath him, he gets tired waving unanswered to exotic creatures, he forces his way back down to earth, resumes pulling her to the playground.

Gloria points to trees and tries to remember names for him.

I was never good at this—linden? chestnut?

He answers with the model numbers of airplanes in the sky. Then it is time to buy water ices at the café. Her old adversary the bird-killer doesn't recognise Gloria with Uri beside her. She gives Gloria a yellow-toothed smile and Uri an irksome rub on the head and the offer of a freshly boiled egg. The waitress's affection is worse than her enmity. Gloria and Uri go outside to lick water ices and slowly walk and shiver happily in the breeze.

Abruptly, he stops walking. On Uri's face is a flushed look of awe. A pair of their soldiers stroll, cupping cigarettes in black gloved hands. His bearing becomes straighter. He hides his water ice behind his back. She averts her features, then doesn't. She is safe with him beside her. She is, for once, impeccably other.

*　　*　　*

At the playground, Uri hugs on to a wooden head of the carousel. Gloria doesn't tire of waving to him each time he revolves past calling to her. It helps her not to hear the shriller sounds from the residential quarter. Finally, he is nearly ready to go home. He leads her towards the park exit, past the handball court where men are sweating, swearing, stripped to the waist, playing.

She has a question to ask him. Gloria doesn't know how to frame it. Who are your parents? Is Zosia your mother? Do you know who your parents are or are you a virgin birth, miraculous, unfathered? But Uri has a question to ask her and he asks his first.

Where are they from?

She would like a compass now, to demonstrate with. This is west, she would point to, where they are from and further, beyond even them, are cities and prairies and once new worlds, impossible sanctuaries. And look, this, the opposite, have you done opposites yet? Black–white, west–east, the east is where mystery religions come from and dusty nomad tribes and love towns and the easterners of course, whose uniforms you wouldn't like half as much, and whose demagogue isn't nearly as mad as theirs; and up, that's north, we shouldn't like to go there, the north is for ice and corsets, repression, snow blindness, midnight sun, frost inside and out; but the opposite to north is south, and that's where I would like to be, bright colours, libidinous pleasures, safety.

The west, she tells him, that's where they're from.

The shadows are lengthening on Uri's forehead. This sunlit day is nearly over. On, Uri, I'll swallow my questions if you swallow yours, it's time to go home, don't dawdle, Madame will be so cross, go! The young prince is cold. He clutches at his groin. His expression confesses that his bladder is full. Gloria is an amateur in the toilet habits of children. He raises one hand for her to take, an entirely unselfconscious gesture that makes her fall stupidly in love with him. He leads her on a detour to a tree. He wants her to direct his penis for him as he urinates. This boy is full of charm. His penis stiffens flatteringly within her fingers.

He wants to button up his trousers himself, struggles, it is too difficult for his untrained fingers, he gets frustrated but his good nature intervenes: laughter overcomes his annoyance. And then he is silent, not moving, mouth frozen in mid-exhalation, a whisper finally fights its way out of him, *Look!*

Gloria clasps the final trouser button, looks around, wary for more of them to feel awe for, to worship. But no. Excruciatingly slow, a tortoise is making its way over leafy thawed ground.

Look!

Its head moves from side to side with the effort. Its feet laboriously shovel earth away with each heave forward. Gloria admires the animal's power of persistence and envies him his shell, which is mottled brown-green and gold.

A tortoise.

Uri runs to it, crouches down, watches it move slowly on. He finds a stick to tap the shell with, smiles, then looks concerned as if he might have carelessly bruised the tortoise and throws the stick away as far as he can. Very gently he lifts the tortoise by the shell—its legs and head immediately retract. Uri peers into the dark head hole, says hello to Mr Tortoise.

May I keep it?

Of course not.

The tortoise is replaced quite crossly on the ground. Gloria tugs Uri on, Uri holds his ground. He insists he be allowed to wait until the tortoise has revealed his head and limbs again. The day is getting colder and older. She hopes the boy hasn't noticed that he has set the tortoise down in the opposite direction from the one it had been so effortfully pursuing.

Uri!

He does not hear her. He peers at the tortoise, he rests stiff leaves on the animal's back. A head eventually peeks out; before it can retract Gloria has taken Uri by the collar, wrenched him around, bundled him away.

Uri marches disgruntledly beside her for the journey home. Tear tracks that he refuses to let her wipe at streak his face.

The boy is delivered into the excluding arms of a holy librarian. Gloria has just time enough to visit the bureaucrat's office and return before curfew falls. She thinks two weeks might have gone by since she first visited him. Everything will be revealed to her now or else the bureaucrat had just been saving her up for a future sadistic treat.

Without Uri she feels exposed, isolated. She walks faster, she keeps to main roads, her hands in overcoat pockets, her legs working fast. She overtakes others who walk usually in pairs, eyes straight ahead, quietly talking through hardly moving mouths. She has covered nearly half the way to Long Avenue when she has to step around a small crowd standing on a corner listening to the latest list of their victories being announced from a loudspeaker. Something detaches itself to approach her. Gloria walks faster.

Excuse me.

So here it comes.

Excuse me. Doctor.

She has to stop. A stick figure in a big dark overcoat stands in front of her, hands in coat pockets flapping. His nose is ugly, his hair curly; even in this light she can read the melancholy in his eyes.

My name, you might remember me, is Zygelbojm.

He executes his joyless little manoeuvre, hops into the air, his feet click twice together off to the side, and he is on the ground again. And Gloria is trying to suppress her surprise and her sensation of immediate peril, and distaste.

Of course. Zygelbojm. How lovely to. I'm afraid. I don't have much time. I have an appointment.

She walks on. He takes hold of her sleeve, and pairs of eyes examine her more closely. Zygelbojm implicates her. Even in the old days he carried himself like an apology.

Just a moment of your time. It is not often one meets old friends. Please.

He won't be shrugged off.

Do you remember Madame Tatiana? asks Zygelbojm.

I'm in a hurry, she says, staring straight ahead while slipping the words quietly out hardly moving her mouth.

Do you think her school is at the same place? Sometimes I think that her school must have closed but at other times I tell myself that there is more need for her expertise than ever before.

That's what you tell yourself.

What do you think? Do you think the school is at the same place?

I couldn't say.

Doctor. May I talk freely?

I'm not a doctor.

We could walk over there.

It is awful, being included in Zygelbojm's notion of a *we*. The place he has chosen to go to is at least relatively a good one. A street market. Safety in numbers, shoppers and time-passers, things to look at, blankets on the pavement, ladies doing the selling alongside street apaches. Cartons of cigarettes, racks of clothes, books, bicycles, toys, soap, milk. Zygelbojm walks her past some recently slaughtered chickens on an oilskin blanket and all she can smell is his fear and hers commingled.

May I talk freely, doctor?

Gloria does not question aloud the notion of *talking freely*. It might lead to technical issues that would keep Zygelbojm with her longer than even the superfluous one can intend or dare. Gloria does reiterate that she is not a doctor nor ever has been nor ever will be, but Zygelbojm merely nods emphatically as she talks, as if to say, *See? You see how sympathetic I am to you? The least you could do,*

DOCTOR! is to return the sympathy . . . So, in the end, it is easier to submit than keep fighting, out comes the old trick: she rolls her right hand towards her heart, gently, with no suggestion of compulsion or coercion, pulling Zygelbojm's secrets towards her self. Does she want to hear his secrets? Of course not. Does she fear infection by his psyche? Not especially. It is a pleasant novelty to feel stronger than someone.

Of course. Talk.

Zygelbojm starts to talk. Both he and she gaze straight ahead (Gloria taking in every stranger's movement, every hint of threat, Zygelbojm seeing nothing) and Zygelbojm talks.

The worst enemy is boredom. The days are like one and endless, except for the nights, which are worse. So you discover ways to pass the time. Otherwise you'd go mad. You're frightened all the time. People are looking at you. So you follow the crowd. Sometimes crowds are bad crowds and they want you for a work-gang but you get a nose for those, and far worse sometimes you run out of crowds to hide inside. The band has finished playing, the audience has to go; the film ends, the credits end, daylight through the exit doors, the ushers shine a torch upon you, you must go otherwise someone in a uniform is going to come for you. Did you know I used to work in the cinema? I had to separate couples who were sitting too close, throw out the under-age boys who had sneaked in through lavatory windows. Happy days. Sometimes even, don't laugh at me, I long for our streets sometimes. There you have no trouble finding the heart of the crowd. You're

*in it all the time, it's easy to be safe. No one looks at you.
But this is all preamble. My father, you know, predicted
that something marvellous would happen and we would all
be saved. This current balmy weather might be a harbinger
of that. It's got something to do with numbers. Excuse me.
It has been a very long time since I talked to anyone. You
understand?*

Gloria looks hopefully around the market for signs of the
crowd that will approach and magically carry Zygelbojm
away in its density. There is no impending crowd, just
eyes.

*I spend a lot of time in parks. I ride streetcars, I sit in
cinemas, but I spend much of my time in parks. And the
station too, people come, people go, it's a safe place there,
away from the trains, but most often in Dolphin Park. You
can hear the forbidden quarter from here, see it even from
certain points. Let me tell you. Once I had a family. I had a
mother and a father and a sister, and my father, blessed be
his memory, may he be inscribed in the book of salvation,
died of hunger, and my mother, blessed be, and my sister,
blessed be, followed him, typhus. And I was left alone. It
is written, I understand, by the sages, I am no scholar as
you know, not like my father, blessed be, I didn't have the
cleverness to understand holy truths like he did, when we
used to pray together I would copy him, move my lips like
he did, sway like he did. He was never taken in by it. But
the saying goes, I am sure you know it: Whoever saves one
life it is as though he has preserved the existence of the
whole world.*

So I decided that at least I could save my own life, that

I had a holy duty to do so. My family was dead. I am not my father. I can't argue with the holy books. So I slipped through a gate quite some time ago and ever since I have been over here, devoutly protecting myself. Sometimes I walk around but most of the time I sit. I sit and I look. And you know what I look at? I look at women. Especially from behind. You know me, doctor, from the old days. I would blush if women were so much as discussed.

I'm not a doctor.

I wouldn't have dared to look at women so openly. I have another confession to make. This is some day for confessions! I admired you. As a man admires a woman, if you understand me. But you probably considered me without sex or human attraction. Admit it. You did.

Nothing to say to that. Please go away, superfluous man.

And maybe I was or maybe it was just all hidden, I can't actually remember. But now I sit and I watch. I expect that you could tell me it is a defensive measure, the gaze of a coward always peeping, always scared to be caught peeping, this looking from behind, and maybe you're right. Who am I to argue with a professional? What I love, above all, excuse me, is the sight of a woman from behind, her arms lifted, her hands holding her hair, about to arrange it, the nape of the neck exposed. I love to see those necks, pale or suntanned, a few loose hairs escaping from buns. The silhouettes of shoulder blades moving beneath fabric. Necks like swans and backs like swords, as the saying goes. The tilt of a woman's head, the movement of her hands, and maybe too, sometimes, a slowly turning chin, the sudden flash of a cheekbone, her shoulders shift, awful suspense, will she turn now? or now? or now? or now? And what, after all this, will her face be like? Because faces and bodies often do not, you know, match.

Zygelbojm opens his mouth and cautiously takes in some air. That little gang over there, of sandy-haired boys with sharp teeth, was it so close before?

Sometimes of course there is disappointment. That charming gymnast's body turns out to belong to a hag. You had expected a wood nymph you get a witch. That's all part of the game. But doctor—

Zygelbojm's voice drops to a whisper, his eyes cast down, his knees stagger, his hands continue to hang limply, chastely, by his sides. He would shrink to nothing if he could. No, not nothing, there is something defiant there, trembling at the core, maybe just a stubbornness beyond or beneath consciousness, a refusal to become nothing.

Doctor.

I'm not a doctor.

I'm not a doctor and I'm not your confidante and I'm not your mother or your sister or your girlfriend. We do not belong together. Your world is not mine. Do you understand me?

This is what I have to tell you. Please. Pretend for the moment I'm your patient.

I wouldn't advise that. My last patient died on me.

Zygelbojm sighs. He will put up with this for as long as is necessary. His indulgence is infinite. If she doesn't

218

submit, the two will stay here for ever until the power of something stronger intervenes.

What do you want to tell me?

I wouldn't be saying this to anybody, asserts Zygelbojm, coquettishly glancing from a sly corner of an eye.

No. I understand.

I was in Hero Park. A pianist was playing, a crowd had gathered, so I joined it. I've never especially cared for music, but it was a nice day and the crowd was good. By the lake, children sometimes getting in the way pushing with sticks, boats, women everywhere, governesses, mothers, waitresses. Sometimes it gets confusing. Too many women, spoiled for choice, but finally I fixed upon one. She was sitting several rows ahead of me. Masculine attire, which suits a woman I think. It seems to be in fashion at the moment. The pianist played and I was gazing. I was staring so hard she must have felt my eyes upon her, violating her neck. You can often tell, can't you, when you are being watched? She kept shaking her head as if a mosquito was disturbing her hair. Twice she adjusted her hat. And I kept staring, greedy, the sight of her, without shame or pity, willing both hands to rise at the same time. Her hair was short, her neck pale and beautiful and vulnerable. I became concerned my gaze might be too uncouth for her, might even destroy it, her beauty, and I had to look away, she must be protected, I was thinking, but I couldn't look away, couldn't do it. And then my gaze became too rough for her to bear. Finally, she turned around to look at her assailant. And this is what I have to admit to you, doctor.

Zygelbojm looks at Gloria, then away, then back again.

Can you guess what I am about to say?

Gloria shakes her head.

It wasn't a woman at all. She was a man!

His voice falls to a whisper.

So this is what I must ask you, doctor. Do you think I am displaying homosexual symptoms?

The former superfluous man gazes dreadfully upon Gloria's face with the blood-absent look of one who desires to be told the whole of the truth but fears he isn't strong enough to bear what it might be.

Perhaps in different times she would have smiled. Perhaps she would even have laughed. Or maybe not; maybe she would always have answered his solemnity with a solemnity of her own. His is the mad glory of the psyche, opposing unacceptable conditions in the world with issues of splendid irrelevance, busying itself with libidinal objects to survive.

I can't, of course, answer the question fully here, right now. We would need to go deeper into things, you understand? Techniques. Dream work. Your early life. Traumas. The nursery.

Of course. But— ? and he stops, a moment of reserve.

But a demonstration drowns everything—a fanfare of trumpets, an unpatriotic anthem, a festival celebrating the glorious occupiers, with belly rumbles of tubas and French horns, as hypocrite hearts swell beneath military-style tunics that Uri might like. And when the demonstration is gone, Zygelbojm is gone inside it, a trickle of water found by the sea.

And it is too late, curfew hangs too close, no visit can be made to the bureaucrat's office today, she must return to the charity house.

14

Supper and orisons are over. Dormitory 3 is filled with women making night-time noises. Again she has been humbled, by every pious genuflection she was made to perform, every look of pity and loathing burningly received from the cold eyes of holy librarians. Zosia was queenly at the top table, Uri inaccessible. Gloria wants to strike back. She stretches on the stairs, steps into the hall, goes quickly down the corridor towards Uri's room. She isn't sure whether what she feels is larkish euphoria or fear. She intends to steal a soldier.

Gloria pushes the door open, a kneeling boy turns around.

She had expected him to be asleep. He is not asleep. He is pleased to see her. He is making his prayers and wants more names to add to his list of souls to save.

So Gloria offers herself, he wants another, so she gives him Solomon Heller, *Another!* the 'Prince', *Another!* Sarah, Mr Mouse, and, finally, Igo Sym, a name that Uri finds agreeable and even comic and repeats over and over until some time after Gloria has told him not to.

He climbs into bed, his nightshirt tailing after. Gloria pulls the blankets up to cover him to the chin.

Does your mother know you're still awake?

He doesn't dispute the relationship. He wriggles sideways to make room and Gloria sits beside him, her back against the headboard.

Read to me.

He holds up a book of fairy tales, and makes it through into the second fable—the third little pig has butchered the wolf, now the hare is beating the tortoise—and Uri's eyelashes flutter, eyes roll up, lids slowly fall, then quickly rise again. The hare complacently rests beneath the branches of a tree, but Uri has stopped listening, his eyes dart one side then the other, no sudden monsters anywhere—he lifts one hand in lordly fashion and she holds it as she is meant to; his lids begin to fall again, his eyes vacate, a final tremble of lashes; his breathing deepens into a half-snore and he is asleep.

Gloria sits there. To hold his hand and regret those (Bernard the hooligan, her brother, her mother, Zygelbojm) she failed to smuggle into Uri's prayers. She tries to retrieve her hand from Uri's. He grasps it tighter, his eyes flicker open, his lips make the shape but not the comic sound *Igo*, and shut again. His hand does not relax its grip, she is his prisoner.

The curtains are drawn. Outside, the street is as loud as it ever gets, the last moments before curfew.

Gloria tries to pull herself away from the child's hand. He grips tighter. Minutes go by. She tries again. He relents.

She goes over to the shelf, this interloper who has

ingratiated herself into a child's heart only to betray it. Face down the lead parade. Ferocious little men aim muskets and spears ready to kill Uri's monsters, the crocodiles and giants and newcomers who eat nothing but boys. Behind her a floorboard creaks, her heart stutters and jumps. Look around, nothing to see, a door, a shadow, today's toy uniform abandoned on the rug. It feels ridiculous to be frozen like this, one hand ready to kidnap a little lead man. If he wakes she is done for. What ceremony is it that requires toy soldiers for its consummation?

She chooses one, not too old, not too prominent, not in the front rank, nor in the back, he's nearly at the middle, far from either unprotected end, a blue musketeer brandishing his weapon in his cracked yellow hands. Backing away from the shelf, Gloria detours to kiss Uri again on the brow. Snores rise from his face, the overspilling of innerness that is adorable in a boy but entirely loathsome in a man, should Uri get the chance to become one.

15

She goes softly down the stairs, into the deserted hall. The house should still be at morning prayers. Gloria holds the musketeer in the same hand that has clutched it through the night, a talisman against dreams. The tune that Damecki was whistling as he left the theatre comes into her mind, the sound is so clear that it seems to be coming from outside her head rather than within it, and slowly she turns, to see the holy librarian and his shadowy friend standing beside the stairs. The whistling stops.

Excuse me. I left something in the chapel.

We'll walk you there.

I don't need you to. I can find my own way.

We'll walk you.

Hindrance has one of those physiognomies that seem permanently mocking. Little looks like everybody else, but in the most extreme way: his features are regular, his hair nondescript, he looks like everybody apart from himself and he is instantly forgettable.

She is marched across the cobblestoned courtyard tantalisingly close to the street door, which is open; the day looks bright.

It would be nice to have a little chat. You don't mind, do you?

Of course she minds. She has no choice. Hindrance leads her to the back pew of the ominously empty chapel. Little closes the door. These men wouldn't attack her? Not here? If rape is attempted what does she do? Resist the attack with unresistance, with utter acquiescence? Or fight? Scratch and kick and scream? Defend her honour, defend her self, which might appear most real when under physical attack.

Madame has been very good to you.

Madame is very good.

Hindrance stares at Gloria, he's alert for any trace of irony or blasphemy.

Are you interested to know why I'm nicknamed Hindrance?

Not especially.

Because up till now that's been my method. A wagon carrying flour loses a wheel—a frenzied dog suddenly rushes into their headquarters—spikes in the street hidden in garbage puncture the tyres of their cars. Getting in the way of a policeman. So sorry, is that a dangerous renegade you're chasing? I'll get out of your way, sorry, oh sorry again, how ridiculous, I'm sorry, so clumsy, oh and there goes my beer, here, borrow my handkerchief, I'll quickly wipe that shirt-front clean . . .

He is very proud of himself and very threatening too.

Up till now?

What is your interest in Madame? Because mine, I will have to tell you, is devotion.

What is your interest in me?

Someone's coming.

Little steps back behind the door. Hindrance walks to a different pew. Gloria gets to her knees. She pretends to be praying.

Zosia enters the chapel, curtsies, crosses herself, picks up the holy book that she has miraculously left behind, crosses herself again, curtsies again. Gloria tries not to run as she goes across to the one-time virgin about to leave at the door.

Zosia permits herself to be accompanied out of the chapel, only looks at Gloria when she realises that she is inadvertently blocking her charity case's way out of the courtyard.

Where are you going?

I'm sorry.

I didn't see you at morning prayers. Your place here is in doubt unless you attend prayers.

I have somewhere I need to be. Only briefly. Paperwork. Bureaucracy. I shall be back for lunchtime prayers.

Do you have a man?

The way Zosia pronounces the word *man*. Do you have a *disease*? So there is something disgusting about you, I had always thought there was . . .

Gloria says nothing, tries to walk towards the street, it's another hot morning. She waits for her stern benefactress to step aside, which she does not. Gloria takes hold of Madame's stiff shoulders, fingertips brush her throat, evade the pimple, luminous in this light; Gloria fails to remember an occasion where her skin has touched Zosia's before, even in parting or by accident. Her breath puffs away a flick of hair that has escaped Zosia's chignon.

The position is held longer than expected. Hip bones touch. Were Gloria bolder, more predatory, more Sym-like, she would—would what? What does Zosia want from her? dread? What would she hate her for? would cast her out of here because?

The moment is lost in the consideration of it. The women break apart, Zosia steps aside repairing her hair. Gloria puts her hands in overcoat pockets, leaves the compound, tightens her fingers around a little lead man.

16

After a last look back at the City Theatre, where an alopecic usher has been entrusted with a blue musketeer to take to his master, Gloria walks on towards the stop where she will catch the streetcar to Long Avenue. It's a pleasant day, still unseasonably warm. She looks for tortoises struggling along. Perhaps all this city warmth is created from her interaction with Igo Sym. Sparks strong enough to wake tortoises from winter sleep. It is good to close eyes, feel the sun on her lids. She tries to remember the tune that Damecki was whistling, and hears her name being called, the sound of footsteps behind; she turns, she expects to see Damecki there, or Zygelbojm again, a second visitation— when the librarian who calls himself Hindrance swings into step beside her. Little emerges out of the anonymity behind him.

Pleasant day. Very warm.

The thick lenses of Hindrance's spectacles magnify the jeering look in his eyes. His nose is always wrinkled as if a bad smell is with him everywhere he goes and he is permanently just at the point of being about to recognise that the origin of the smell is himself. His arms and legs do not move quite in sympathy with one another.

Shall we walk together? Or catch a streetcar?

What do you want?

No no. Your decision. We'll escort you. The city is a dangerous place.

I don't need you to.

I say we should catch a streetcar. How about this one? What do you think?

He makes her hurry across the road through cars going past. The almond smell of diesel. And a streetcar arrives. It's painted yellow, instead of the customary red.

Where does this one go?

Not to Long Avenue, to the dubious comforts of a bureaucrat's office. And not to the western suburbs, the charity house. Yellow means that it passes through the forbidden district, on its way to the industrial district where glass factories used to be.

The wrong way.

Gloria steps aside for other passengers to climb on board. Hindrance pushes her forward. Glumly she accepts a ticket palmed to her by a passenger disembarking. She tries to stand at the middle of the car; Hindrance pushes her against the observation glass at the rear.

Where are you going?

Wherever you are. I only want a chat.

Gloria holds on to a rail for the journey. Hindrance surrounds her with his long arms. Little rocks on the open platform, the city hurtling past. Gloria looks out of the window as if there are many delightful novelties she might be interested to see.

What do you want to chat about?

Igo Sym.

Who?

Very good. I knew you were right for the job. Very good. But you needn't bother with that kind of thing, we've been following you for days. I intend to meet him. The only problem is, he doesn't want to meet me. He even has two soldiers with him at all times, to turn away unwanted guests. I need as it were a sponsor.

Why do you want to see him?

I am going to ask him to stop collaborating with the enemy.

And if he should refuse? If he should laugh at you?

Will he laugh?

No. He won't laugh. But you won't be able to persuade him.

I will be patient and sincere, and pious and patriotic, and trust to the righteousness of my cause that the traitor Sym might see the error of his ways. And if he laughs at me—

He won't laugh.

And if he laughs at me, or sets his gorillas on me, or even politely (I hear stories about his politeness) offers me a cup of tea before sending me back on my way, then you know what I'm going to do to him?

Cut off his hair?

I'll take out my gun and shoot him until he's dead. I carry a gun. Do you want to feel it?

No.

He takes her hand. His touch is light, but insistent. He

makes her feel the object protruding beneath the thick cloth
of his trousers.

What's your real name?

What's yours?

Gloria is reminded of a duelling movie the 'Prince' once
made, two heroes in military tunics glowering nervous and
arch at each other, almost touching, on a scrub of land
signifying a mountainside (which was, in fact, a butterfly
meadow near the Glade). The tension was awful. Close-ups
of the two men's faces, flickering eyelids, twisted mouths.
A bird flapped out of a bush, startling the doctor and the
cameraman, the camera whirled to follow the bird lifting
into the sky and then, as if reluctantly, returned to the
two men who hadn't moved except to raise guns pointing
towards one another's heart.

She tries to penetrate Hindrance's jeery look. Peel it all
away, reveal what's beneath the mockery. Fervour, cynical
piety, disgust, pride, loneliness, what else? Shame? Lust?

I can't help you. Look. I want to get off here. It's going
the wrong way.

He doesn't move away. His arms stiffen either side of
her.

*Do you know his mistress? What is her name? Where
does she live?*

She has wide-apart eyes. That's all I know.

Trust us.

I don't.

What do you want? We'll pay.

I don't want. I just want to get off here.

One of Hindrance's hands presumes to touch her.

Does Zosia know what you're doing?

Do you think anything goes on without her approval? Do you think you're under her special protection?

Saxon Square flits past, unapproachable. There goes the large wooden V. Yes, she had rather thought she was under the virgin's special protection. She hadn't realised that Sym was under such threat. With her resistance she keeps him alive.

I want to get off. I can't help you.

There are three in the squad. Myself, Little here, and the third one is codenamed Grey. This is how it will happen. At his apartment in Willow Street: Hindrance, Little and Grey. Little will keep watch-out on the stairs. Hindrance will fire the shots. Grey will be the witness.

How very interesting. I'm not going to help you.

Then I have to threaten you.

He does not seem disappointed to have to be doing that. Little, holding on to the rail with both hands, leans out, head back, face smiling in dizzying space.

We'll do it anyway, without you.

Is that your threat?

No. Promise. We'll make sure you're not allowed back. We'll make sure you go where you belong.

Is her provenance that obvious? Did the others all know all the time? She had been assiduous in brushing her hair away from her forehead, in making her eyes look stupid and cheerful.

His hand is still on her sleeve. It is hard to believe that he has a body beneath his clothes.

And we'll denounce the boy. For what he is.

What is he?

He should go back with you, where you came from.

The 'Prince' then is his father. She is glad of that, she had hoped so. Behind her, approaching, is the forbidden district. Out of the window she watches the last other apartment blocks pulling away. The city turns grey here, the final stretch before the forbidden district.

Why are you smiling? Who do you work for? Who tells you what to do?

Nobody.

She wishes there were somebody.

People have been keeping watch on you ever since you first came to spy on Madame.

I don't think so. I'm not a spy.

You knew Madame had a child. You must have known or else you wouldn't have had a hat to give to the boy. Who briefed you? Them or the dreks?

It was accident only. A boy at a checkpoint lost his hat. I picked it up. I happened to have it when I visited your Madame. Fortuitous.

Hindrance sneers. There can be no accidents in the world of the conspirator: God and the Devil work in opposition at every moment in even the humblest material.

Gloria ducks under Hindrance's arm. She moves towards the open platform. At the final two corners the streetcar will have to slow down, she has two chances to jump off. Little ignores her. He is still leaning back smiling, the psychoactive properties of streetcars are making him giddy. Gloria shuts her eyes too. An ocean liner is what she sees, streamers, trumpets. Hordes on the shore whom she waves at as if there were friends wishing her well in the crowd.

She gets ready to jump.

Hindrance is taking hold of her. His hands are on her shoulders, his face is pushing itself against the side of hers, no one on the streetcar notices or cares, but he should be easy to resist, he is a paper man, his beard scratches her face. He braces himself against the rail for support, her ear tilts his glasses away from his nose. There goes the first corner. And there goes Little, lightly stepping off into space, landing on the road, half jogging, still smiling. She fights Hindrance away. He grabs her again and tugs her back towards the rear window, and coughs, and awkwardly steps around her and off the streetcar at the final corner before the forbidden district.

The streetcar accelerates. The other side recedes. She watches the sunlight bouncing off Hindrance's spectacles, which diminish away from her. There goes the road, the checkpoint, the barrier, the notices announcing disease and punishment, the guns and colours and policemen—and an immediate crowd surrounds the streetcar, which lurches to a stop. In the glass Gloria sees the reflection of soldiers inspecting the papers of the few passengers left aboard. She steps off, into the crowd.

Part Three

TORTOISES

I

Gloria goes to the family apartment not entirely out of choice. Gloria goes to Valour Street partly out of habit, and some nostalgia for a person she had once been, who had lived in this quarter of the city, fighting family wars, surviving family romances, which in that relatively innocent time had seemed to be important.

But mainly she goes to Valour Street because that's the direction the crowd is going in, and it is easiest to go with the crowd. Sometimes she lifts her feet off the ground, lets herself be carried along, far better than any streetcar. And in this tight mass there is security: the closer together the bodies are packed the less intimacy there is, no space for pickpockets or bespectacled men with half-dead hands and bad intentions. She is invisible here, she is nothing here, she is just like everybody else. The relief, again, of having an us to belong to. Zygelbojm should be here, he would like it better here. And it doesn't matter that the crowd-world around her crawls with insects and stinks of herring and sweat and shit, she will soon learn not to smell anything just as she is learning not to hear the beggars; already she can't tell, over the thud of the blood in her ears, over the harsh rumbled voice of the crowd, what is being pleaded for.

Gloria struggles away from the crowd to enter the apartment building on Valour Street. (Her elbows are useful instruments to cut a path with—she is becoming a surgeon of the crowd.) A man trudges ahead of her up the stairs. She follows after, passes him knocking on the door of the apartment that the Limes used to live at; Mr Lime was her stepfather's antagonist, his youngest son was the first boy she ever kissed. She carries on up the stairs, hears five bolts unlock behind her, a following din of complaint. She climbs on, walks along a dim corridor to a corner apartment. The nameplate Streamwood is still beside the door. Her key still fits in the lock.

In the living room a thin malcontent wearing a green police uniform that was made for a bigger man sits in one of stepfather's horsehair chairs. His cap is at the other end of the table, by the telephone. In front of him are two piles of canvas army belts, with a metal bowl in between. One by one he lifts a belt from the left pile, dips it into the bowl, pulls it through and out—viscous stuff has been smeared more or less evenly over it—and then places it in the growing pile on the right.

Brother Daniel wears a flashy gold watch, diamond rings on two of his fingers. His armband shines as if it has been coated with gilt. Patches of scalp dully gleam through the curly remnants of hair. Every now and again he wipes his mouth with his sleeve. The third time he does this he senses that he is not alone in the room.

Daniel turns his head fast to see her. The look of irritation is surprisingly replaced by pleasure.

I knew you'd be back. As soon as you heard of my prosperity.

His prosperity doesn't seem to agree with him. The only parts of her brother that look truly alive are his trembling gloved hands and his wet lips and the red shaving rash that rages over his throat and chin.

Where is everyone?

He tells her. Stepfather is dead. Mother is safe. A hooligan came from Heller's headquarters shortly after Gloria *ran away*. He plucked mother away and sent her to safety in the west. Stepfather heard the hooligan coming, feared for his life, and ran downstairs and hid in the laundry room until he was gone. Daniel too was offered a kind of safety.

The hooligan wanted me to drive for him. He'd got hold of Heller's car. You think! I was a lawyer. I'm not anyone's chauffeur. Mother is safe, but lonely. I get postcards. Stepfather died of the typhus plague. But not me. Do you want one of these? It'll protect you.

I haven't got any money.

It's a miracle cure. You can't afford not to have it.

The telephone rings. Daniel slowly gets up, walks around the table to answer it. He nods as he listens, doesn't speak, until the end, when he says, *Yes. I'll pass that on.*

There are only two working telephones in the entire building. I've got a lot of irons in the fire. How much salary do you think a policeman gets? Nothing, that's the answer. Do you think I could afford to do the job just for prestige? I have to use my initiative. Man can't live by bribes alone.

Do you remember Sarah? Is she still in the quarter?

A sly expression briefly rejuvenates his face.

Heller's tart? I know where you can find her.

She is almost reassured by the slyness, and by the return of his old self-satisfied scorn.

What I also know is that you'll catch the plague and die and when you do you'll only have yourself to blame.

A knock comes on the apartment door. Daniel doesn't appear to notice.

Should I get that?

Don't bother. It'll be some busybody. I'm not expecting anyone.

Where can I find Sarah?

There's a place called the Beach Bar. It's on Chestnut Street. I expect you'll want to stay here. You can if you want to.

This is as close to tenderness as she's ever known from him. If she begs him for a favour now his exultation, and intimacy, will be complete.

My old room?

No, he concedes. *A family is in your old room. Regulations. But people know to keep out of my way around here. You'll have the run of the rest of the place, just like me. You can do the cooking. Take a walk now. I'm busy. When you go, knock twice on Miller's door upstairs. Twice. If anyone answers say that Miller's got a telephone message and the usual rates apply. If he offers you money, don't take it, it goes to me. I'll know if you try to cheat me. You'll want to go to the Arts Club tonight. Everyone'll be there, I can get you in. Where's your luggage? You haven't got anything?*

He turns his attention back to his miracle cures. Lift: dip: pull.

2

Gloria presumes her brother knew that swimwear must be worn at the Beach Bar and Restaurant. This is, says a woman custodian with savage buck teeth, the strict and absolute dress code. Gloria has to hand over her own clothes and pay an extortionate amount to rent a baggy bathing costume and a green sun visor. Only then is she allowed in. An apartment building used to be here, now it's a patch of grass, four bomb-blasted walls, painted into an imagined tropical beach.

She is the only patron of the establishment. Gloria is invited to sit in a deckchair and the waiter leaves his guitar in a corner painted with waves and palm trees and dolphins to ask her if she wants to order a cocktail, which, she supposes, she does. Despite the heatwave the weather is still too cold to be sitting out like this, but it is preferable nonetheless, the quiet make-believe tropics, away from the crowd. Gloria is convinced that she has enemies everywhere. Even if she didn't, this would still be preferable. There are half a million case studies in disintegration out there, but Gloria has given up psychology. Behind the walls of the Beach Bar, you can will yourself swiftly into delusion, hear the crowd outside as the sound of the sea. Maybe the entrance fee wasn't extortionate after all.

The waiter brings her a tall glass into which something very muddy and treacly has been poured. She asks if she is permitted to borrow her overcoat back. He tells her, with some sympathy, that she isn't. He returns to his corner and picks up his guitar.

When Sarah arrives it's in a bathing costume that's elegant and fits her. The waiter constructs a deckchair next to Gloria's without spilling a globule of the cocktail he carries. Sarah's legs are long and goose-bumped. Her face is unpainted. Her hair is almost entirely grey. Even so, she looks younger than before. Gloria asks questions. Where were you and why didn't you meet me and what's been happening to you in the time between? Sarah shakes her head and tells Gloria that the waiter used to be second violinist at the City Philharmonic.

Are you hungry?

Always.

Sarah defers all Gloria's questions, and Gloria answers any one of hers. This means that Sarah is the stronger.

Sarah takes another sip of her cocktail. Her mouth puckers around the straw. Her cheeks suck in. Then she stretches, stops.

Look, she whispers. *Another.*

Gloria looks sharply all around, have her enemies followed her here, too? Is that Hindrance Sarah has seen leering over crooked walls? But there is no one, only the waiter, he bows his head over his guitar, long fingernails pluck at strings, music rises up, a modern lament.

Then Gloria sees, from the brightest patch of the beach, a pair of cautious, dark, not unbenevolent eyes gazing unblinkingly back. It's a tortoise, making its excruciating journey across the beach, attempting, foolishly or heroically, Gloria can't decide which, to mount any rock that blocks its way.

Where do these tortoises come from? Is it because of the heatwave?

Sarah gets up, elegant stalker, she follows the tortoise and picks it up, cradles it back to her chair, stroking its shell as if it were made of fur.

I could take you somewhere else if you liked. The food isn't very good here. I could take you somewhere with more case studies.

The prospect of going anywhere inside this city does not excite Gloria, except into repulsion.

I've given up psychology. Heller's death gave me that much, at least. All I want is a place that's quiet and warm and safe.

Yes, me too.

Sarah looks at Gloria, as if for the first time. There's something regretful in her voice.

Heller's not dead.

Of course he's dead. It was his apotheosis.

Did you see him dead? Did you see his body?

Sarah has the clear-eyed look of a missionary. She is dispensing revelation and is curious, in a distanced loving way, how the soul previously in darkness will receive it.

No, not his body, Gloria has to admit. A tartan blanket covered it, it was the one he used to have in his car. Remember it? Sometimes we sheltered underneath. Drank vodka or was that with Bernard? I don't remember. Do you remember the hooligan? I used to wonder what became of him. Is it true he has the Buick? My brother said.

Heller feels bad about what happened.

His capacity for feeling was doubtful even when he was alive.

Heller's not dead.

Sarah is repeating this with such utter candour that it is either, yes, the world-shaking truth, or else absolute symptom of her insanity and either way to be attended to.

Where is he now?

I don't know. Mostly he sends messages through intermediaries.

Mostly.

He might even be out of the country by now. I like to think that he's nearby somewhere, watching over.

Of course. I would like to think so too.

He's not dead. He used you, Gloria. He feels bad about that.

(Why say *you*? Why not *us*? Because Sarah belongs to a different, superior category, which madness or complicity has elevated her to.)

He showed all the signs.

He was a good faker. They were going to close him down. After he disappeared most of his associates were arrested and never seen again. A body was buried in the graveyard. His own psychologist was a believing witness to his suicide. Who's going to doubt?

You knew this? You were part of this?

It's a good way to hide, isn't it? Being dead.

The best.

Thoughts, accusations, now tumble in.

You knew all the time he wasn't dead. That means the two of you were in on something together. You never intended to meet me. And you sent me over to the other side, a goose-chase bureaucracy. I was on my own there. Superfluous. Isn't it a little inhuman? I'm sorry. I'm starting to feel very sorry for myself.

Heller thought—

Oh of course.

Oh of course, *Heller thought*, Heller is dead and in his place Sarah has raised a magical creation strong enough to carry any guilt accruing to her.

Heller thought it would be quicker, easier for you. You shouldn't even be in the city now. Why are you here? There was money waiting for you, travel documents. At his lawyer's office.

I went there. He told me I'd arrived two weeks early. The wrong date.

Probably he was trying to cheat you. Hope the city swallowed you up. He'd keep the money for himself.

It nearly did. But. I remember he warned me against a man he called a rat-catcher, he gave me a ticket to a charity house.

I said I thought he was trying to cheat you. I didn't say he was bad. Why didn't you go back when he told you to?

248

I don't remember. Something got in the way. I don't remember what.

Brother Daniel will know the truth. Gloria needs a reality principle third, Daniel or the hooligan Bernard or best of all Heller himself, stepping out of the shadows, dressed all in black like Sym, doffing his cap in an awkward flourish, only the dents on his face revealing the impressions of his fall, *Yes yes I'm alive. I tricked you. I was cleverer, more ruthless, more cohesive than I led you to believe. Everything she says is true.*

I have to say, I don't believe you.

Sarah is getting impatient with her. What does the missionary do when the savage refuses to accept revelation? Bring out the instruments of torture?—the black iron shafts wrapped with remnants soaked in paraffin, ready for the flame.

We'll go together to the lawyer's office. I don't like going over but I'll go with you there.

Gloria has won at least a concession of a *we*.

Come then. I'm ready. I don't have any luggage.

We'll go to the bureaucrat lawyer's office. Prove to me your truth. Produce evidence of Heller if you can. I'll believe him when I see him. But Sarah will say that Heller can't possibly be produced; he is all very sorry et cetera, but it's a question of security, not just his.

We can visit the bureaucrat, receive my reward, find Heller together.

He won't see you. He—

Yes, I know. I can guess what you might say.

This is infectious. Gloria's own imagined Heller now

goes on to say, *What's her motive in all this? Dead or alive I never did find that out.*

The two women put aside muddy cocktails, remove sun visors—music tremolos under the distracted fingers of the guitarist—step away from deckchairs. The tortoise is asleep. As the buck-toothed custodian is approached the sound of the crowd outside gets louder.

Sarah holds the tortoise to her breast. It gazes sleepily up at her with an expression that is disarmingly close to kindness. She instructs the rickshaw driver. He whistles as he pedals.

How's your child?

Sarah ducks her head. *I don't know. It's better for him.*

What's his name? Is his name Uri? Does he have copper-coloured hair?

That's not his name. His hair is black. Why?

I think I know a boy just like.

I'm sorry, Gloria, I am. I have to look after myself. It's all anyone can do.

Gloria shakes her head several times, to try to clear it, to find some words, or maybe just for something to do. She lifts the collar of her coat over her chin and shields her eyes with a hand.

Are you trying to look inconspicuous?

This sun is too bright, that's all.

Her head slowly finds a place on Sarah's shoulder. An arm surrounds her with sheepskin. She feels more like crying than ever. The tortoise slowly turns its head to look at her, somewhat sceptically.

Turning the corner into Market Street, the driver stops pedalling to let a streetcar rattle past. It's the same one that Gloria took into the quarter, making its return journey or its return return journey. Over on the opposite pavement a beggar boy's rickety legs have refused to carry him any further. He struggles to get up, he falls down again, into the useless shade of a tree. Two sisters pause to watch him before mother tugs the pair away. Outside an antique shop a small sub-crowd has temporarily broken away from the main body to look in, faces to the glass. The rest of the crowd pushes interminably along. Gloria wonders if her time would be best spent investigating the hidden laws that govern the movement of crowds.

Maybe it is something to do with the moon, like tides.

What is?

Gloria hadn't realised that she'd spoken the thought aloud. The driver stands up from his saddle to pedal faster, he catches up with another rickshaw. The two drivers fall into conversation and the same bicycle rhythm. The passengers in the second rickshaw both wear prosperous jowls and council armbands. The councilmen glance at the two women, then away, then back again, staring now like sinister enemies. Or maybe it is interest in Sarah that these councilmen are registering. If you can afford a rickshaw, you can afford lust.

How's Heller's digestion? Does he burp a lot?

Sarah doesn't answer. She is getting more nervous as the rickshaw approaches the gate. Gloria feels her anxiety grow.

It's inconvenient to go over. I run businesses for Heller

*in the quarter. And a nightclub. Heller says you took him
to a nightclub once.*

Yes. I think I did. He didn't like it very much.

Sarah withdraws her self; she raps the tortoise on his
shell; he blinks once and immediately pulls in head and
legs. Enviable.

The rickshaw comes to a halt near the gate at Vine Street.
That might be a look of malice in the rickshaw man's eyes.
Or just resentment that he hasn't received a larger tip.

3

The gate is better fortified than it was last time. Fresh signs on the high wall, print still wet, announce that any newcomer caught unauthorised on the other side will be shot. Gloria is the wise one here. She feels Sarah's trepidation grow. She tries to instruct her in the ways of the other side.

We'll catch a streetcar, you can expect to receive a ticket in your hand, surreptitious. It's a form of resistance. Are you listening?

Yes.

And it's always best to stand. If they do one of their inspections they always start with the passengers sitting down, I don't know why.

An electricity man walks through the gate. The line crabs forward. Sarah clutches her tortoise tighter. It is comfortable in her arms.

I hadn't been expecting this. I thought I'd be in Forest Street tonight. There's a première.

My brother said something about it. He said he could get me in.

He probably could. He's become quite influential.

Tell me about your child. Did Heller discover about the son?

No, the word comes harshly, a warning that some things mustn't be told, even to ghosts. Of course Heller did not find out about the son. The tycoon is dead and Sarah's Heller is the shadowy creation of her need for him to be alive, her persevering need for father. Sarah's husband will have been older than her too; Gloria imagines for her a more provincial, more rounded version of Mr Mouse.

Or Heller is as clever (and Gloria as foolish) as Sarah says he is. Gloria does not yet feel any joy in the possibility of Heller having stayed alive.

The gate is closer. And it is a gate now, black metal topped with barbed wire. Two green policemen block the way. They look better in their uniforms than Daniel ever could. A few onlookers gaze idly through the bars. Is that Hindrance there? the sun on his spectacles, and the man obscured behind him will be Little. She can't see the third member of the assassination squad, the mysterious Grey. She looks more closely: Hindrance's malicious face dissolves into the face of a stranger. A barefoot ragged boy jostles into her and away. She has to hold on to Sarah's arm to catch her balance.

You don't need me. I'll telephone the lawyer. He'll be cooperative.

Sarah and Heller are the two most sensible people Gloria knows. No. Knew. Gloria removes her hand. She must resist being sucked into a shared delusion, yield herself to a mad dance for two.

When Gloria visits the bureaucrat, in the moment of his

greeting or rejection, it will be revealed whether Heller is
still alive, whose world she is living in. Sarah is past Gloria's
help. She is looking after herself most efficiently. Mad or
not, she doesn't need Gloria. Igo Sym does. Uri might.

She checks her pockets. If the boy was a pickpocket he
didn't get anything; she has two gold coins left.

I'm going to telephone the lawyer.

No. Not now. Wait. We're almost at the head of the
line.

And *NEXT!* is called out, and Gloria steps forward, and
Sarah steps back. Gloria's documents are held up to the
light, taken away for numbers to be checked against lists
in the sentry box. She is allowed to proceed. Heller's old
forgery still holds. Sarah and the quarter are left behind.

There is immediate relief in the escape from density.
The quarter was something entirely new, evolving ugly
fast in concentration and quarantine. Gloria's body lifts,
she feels her flesh as her own again, her muscles relax in
the breathable air of the other side.

Her disappointment is easy to push aside. She had not
truly expected Sarah to come over. If she were to write
Sarah's story it would be a history of absences.

She tries now pretending this thing is a dream. Follow
the apparent rules and hope that the slippery world does
not suddenly metamorphose into something contrary.

Gloria rides the streetcar back to the charity house,
holding a creased blackened ticket in her hand. When
the streetcar reaches her stop she passes the ticket to a
passenger getting on, a perfect sleight of hand that makes

her more confident, as if she belongs here; she knows how to practise its ways.

She will visit the charity house, collect her bag, kiss goodbye to Uri, and maybe Zosia, then return to the bureaucrat's office to be readmitted to her destiny. Igo Sym will have to seduce and be irritated and flourish in his uniform without her. She will send him a postcard from the south.

4

There is mayhem in the charity house. Empty spaces in the chapel. Empty chairs at the top table in the refectory. No Zosia, no Uri. An undercurrent of murmurs. Gloria wonders if the boy is sick. Henry, his supposed uncle, was always catching chills. Maybe she had been out with him for too long on the park expedition, needlessly exposed him to too many city infections. She feels confident enough to go to his room. The way is barred. Two librarians, a male and a female, block her way. The female tells her Uri is to be confined to his room today. Why? Because he has committed a crime, a series of crimes. What are his crimes? Gloria is not permitted to know. She is permitted to wait outside Madame's office door. Hindrance passes by as she waits, he lifts an eyebrow, mockery and threat.

Madame finally consents to talk to Gloria. Madame is haughty, furious.

What has he done?

I will tell you what he's done!

Zosia shivers with rage more uncontrollable than Sym's, less eternal. The pimple on her throat has never looked quite so scarlet, pearly white, as she grabs at Gloria, tugs her along a corridor. Holy librarians step alarmedly aside—Zosia reaches Uri's door, turns a key, pushes open the door.

The boy in his nightshirt is silent, heroic, on the bed. He looks away from his intruders. If Gloria could see his face she knows she would see tear tracks down his cheeks, a mouth set firm.

One of his soldiers is gone! The soldiers were my brother's before him and my father's before that. A sacred possession, lent to the boy in trust.

But—

That's not his worst crime. He refuses to confess. He refuses to say what he's done.

Zosia storms to the bed, makes as if to swipe the boy's head. He hardly flinches. Despite her rage, she doesn't have the heart or the appetite to hit him. The hand falls uselessly by her side. He is taking Gloria's blame. Mute, martyred Uri. Gloria clears her throat. He signals—with just the slightest turn of his head, the merest flicker of his long eyelashes—that she is to be silent. It is the most poignant look. He knows that she is the culprit and he trusts her. Whatever she might have done with his soldier he will defend her for it, interpose his body between danger and her, take with his slender flesh the arrows that had been meant for Gloria.

Zosia closes the bedroom door and locks it again, stares at Gloria.

He has never behaved like this before. You have unsettled him.

There is no argument to make. It's clear that it's not just

Gloria she blames, it's everyone who belongs to her parasitic newcomer tribe. Zosia allows Gloria one last glare, a final bolt of fury; she swallows, her pimple furiously lifts, threatens to explode, and slowly lowers again on her throat, and Gloria must go.

5

This is the path she takes, to elude Hindrance and Little, and any other malevolent pursuer. She announces to a corridor wall and several uninterested librarians that she is going to Dormitory 3. Then she goes instead to the courtyard, passes unmolested out to the street. She walks fast, she reaches a corner, loudspeakers bark at her denying any break of a pact with the easterners, there's the usual mood of complicity in the pairs of men strolling, sweating in furs.

Gloria catches a streetcar, she gets off at the first stop, crosses the street, slips down an alleyway, through a courtyard and on to Frost Avenue, where she catches another streetcar going in the opposite direction. Her bag is still in Dormitory 3, her destiny at the bureaucrat's office, and Gloria has chosen.

From behind a streetcar window she looks for assassins. She does not see assassins. She sees a prostitute on a corner near the meat market looking severe and unapproachable, even while being approached by a client, even while leading him by the lapel into a narrow turreted building. She sees a soldier pretending to be a scholar, hunched over a wheelbarrow of second-hand books, the glint of something metal shines as the breeze flaps his overcoat open, a blade or a medal, doubled by something alert in his eyes.

Frost Avenue becomes Parliament Street. The road widens, ruins diminish, she is in their part of town. She climbs down from the streetcar at a stop just short of Theatre Square. There is space to stroll in this version of the city, to breathe; her paranoia increases quite comfortably, with a corresponding exhilaration. She walks down side streets, criss-crossing, and then returns along the boulevard, hardly ever buffeted, past a cinema, a grand café, a milliner's. Gloria stops, once, at a jewellery shop in the arcade in Theatre Square, where she holds an amber necklace up to her throat and examines the mirror for threatening shapes behind. There is nothing to be scared of, thumbprints on the mirror, the window blur of sunshine in Theatre Square, a weary shopgirl advancing.

As she reaches Willow Street, as she walks past where the Tip Top Club used to be, the freakish sun warmth is lifting away from the city, street lamps are flickering on, and there is no sign of Hindrance or Little or the other, mysterious third.

6

Igo Sym is restless, she has infected him with her own
mood. He wants to go out, he doesn't want to go out. He
fiddles with buttons on his shirt. He picks up a magazine
and shows her a photograph of a medievalist villa in the
mountains. *What do you think?* he asks. *It's been made
available for me.* Gloria waits, sipping tea, her legs together
twisted away from the angle of her head and shoulders, the
old professional stance.

He had been irritated with her when she arrived. She
had come so late, he'd been expecting her in the morning,
he'd been stuck inside all day, had to cancel important
appointments, had to argue with—and then he caught
himself, she watched him disapproving of the tone of
his voice, of himself, which culminated in him making a
glamorous move for Gloria's coat, in guiding her swiftly
down the half-staircase into the living room.

Gloria had never experienced Igo Sym's irritation so
directly before. His tone was shrill but his face was perfect throughout, improved even—the flicker of lust, the
trademark look both casual and cruel. The living room
was innocent of any signs of his irritation. Most men's

pathologies exert outwards, the rubbish basket kicked, the cigarette box scattered. Sym's living room was undisturbed, immaculate.

When she returns to the charity house she will have a blue musketeer hidden in her hand. Sneak into Uri's room, slip the soldier back on the shelf, release the child from his martyrdom, a toy miracle. She has been given the opportunity to choose, so she has—she's intent on discharging her responsibilities one by one, beginning with the lightest.

I met your actor Damecki.

Oh? A look of displeasure. He brushes away something imaginary. *What did he ask you to do? Plead his case?*

Yes.

Damecki's a buffoon.

The 40 Husbands of Madame Ilona is to begin its scheduled run. *Drunk Walter* has finished. Damecki was twice offered roles in the new production, but he turned each down as unsuitable for his status, imagined, his reputation, self-sustained. Damecki has made himself, Sym tells her, superfluous.

He can cross his eyes at will. That's it. That's all he can do. And sometimes he's able to remember his lines. Do you remember him from before? Of course not. No one does. He claims he had a speciality playing drunk peasants but I'm sure I never heard of him. And then he got a break. He got a break because his country was invaded, because most of his betters in the profession are in cemeteries or labour camps or washing dishes in restaurants, because it's supposed to be unpatriotic to be involved in my productions. The good of the nation. I am, you know, regarded by some as a traitor . . .

Gloria lights one of Sym's cigarettes, murmurs her shock and surprise. (No! Surely not? I had not heard.)

But none of that bothers Damecki. I'd have more respect for him if it did. The joke is, he thinks he's a star because of his gifts, only now recognised. He wants the world to remain at his feet but now the party's over and he can't bear it. He thinks I can't stand his success so am set on destroying him?

Something like that.

My resources are limited. I don't like grumblers, least of all when I'm doing it myself. Damecki will have to find his own way. These are new times.

Sym glances at himself in the looking-glass.

Do you feel guilty?

Guilty? No. I don't feel guilty.

Sym's philosophy: One Does What One Can. Zosia has the bullock and the sword for her family crest. Sym would have military epaulettes and—? Gloria wonders if it is possible, for heraldic purposes, to picture charm. With sandpaper beneath.

Do you worry that some people regard you as a traitor?

Am I so dependent on the good opinion of others, you mean? That's not the reason why, Gloria.

Sym takes away the tea things, which he then brings back in, a filled pot, the pair of china cups freshly washed and warmed, a pitcher of milk. A ginger tomcat pauses on the gallery to observe. It licks its front paw. Gloria relaxes a little in her chair.

Sym half reclines on the couch. His head is supported by cushions, one foot is on the floor, the other rests on the far arm of the sofa. He cracks his knuckles. He looks down at his fingers.

She wants just to say, May I have that soldier back? the blue musketeer, and then my life may move on. But first the case of Sym must be attended to, and then the cases of Heller and Sarah and maybe even of Gloria.

I don't usually do that. It's a habit I gave up when I was a child.

I don't believe you ever were a child.

Not even when a charming boy mangled his own name so Hugo came out as Igo; even then, there was a separate egoistic consciousness, watching, applauding.

The charming man sits forward. The trouble on his face is beautiful. *Will you help me?*

(Oh yes. Just ask me a second time and I'll say yes.)

I've given up psychology. I think I told you.

Yes. Yes of course. Is it because of your gangster? I won't ask. But what if—If a psychologist were to treat me or someone like me. If a psychologist like you were to treat a patient like me, it's possible to talk about it that way, isn't it? What might her treatment be?

Parlour games with Igo Sym. Most enjoyable.

Except, just once, she would like to be the teller of symptoms. She would like to exchange positions with Sym and lie down on the couch and pour out her own heart. Listen. This is how I desire, and these are my unhappinesses. Listen to me for once, this is how I am troubled, by the world and uncertainty, and in my self,

oppressed by fears and bad friends and paranoiac thoughts
and unsuitable men. All I want is to go, somewhere, south
and hot, I don't know the name for it.

Gloria?

Yes. Tell me first. What your hypothetical patient hopes
for, for himself.

He and she are approaching the big thing. She imagines
an incident. The war before is nearly over, young Lieutenant Sym is on the battlefield, his uniform goes strikingly
well with the colour of the stallion he rides. A bomb hits,
a long-range artillery shell speculatively launched, with
horrific consequences. Sym's horse rears, the young lieutenant is thrown, into the mud, covered in equine blood,
surrounded by the bodies of his friends. Later, at evening,
or the next day or the next, the burial teams come, and a
hand moves, disturbing the still landscape of carnage, and
young Lieutenant Sym is pulled out, shivering, weeping,
the single survivor who, of course, cannot deserve to be.

Or he wasn't a lieutenant at all, that was imagined, he
was a fetishist always; in someone else's borrowed uniform,
the audacious young corporal was play-acting. He liked the
feel of good cotton against his skin, he liked the admiration
in other men's eyes. Meanwhile a dangerous mission was
being organised. A corporal was pressed to volunteer, and
while Sym was busy practising his officer's salute behind
the enlisted men's mess, his best friend was sent instead,
and died instead.

Or there was never a big thing at all. Maybe, when
the war before ended, young Lieutenant Sym investigated
analysis purely out of intellectual curiosity, as he claimed,

and the only reason he came to her was that she had the same first name as a woman he happened to be besotted with. That could have been true once, but not now—the woman rejected him, and even then he carried his constant irritation within him, a chafing internal rubbing that by now has worn some vital parts away.

Tell me. What does he want?

Just to be cured, says Sym. Said so simply, by an actor. Play-acting the penitent or not, it makes her unchilded heart go out to him.

She can find it now. What Sym has been keeping back even from himself. (Is it fair to demand candour when she is keeping so much back herself? There are two traitors in this room.)

His hands on her, his gift like electricity—Is this seduction or just extended courtesy? He reaches for her, no that's not what's happening, somehow he's made her reach for him, she's touching his face, fingertips to skin, like she practised with his cigarette card image as a child, and his lips graze the side of her neck, her throat.

Why isn't he holding her any more? Because there is someone knocking at the door and suddenly irritated Sym gives her *that* look again, the flicker of lust, the trademark something casual and cruel, and he is smoothing down his robe as he walks to the hall.

There is always recompense, few wounds are truly disabling. The secret of a great screen lover: when he wanted to seduce every woman in the audience, he looked at his co-star and remembered when she most recently fluffed her lines, or the script girl who had given him the wrong prompt, the director making a mistake with the camera set-up—he remembers all these annoyances and his eyes glitter, his lips part, and in the darkened auditorium a hundred women swoon.

But Sym is at the door and Hindrance will be behind it. She had been followed after all, despite her amateur precautions. There is no escape route. Rush to the window and Hindrance will be there, breathing condensation on the other side of the glass. Come away from the door please and don't open any cupboards, he's waiting behind every opening, hiding in every hole. Hindrance is hanging like a suit in the bedroom wardrobe, he's in the basement, in a pile of coal, patiently waiting with his chin pressed to his chest, his arms wrapped around his knees, the sinister mocking expression still visible through the soot on his face. Just stay with me, don't open anything please, least of all a door, forgive me please. You could carry on seducing me if you liked, your gift of hands, and tongue too, I've always supposed. Up on the gallery a large tomcat pads past.

The chance is over, and she can try blaming Hindrance for it. Sym unlocks the door, pulls it open. And outside—she has never been relieved to see black uniforms before—are two gorilla men, Sym's bodyguards, who peer in at her, ogling, adjudging. She sees their quick disappointment, they are probably connoisseurs by now of their master's women, and they see her as a poor sort of catch.

Sym issues an order. He closes the door, returns to the couch.

I've got rid of them. They won't come back. You were about to tell me about treatment?

Was I? Your hypothetical case. Yes. The patient. What symptoms does he present? She would ask him what he considers his problem or problems to be, but first, before any of that, tell me please, what happened to the soldier. May I have it back please?

Which soldier?

The toy soldier I gave you.

You want to know what happened to your soldier?

Yes. No.

She was saving this for last, her highest priority; but the urgency of Uri's case has made her impatient.

Yes. What happened? Why did you need it?

I'm sure I said why. Didn't I? I don't remember you wanting it back. Did you say you wanted it back? I should have invited you. You'd have liked it.

Liked? Liked what?

Last night. At the Bristol.

He is about to tell her a story. She begins to relax.

Who was there?

Administrators. Officers. The military governor's assistant. The deputy chief of police. Some epidemiologists here to study plagues in the forbidden district. An ethnographer. A guidebook writer. A pianist playing jazz. A couple of actors.

Actresses?

Actresses too. And your friend Damecki. He arrived late, out of breath, out of temper. Two women were with him at the start—

And at the end?

Don't be impatient. Do you have somewhere you need to be?

No. Not at all. I'm sorry. I have nowhere else to be.

She ducks her head, she could be blushing.

The women—Damecki had two women?

Could have been twins. Local girls. Doing well out of things, like Damecki.

Except Damecki isn't doing well any more.

No. He's not. And as a result the girls were losing enthusiasm for him. It didn't take much to—but I'll get to that. The climax is the fortune-telling. Your soldier was on the mantelpiece above the fire. Someone pointed to it and said it was in better condition than the people who had tried to defend this city.

People? They call the others people?

It's Sym's turn to redden. Only newcomers call the others others. She has just revealed her own provenance—what he has probably always suspected is now verified. Igo Sym knows her perfectly well for what she is, despite her regular features and good nose and perfect intonation. It's nothing to do with hair, or a look in the eyes. And he doesn't hate or blame her for it.

Sym licks his lips, he looks away. *Sometimes. Sometimes barbarians. Sometimes manure. More often pigs. That reminds me. The deputy of police told a story.*

He's about to tell it to her, she can see him settling to tell an anecdote and it'll use up the time he and she have been allowed, so this is what is going to be talked about during the wait for his assassins—or maybe not, it doesn't matter, as long as she can keep him talking, about anything, toy soldiers or war traumas or deputies of police, nothing else can impinge upon the sanctity of the confessional, psychologist and patient.

The deputy of police was at the train station. He was on the platform. A train had come in from the farmlands in the east, his men were searching for contraband. They called him over to the final carriage. A group of peasants there, sitting like a funeral party, glowering, like the peasants usually do. At first sight it was one man and three women, nothing special. But the dogs were going crazy, barking, pulling at leashes. The dogs, the deputy said, are never wrong. And the dogs were trying to attack the furthest peasant woman, by the window, in the shadows, blind pulled down. Usual outfit—scarf, shawl, overcoat, big boots. Sitting entirely still. Not a flinch from the dogs' attack. At first the deputy couldn't work out why his men were all laughing. Then his eyes adjusted. She wasn't, that one in the corner, what she appeared to be. Not a woman at all. A pig had been dressed up as a peasant woman. A fortune to be made on the black market if she'd been smuggled through.

What did your deputy do?

Confiscated the pig. I'm sure, although he didn't say, his men sold it themselves on the black market.

And the peasants?

They let the peasants through, didn't have the heart to make any arrests.

What's the moral of this story? In suitable circumstances, they are capable of mercy? They have a sense of humour?

Or the moral might be that all self-knowledge is inherently comic—what do the others look like? the others look like pigs and pigs look like others, therefore that is how pigs and others should always dress, interchangeable. Someone once told her that to their ears the others' language sounds like broken glass in the mouth.

By the time he'd finished the story the first of Damecki's women had left his side to sit by mine. I didn't invite her to.

(Oh, it was just the comic turn before the main, erotic story.)

He has paused for breath and she is silent, deliberately, even if it kills him. She refuses to ask for details. Jealous Gloria doesn't want to hear about the movements of Igo Sym's heart and hands and mouth.

There's a young man in town to research a guidebook. I don't remember his name.

Gloria doesn't say that she might have met this young man, that she doesn't remember his name either.

The guidebook writer had somehow appointed himself factotum for the ceremony.

Ceremony? What ceremony?

The point of this story. You are listening, aren't you?

Of course. Go on.

She hadn't noticed before or he hadn't chosen to show her, the muscles on his arms. He rolls up his sleeves, hard veins cut along his arms.

The company gathers at the fireplace. The pianist plays a local ballad that the locals aren't permitted to hear. Skirts are smoothed down, jackets removed, bottles of

*plum brandy, one of the actors performs a drinking song.
I have both Damecki's girls beside me now. Without a
word each one has declared herself utterly available to
me. Damecki opposite is furious, fuming. The girls have
loosened clothing, stretch like cats. Then the ceremony.
The guidebook writer passes the fire tongs to the deputy
of police and then hands him your little red soldier. The
deputy grips the soldier with the tongs and holds it over
the fire—*

No no, Gloria stifles the shout, that's Uri's man, you
mustn't do that, this is awful, far worse than whatever
acts you perpetrate with local floozies, I had no idea your
ceremonies could be so cruel. And for another thing, even
more unforgivable, you've forgotten the colour of the lead
man. She hears a rattling at the window. Hindrance. She
shuts her eyes. Keep talking, Igo.

*The flames reach up, the soldier melts. Someone pushes
forward a surgical bowl filled with water—*

An odd angry noise escapes from Gloria's mouth. Sym
puzzledly reaches across for her arm, seeking to reassure—
she shakes him off. For once the electricity does not
touch her.

Go on, she coldly says and wonders if that's desire which
she is seeing for the first time in his eyes.

*The colour goes first, then the edges, then the centre,
it loses all resemblance to itself* (Yes yes, that's exactly
how I am learning to feel, without substance), *the deputy
drops it in the water. Instant transformation. The lead is
suddenly solid again, an extraordinary new shape, spiky.
Everyone comes out with interpretations, like when you're*

lying under the sky on a fine day, making shapes out of the clouds. It's a map, someone says. It's the insignia of a commander, someone else says. It signifies promotion, he's to be a deputy no longer, a new posting will be in tomorrow's order papers. The deputy looks pleased, says he wouldn't mind leaving the Wild East behind. His woman protests. Sweetheart! A blonde local girl, she covers his neck with kisses. Then the guidebook writer takes the apparatus to the next person. Everyone has his turn. The same procedure each time. Tongs, fire, liquefaction, the sizzle of metamorphosis, interpretation, laughter, solemnity. One of Damecki's women has her hands inside my trousers. I don't know which one. Skilled fingers.

It is heartless—despite what the pig story professed to teach, they have no capacity for mercy. They are unsparing. No wonder they are conquering the world. Poor Damecki. Like herself, he has no chance against them. None of us does.

Oh she could list Sym's crimes. He doesn't know which woman is caressing him. He has no libidinal interest in Gloria unless, maybe, she continues to coldly resist him. He murdered Uri's soldier again and again. She could ask him now whether the soldier carried a musket or a sword and he would have no idea what she was talking about.

Each new shape is unique. The epidemiologist shapes what looks like a flower, the company ponders, interpretations are thrown out. Laughter. Get me another of those soldiers, Gloria, and I'll play the game with you. It's very enlivening. Future-gazing. Choosing destinies. Damecki has his turn, he's sullen, his eyes are wild. He casts his

274

shape, it looks like nothing at all. How typical, says one of his former women. He wants another turn. Heads shake. No second chances in this ceremony. Damecki is nearly in tears. He has lost his women and his future. The nugget of lead moves on.

What shape did you get?

A heart perfect and true.

How sweet.

Everything is awry. The gap on Uri's shelf, how will it be explained to the boy? Your musketeer flew to Valhalla while you slept or wherever it is your dead immortal heroes go.

No. Actually. It was something else. Made Oscar blush. That's his name, the guidebook writer.

He should blush. Were Oscar as diligent a guidebook author as all that he would be out investigating local customs instead of perpetrating imported practices. Visiting the Forbidden District with a mask over his face to protect against disease, noting down the most obvious manifestations of barbarism and inferiority. This is what the dreks do with ritual baths, with facial hair, these are the barbaric slaughtering rites, this is how the dreks hide in the laundry room and catch the plague and die. He should blush. They should all blush.

Tell me about Damecki's women. How was it?

You want to know?

Of course.

He is smiling at her. And even if it's mockery, she is smiling back. Wait for it to come, a dryly described tableau of libidinal abandonment.

I sent the girls home. I spent the night here alone.

The why she kills on her lips. As long as he says nothing more and she asks nothing more, together Sym and Gloria can pretend he did it for her.

What's the matter? Why are you looking at the door? Are you bored?

No, nothing. I thought I heard a sound, that's all.

You still haven't answered me. How would she treat him? His hypothetical psychologist.

The first step is to name his symptoms. The second is to uncover the causes of the symptoms.

And that would be done (he lifts a hand to his remarkable mouth to make the merest suggestion of a yawn) *by talking about dreams and what father did to mother and when the patient first played doctors and nurses with a neighbourhood girl.*

Not at all. One does not necessarily believe any longer in the talking cure. One might decide to use more advanced techniques. Which is to say, one manages the patient more actively, makes frequent verbal interventions, refuses to allow the sessions to be dictated by the rhythms of the patient's perhaps overpowering ego. Nor, I might add, does one have the luxury of infinite time.

There is no time. Only the present event, which ends, ghost-living on in memory, which decays. So she must extend this moment, make it last for ever. She and Sym, two episode-selves, cross-infecting quietly in a room in perpetuity.

Between the two there is enough breath; when he stops speaking she must start, allow no beats in between, no cue for Hindrance to enter, it can be done, the others won't intrude. Fill each gap, join it all up, don't allow any beat to pass without the sound of my voice or yours.

Just tell me what happened to you, which cataclysm it was that struck you and were you truly in love—and when I say love all I mean by it is a largening of the heart, a rush of passions with someone not you for the object, an obliviousness to tact—were you in love with Gloria the Astonishing? And I know you are kind and charismatic and stifle anguish within you for communal benefit, so maybe I can help, I'd like to help. And if there is any time left at the end you can teach me to play the musical saw.

She relaxes her vigilance. Several beats of non-talking are allowed. She hears the cat somewhere lapping his milk.

He finally says, *I don't know, what happened. I don't remember being changed. I remember things getting worse. Harder to get through the day without feeling as if my stomach was eating itself. Can you cure me?*

I'm not promising to cure. I might be able to help.

Help me then. How can you help?

Active intervention. What I was saying. A channel to the unconscious must be established. Dreams yes, but more. One—or rather two, both, you and I together—would work towards heightening the tension in the sessions. I might even perhaps make certain prohibitions.

Prohibitions?

In a case like yours, sexual relations for example. No lovemaking to be permitted, or even any relief allowed in masturbation. Use the thwarted libidinal energies to turn

inward. Then the discovery can be made of what caused
the original narcissistic wound. If there is one.

And what about the psychologist's libidinal energies?

These might be usefully employed also.

*There is something outside. I can hear it. Your ears must
be sharper than mine.*

Footsteps outside, and a heavy silence, and the knock
which finally comes. And then as if to make up for the
delay, two more, quick loud knocks, then a third and a
fourth, softer, each sounding further away, like echoes. Or
maybe the chance is not over. If she could get to the bottom
of it all, cure the disease Sym suffers in his heart, then he
might live and the wolves be vanished and her reward will
be the promised orgasms of long ago.

Come back, Igo. Look at me differently. Touch. Here.
Sit here. I want to be whispered to, adored. Forget for a
moment what's outside, look at me, forget what happened
yesterday or tomorrow, forget that sound, that's only
an echo. There's nothing outside, this beauty is dying.
Touch—Look. If I lift my hand like this the shadow of
my flesh rises to meet my fingertips, pull my hand away
and it's gone, touch me rather, we're almost out of time.

Don't answer it.

He smiles, he misinterprets the panic in her voice. He
likes the chime it makes with the drawing-room seduction
scenes he would have played dozens of times.

*I told you, they never leave me alone. I'll get rid of them
and then we can go on. Pour yourself a drink. I'll have one
as well. You'll find ice in the kitchen.*

He's not irritated this time. Up the half-staircase into the lobby he goes, two stairs at a time, he checks his tie in the hallway mirror, straightens the lapels of his oriental robe, returns his hair to its perfect order, ignores her warning call of his name—he's too used to the sound of his name in the mouth of an excited woman. Sym releases the lock, turns the knob, opens the door, his brow tightens, lips purse, *Who?* And this isn't what was meant to be.

Hindrance and Little, with revolvers in hands, wave Sym back down to the living room. (Little looks suave by proximity with Sym; Hindrance never, he stumbles against a corner of the sofa, the gun shakes, both Sym and he wince.) This isn't what was meant to be. This most active of interventions.

Sym is told to sit down, back on the same cushion of the sofa where he and Gloria had been discussing suffering and transformation. He doesn't look surprised or disappointed, just watchful. The legendary Grey is not here. She wishes she could pass the reassuring message to Sym, but he isn't looking at her. When Grey arrives she will have to act. What can she do? Sym is courteous and kind and sympathetic, a hundred men are worse, profiteers, blackmailers, rat-catchers, bureaucrats, why choose the star for extinction?

Hindrance raises his revolver. Little goes back to the opened apartment door, he peers down at the staircase.

In the name of the republic we are commissioned to pass sentence upon you.

What are you doing?

Be quiet.

But Grey's not here yet.

279

Shut up!

She herself disapproved of the whining tone in her voice, feels some sympathy for the others, how noisome, to have this complaining female along. A hand presses roughly against her mouth and nose, fingers taste of coal dust and moth balls. Her lips are squeezed against her teeth, Hindrance's hand pulls her docile.

As representatives of the district government plenipotentiary, and in accordance with articles 77 and 226 of the Penal Code we sentence you to infamy for the crime of cultural collaboration with the enemy, and we sentence you to death for the crime of treason.

Sym performs the kindness of not looking at Gloria, of not reproaching her. It is unfair. So many things are. Hindrance lets her go. She half falls against the coffee table. Hindrance looks at her, whispers the word *Grey*, and this must have been the codename she has been known by since the beginning, when she was first followed going to visit Igo Sym, since she first met Zosia, after she passed over a harmless navy-blue cap.

Hindrance looks at Sym again and raises his hand. Sym clicks his tongue. He has a pained expression on his face. Hindrance shoots and Sym starts to look a little pleased with himself, as his body slips down, as his hands try to clutch on to the arm of the sofa—remember, Igo, please remember how to remain on sofas—but he's missed it, his legs are folding neatly at the knees, his shoulders are towards the foot of the sofa, he's smiling again, most amiably, when Hindrance shoots again, unnecessary, the sound makes Gloria jump, although she should be used to it by now, the explosion of gunfire, the percussion of bullet into chest, and Sym's head goes back and bounces forward again from the sofa.

I pronounce you cured.

She doesn't know if the dying man has heard her. The air is still wild from gunfire. Igo Sym's lungs are loudly churning, with blood, extraneous fluid, somewhere a cat is drinking—and then the moment is over: Sym is dead. Hindrance touches his fingertips to the snout of his gun, flinches, presses his fingers further against the hot metal, watches his skin blister.

Thanks for your help, Gloria. Don't bother returning to the house. We'll turn you in if you do.

Where should I go?

Thanks for everything. We could never have done this without you.

Suddenly the assassins are running away, clattering down the stairs, catching breaths, shouting, exulting. A satisfied cat licks its lips with a pink abrasive tongue.

She slowly follows the others down to the street. She is alone.

7

A star falls, the city must be punished.

What shape would it have made to an aviator watching from the sky?—a flower? a heart? a star? Black police and blue police herd their prisoners out of all the places that had been assumed to be secret, the clandestine schools and covert libraries and charity houses and underground cafés.

Everything is known, all renegades are photographed, secrets kept in duplicate in unindulgent silence. Maybe this had all been planned anyway, waiting for the excuse that Sym's death provided. But Gloria can't imagine why they should need an excuse.

She looks for him to save her, Sarah's hiding hero, in the shadows, through every window, at every slightly opened doorway, the ghost of a smile beneath an incongruous military cap, mild blue thyroidal eyes, thinning fair hair.

Igo Sym is dead. Punish me.

Gloria walks on, making towards Long Avenue, the bureaucrat's office, and every few minutes she sees them at work, in city squares, arresting others, outside apartment buildings, pulling old men down steps (assistants following after, carrying paintings and candlesticks). Gloria drifts through as if untouchable, as if, at last, invisible. They seem to be arresting anyone who isn't a peasant or a worker; blocks of well-dressed others stand under guard by park gates, outside factory walls.

Did any of these soldiers melt men with Sym? The one over there, directing that round-up, he could be the deputy hoping for a foreign posting. The one with the sweetheart and the pig anecdote. Some crimes are forgivable. You tell me the details of your crime and I'll tell you the details of mine.

And Gloria continues to walk.

Without Uri she is exposed, isolated, terrified. Sitting at a cold café table, sipping a coffee, she closes her eyes, tries to show herself as someone enjoying her right to a drowsy warm spring evening. She doesn't believe in it herself, she doubts her ability to show it to others. She continues to walk.

She turns the corner into what used to be called Saxon Square, and Gloria walks into a round-up. So here they come. The agents of retribution.

A man in a black uniform bars her way. He shakes his head. She shakes hers. She tries to look politely baffled, she makes as if to go on; he stops her again, and, holding her frozen with a mime of his hands, he steps aside revealing the crowd behind, standing neatly in rows of ten, waiting to be told what life is to become. A bad crowd, Zygelbojmian. The arrestees are most distinguished in manner and dress, that one wears an evening gown, that one a pinstripe suit, that one, unmistakable, a coffee-house philosopher, yellow-stained white hair.

Briefly, her face and her alibis are examined. *Where do you live? What's your name? Your occupation? The school you attended? Your father's occupation? Your grandparents' religions?* She gives him answers, 147 Long Avenue, Gloria Wood, psychologist, the City Gymnasium, movie producer, oh Catholic each and every one.

They tell her which line to get into. Gloria walks towards the block of prisoners. She looks up to the sky and wonders whether the desire to be punished is independent of the capacity for guilt. There are no aviators watching from the sky. The clouds are like wolves. The air tastes human.

They will get what they want, it is inevitable, all the power is on their side. Everything is moving in their direction. They will strip her bare inside and out, they have awarded themselves the right. So stupid to resist, she will never know what Solomon Heller had planned for her, and now she is just to give up, give in, give them what they want, and then maybe she might be allowed to get on, whatever it could be they have decided for her.

She tries to take her designated place at the head of one of the lines and receives an elbow in her ribs from a regal-looking man in a dinner jacket. *Get to the back of the line! I was here first*, he says, and he puffs himself up, makes his chest big, lifts his narrow arms, proud man defending his rights.

So she walks around to the back of the crowd. She looks for a place at the end of a line, suitable for latecomers. There's a space, she's nearly at it, that'll be her position, beside a handsome woman with clay spattered on blue denim. This is where she will stand and wait for destiny to be revealed. This isn't so bad in a way, a relief almost, not to have to make any more decisions, not to have to constantly connive at survival.

A man near her says something as if to himself. He speaks again, and this time she realises he's speaking to her, he's talking for her.

Keep walking, you idiot. Walk on.

Leave me alone, she thinks, is your life so easy that you have the luxury to worry about mine?—but then, yes, probably yes. This wouldn't have occurred to her but he's right. Once she's in line she'll be there for ever, committed. So she does keep walking, she reaches the place she was aiming for, at the rear of the shortest line, and she walks past it—and no one meets her eyes so she will never know the face of the man who saved her this time—and she keeps going, her hair is shivering, she's anticipating a blow to the back of her head, men with shovels, men with guns, but no one is watching, she's almost out of the square, there's Marsh Street, there's a stretch of Heller's wall, she doesn't dare look back, she takes her first step out of the square, a gap in the wall invites her on, she keeps walking, she looks back. The crowd and the square disappear behind the corner. She is, she feels, for maybe the first time in her life, free.

8

A sad-eyed comedian, Rappaport without his Rappaport, sits on the apron of the stage, working a toothpick between his teeth. He wears a long dark overcoat, its sleeves sewn with eccentric rainbows. On the backdrop curtain are a night-time sky, oriental towers, twinkling stars. Rappaport examines the horrors on the end of his toothpick, then turns his attention to the audience filling the Arts Club. The tables are crammed, the bar space is packed too tight, everyone's dressed in best. A spotlight transforms Rappaport. He stands up—as he moves, the rainbows separate into different-coloured armbands—he hides behind the backdrop, looks out, nervous, feral.

Have they gone yet?

The audience's laughter infects even Gloria. She is a drowning woman's lunge away from the bar, standing as if this is where she has chosen to be, between the legs and elbows of people laughing on comfortable stools. The maître d' sent her here. Her brother's name got her in through the door and into this narrow space. *The policeman?*—more an announcement than a question. The maître d' is talking to more important customers now, wearing his better monocle.

Tortoises

Have they gone yet?

More laughter. Some jokes are improved by repetition.

Members of the band are taking positions, unpacking instrument cases, squeaking chairs. Rappaport's sad cold eyes appear to take in everything and everyone. Hot shots, councilmen, crooks, beauties. Gloria is squeezed between a heavy-faced woman who looks like an heiress who lost her legacy too long ago, and a dapper man, good face, he looks very suave.

She is being jostled by elbows and arms and burning ash every time someone near her moves a glass or sucks on a cigarette. Gloria looks out for the unhealthy shine of her brother, the gold of his watch, the jewels in his rings, the gleam of his scalp through remnants of curly hair.

Rappaport moves forward to the front of the stage, the spotlight nervously follows. He takes a final look at his toothpick, grimaces, and tosses it away, and—CRASH! A cymbal crashes, startling everyone in the audience and it seems Rappaport himself, who jumps, looks all around, alert for any movement, threat, noise, enemy percussionists. His eyes interrogate members of the band who shrug, smile, adjust clothing. The drummer resists deadpan, he holds the cymbal noiseless and steady. Rappaport bristles, cartoon fury, then relaxes. His face resumes its customary sorrow.

The comedian appears suddenly to remember something. A look of concern. He slaps his forehead with an open hand. He pats all his pockets, trousers, shirt, overcoat. Finally he finds an envelope in one pocket, a pair of spectacles in another. After fixing the spectacles to his nose, he experiments with different reading distances; the most comfortable one is with his arm fully extended, his head pulled achingly back; squinting, he reads the words on the envelope, makes a look of disgust and abruptly tosses the envelope away. Another CRASH! Rappaport hops into the air, nearly slips over on landing. After he recovers, the outraged comedian puts his hands on hips. He pouts, examining the evil laughing world in front of him. He never really needed a stooge, he can play both parts of the act himself.

The brandy is good and the people around her are becoming more interesting and attractive with every sip. The suave man is offering Gloria a cigarette and a flame to light it with. He looks pretty good, he knows how to wear a dinner jacket, his shirt collar is pressed and clean, his hair is all his own. Something sweet happens when he tries to smile. His teeth are agreeably crooked. This brandy is very good.

Rappaport has discovered a feather in yet another pocket. He flicks it into the air, watches with assiduous care its rise and descent and catches it between thumb and forefinger. He does this a second time, a third, a fourth. Then something about this procedure annoys him. He flicks the feather into the air again, looks increasingly disgruntled, the feathery path offends him. He catches it, he wraps a fist around it, takes a short run up and—CRASH!—throws into the ducking crowd.

Rappaport looks more scornful and sadder than ever as he slowly opens his fist to reveal the feather still in his hand. It is a mournful kind of pleasure to fool such stupid people as the percussionist, as the audience, as himself.

The barmaid has plump cheeks. She knows everything and understands everything. She refills Gloria's glass with brandy and shakes her head and smiles, *This one is on the house, enjoy the evening, look, excuse me, over there, you're being called to your table.*

Rappaport withdraws from the stage. The band settles into a rough modern waltz. Gloria makes her way through to the busy table at which her brother is standing, yelling orders at a waiter.

Policeman Daniel makes the introductions and orders food for everyone and then has to sit down, wiping his face with a handkerchief as if the effort of being part of this happy crowd costs him too much. Gloria receives and performs handshakes and smiles with well-dressed, energetic men and women, yes yes you too, Gloria, I'm Gloria, yes I do have the misfortune to be his sister, ha ha, how was he as a boy? oh the stories I could tell, but what was your name and yours and yours? I haven't really remembered any. Yes première, yes how exciting, I'm excited too. Hottest ticket in town.

The music is good, much better than the food, thin turtle soup and dubious meat covered in sauce, and Daniel has his eyelids half closed as if the best way to control things is by regulating the light he allows into his eyes, and a man with a military air who's sitting next to Gloria takes the waiter by his apron. *Is this horseflesh?*

No, the waiter is shocked, he touches his chest proximate

to his heart, *of course not, this is beef, not even beef, that's far too crude a word for what it is, really, it's veal, brought in at great expense and ingenuity from the surrounding countryside, if you want to know the story, the chef has a cousin who—*

Of course it's horseflesh, says the man, who appears to be a connoisseur of flesh of all kinds, and how Gloria wishes the 'Prince' were here, she'd trust his arbitrage. *You can tell by the yellow fat.*

That's not fat, says the waiter, *it's gravy.*

Of course it's fat, says someone else, *you don't think you'd find any meat here? Don't talk to us about meat.*

It's all gristle and fat, that's all it ever is.

Yes, says the waiter, *I know that's fat, what I meant was, the colour of it is because of the gravy.*

Someone tosses a crust of sawdusty bread at him. He builds a quick tower of plates, his eyes flick disdainfully elsewhere, he sweeps everything away with a flourish, the string of his apron as he departs is like a tail.

It's a gossipy table she's at. Whispers, pointing fingers. *You see her? Look. Look. She's with the Pinky brothers tonight.*

Who's she?

It's Sarah who's being pointed at. She's at a nearby table, with the tortoise in her arms.

That's only the owner of the Melody Palace. The so-called owner. They really own it.

Look. There's Stash. Wave him over.

I'll buy a bottle of champagne for whoever can identify all of Rappaport's armbands.

At the least favourable table in the establishment, in an uncomfortable alcove by the toilet doors, is a ragged bunch that suddenly erupts into noise, shrill apocalyptic good cheer.

Shouldn't be allowed. Puts you off your food, says a woman wearing a black half-veil.

The expert on meat keeps taking Gloria's beret off and presenting it back to her as if this is the greatest joke. He wears a military kind of moustache, and a brown ribbon ostentatiously dripping out of the breast pocket of his tweed jacket.

Have you heard about the naked refugees they marched into the quarter the other night? Whatever village it was they were clearing us from this time. No one was allowed to wear clothes for the journey. Anyone who put up a fuss they shot.

Heard about it? I was the one that told you.

Look. There's Stash.

See if you can get him over.

Do you want protection? asks gimpy Daniel of a man in a stylish business suit. *I can guarantee protection.*

He strokes his crumpled policeman's tunic. His appearance is essentially comic. He would make a perfect new stooge Rappaport if one were required. Everyone, though, is polite to him. Nobody laughs.

I want to tell you my tortoise joke, says the military-looking man to Gloria. *This is how it goes. One day the king of the tortoises—*

On the other side everything signifies its opposite: virgins are mothers, librarians are assassins, kindness means cruelty, therapists murder patients. But maybe here it's all different. If he were on the other side looking like a commander of the underground, he'd reveal himself to be an informer or a pacifist. Here, maybe, appearances don't deceive.

Have you heard the news? They've had a clampdown. Some big shot got himself killed on the other side. They've arrested hundreds of others. Sealed the quarter until further notice. The price of potatoes is rocketing.

The king of the tortoises invites all the western leaders to his court. He's worried about our predicament, you see.

I heard they sent a photo crew into the quarter. They're going to choose twelve of us.

Choose? For what?

Commander Brown Ribbon raises his hands and his eyebrows—what can one do with these chattering people? *So the king says, after coffee's finished, the dancing girls dismissed, the king says, Something must be done! A pact! Rescue those good folks in the residential quarter. Expeditionary forces must be organised.*

For ethnographic purposes. I've had it on very good authority. Solomon Heller himself is involved.

What do you mean, Solomon Heller?

Yes, what does he mean, Solomon Heller?

He threw himself out of a window and died.

He's not dead, everyone knows that. He fooled everybody, he's pulling all the strings.

That's right.

No it's not, says the woman with the half-veil.

He killed himself, says Daniel, with understated authority, with the solemn joy of reporting the defeat of a man whom everyone had thought to be strong.

I heard, it was all a trick, he did get over, set himself up on the other side, and then got shot in the street.

No, he's alive. He's pulling all the strings.

He killed himself, repeats Daniel.

Daniel went to the funeral, the woman says this so proudly she must be his mistress or intends to be.

Dissent is murmured but no one wants to prolong an argument with Daniel.

Lucky Solomon Heller. He has at least become myth.

What ethnographic purposes?

They want twelve of us for a museum in their capital.

And they're going to choose you?

They have to choose somebody.

With your appearance?

Why not? Why would they want someone who looks like them? It's for ethnographic purposes.

Listen to me: The western leaders say, the armies of the west will get there first, but the tortoise king says, No, the tortoises will get to the city first. And the wager is struck.

I've had it on very good authority.

We're bent on world domination. All their propaganda says so. No peace until the last of us has disappeared.

Except for the twelve. Stick with me, if you stick close enough they might choose you too.

Oh. Stash has gone to the bar.

Daniel doesn't like him, says the woman with the half-veil.

He thinks he's so special, a big shot, the king of virtue.
Ssh. People are looking.
People are looking? People are LOOKING?
Daniel is suddenly belligerent. He stands up, the business-man pulls him down again.
How has he offended you so much?
Because he used to be a cop like me but the cop life was too ugly for his poetic soul. It gets you a good enough living and sometimes you have to look a different way sometimes, but he couldn't do that, couldn't compromise his bleeding poetic heart. And oh the fuss that was made by his well-placed friends. Stash, what have you done, and Look look at what Stash has done, you've resigned, you're giving up relative safety, please reconsider, fucking hypocrite.
Why did he do it?
To make the rest of us look bad.
Gloria twists in her seat to find the object of Daniel's rage. A short young man is standing a little apart from the crush at the bar. He wears round glasses, a bulky suit; he's listening half amused to a taller woman in a white dress who has her hands on both his shoulders.
Daniel's right. Not everyone has wealthy patrons.
Not everyone's a poet.
Poet! What a poet! Oh his words are so moving. What a talent. I'll tell you what he has a talent for, getting a free ride.
Ssh. Trying to listen to the music.
Ssh yourself. Go fuck yourself. My policy has always been to make friends with as many of them as I can, they're

not so bad when you get to know them, you never know when well-placed friends are going to come in useful.

Got to feed the jukebox, agrees his woman. *Pay the piper.*

He would have approved of Igo Sym, Daniel would have, it's always been an awful waste of his ambition to be limited to this narrow, forbidden zone. Indignation has fuelled her brother with a crazy new burst of energy. Daniel is ranting again. Brown Ribbon gent impatiently waits with his punchline.

I'm just as good as him. Look. You know the question-naire that's going around. I've been asked to fill it in too.

You? Brown Ribbon can't keep all the surprise out of his voice.

Yes me. I've been asked.

What strings have you pulled? says Brown Ribbon. *Only joking.*

Without looking at Gloria but, she presumes, at least partly for her benefit, Daniel brags, *I don't usually get involved with local projects, but it's only the elite who have been asked, intellectuals, makers and shakers, men with influence. It's tiresome, of course it is. A lot of questions and some are really absurd. It's a chore. Look.*

He pulls a stapled pamphlet out of his tunic, wipes off some of the surface grease.

Listen to these ridiculous questions. How will the exile of our people be brought to an end? What role will we play after the war? What is the cause of the heartless indifference with which people walk past corpses in the street? What shadows have been revealed in the course of our present predicament? I ask you: shadows? What is that supposed to mean?

It's a metaphor.

An analogy.

I don't have time for analogies.

You describe one thing in terms of another, thereby casting light on both.

What's the good of that?

Tentatively, hoping not to offend Daniel, even the woman with the veil disagrees. Everyone at the table except for Daniel and silent Gloria concurs that analogies are useful and satisfactory mechanisms for making sense of things. Images get offered up, to describe the present predicament.

It's like a movie.

It's like a bad dream—

It's a boat at sea, that's what we are on, on turbulent seas.

At night.

A leaking *boat at night—*

—on turbulent seas.

A leaking boat at night on turbulent seas, and there's a storm.

A hurricane.

It's like a—

Gloria agrees with her brother. She has no use for analogies either. To attempt now even to use the watery metaphors of depth psychology, with its channels and dams, would turn her mouth dry. Gloria stays silent. She awards smiles to each speaker, for every analogy offered; she keeps her own thoughts to herself. Daniel covers his mouth with his hand. The joke-teller reminds her of himself with a hand on her leg.

And now the tortoises have won! The tortoise commandos are already in the city. The big forces and artillery are just outside. Any day now we're going to be bombarded with flies and lettuce leaves. The westerners of course are a long way behind.

Things are things. Shit is shit. A sickly policeman is a sickly policeman. A dead tycoon is a dead tycoon, whatever else he may have become. And brandy is brandy. Wood chippings were in the bread but this is certainly brandy, as authentic as Brown Ribbon's irritating expressions of libido. Fill it up, yes, my appetite for brandy has no bottom, ha ha, thank you, that was a very funny joke and you're a very amusing guy, I'll put my beret back on again and I'll even laugh for you, and Sarah's hair looks yellow in the light—Sarah, can you read the message in my eyes? I didn't see him, I killed a man but that still did not reveal Solomon Heller to me. Ha ha thank you again. Very funny. Sarah cradles her tortoise beneath her chin, she coos at its ancient penile head but it quickly retreats into its shell, which makes her crossly rap the shell and a heavy man leans towards her and says, *How charming, a pet tortoise, does he have a name?* and Sarah looks even angrier than before, and says, *She's a girl. Actually.*

The military man's hand is on Gloria's leg and he's announcing, *I know another joke. This one isn't about tortoises.* But someone else is telling him to shut up, because the show is about to start.

Spotlight on the empty stage. The band swings into a waltz. Actors in scarlet uniforms step on to the stage holding hands high with silky women dancers. And, wearing golden earrings, in flowing crinoline cut low at the bust, it's our plump star (*Vera!* her audience can't help invoking her name). Vera takes little steps forward, folds of pale flesh are squeezed between the straps of her dress and her powerful arms; she waits for the enthusiastic applause to die down, a diamond catches the light in her short black hair. She starts to sing. Her voice is very low and grand and husky, cracked with regret, spoiled by knowledge.

> *It's my first ever ball*
> *For sweethearts*
> *This waltz*
> *A deeply cherished memory*
> *The waltzing throng is a brilliant blur*
> *The spinning walls, the whirling floor*
> *It's my first ever waltz*
> *It's my first ever ball.*

An ardent young lover steps forward, his uniform is blue, his military cap worn jauntily on the crown of his head, he carries flowers and a cloak that he sweeps around her. Behind Vera and her young lover, the couples turn facing. The dance begins.

For a moment there's nothing to cry about or talk about, just listen to a woman's voice, to a violin and a piano and a drumbeat. It feels quite good, this night, so let that veiled woman beside me stroke the inside of my forearm, but close my legs tight at the knees because I want that man to stop, yes yes you're very sensuous, what a lover you must be, and my brother's being nice to you so you must be important somehow but stop it now with your hand. I think that's enough, for the time being at least, I'm new to this scene, I don't want my reputation to suffer. Give me another cigarette. And yes I do want another brandy and I'll want another after that, line each one up or better still, yes, thank you, intelligent barmaid, what a mark of favour, leaving your station to serve the table with drinks, but I'm sure you've got a way of putting extra on the bill.

And Daniel is standing, shakily buttoning up his green policeman's tunic.

I am a little tired, maybe I'll go home.

The woman with the veil knows him better than Gloria does—she gives Daniel a quick flattering look of bereavement and sexual disappointment before losing herself again in the music. Gloria makes the mistake of speaking.

I'll come with you.

No. Enjoy the show.

A look of utter hate from her brother as he struggles to his feet. It would be impossible to make him understand that she wasn't being pitying, she would be quite happy to leave, and it's a matter of practicality, he needs somebody to go with, by the look of him he's not going to get home tonight. He's drooling and he keeps missing his mouth when he tries to wipe it.

There is relief though after he's gone, everyone relaxes a

little more, no need for phoney politeness to the unhealthy little hectorer, and no competition for the stage. All attention finds its home on Vera singing a tango.

> *Let me race the wind*
> *Let me see the world in a dreamlike daze*
> *Let me see Morocco*
> *And the Orinoco*
> *It feels so good to be alive*
> *See the world go slowly by*
> *Drinking bitter sweetness in the tropical night.*

And Commander Brown Ribbon is offering his hand to Gloria and Gloria is taking it. He leads her away from the table, he's chosen his moment well, everyone in the Arts Club is still, almost frozen, eyes to the stage, Sarah doesn't respond to Gloria's touch as she is led past. He leads her out of the main room, past the bar, through flickering pools of light from the carbide lamps on the walls into a small back room that smells as if it has been used for this purpose before.

Feel the cracked leather of the couch beneath buttocks. The grunting man pushes into her, rough face against face. Senseless endearments drip from his mouth. His hands hold her skirt high. His body drums into hers. When she moves towards him his ardour increases—move away and he slows down, there might even be a consequent unstiffening. Gloria has given up any hope of an equivalent pleasure to his, no exchange is taking place here, so why then does she not just keep thrusting forward, push this event speedily along to its solitary conclusion? It's a perversity to make it last.

Vera is singing a lullaby; it sounds unconvincing, her voice is too nightclub-raw, too many cigarettes, too many drinks, but Gloria can't hear it properly anyway, the stage is too far away and Commander Brown Ribbon is breathing so heavily.

Imagine who else it could be here—pinch a fold of skin on Commander's neck, let it escape, watch the blush caused by her fingers slowly disappear, his hair ends in a thin twist like a biscuit wrapper, Mr Mouse had that too. But it should be Igo Sym, here, with her, open his grey-blue eyes, make him live again. He would honour this occasion with orgasm, with cat fur; with him she would feel more than this discomfort, tolerance, irritation; glimpse more than this sticky snaky path, lost now in the clouds, up towards unavailable pleasure.

The return to propriety is amiable. She helps him with his tie. The unexplained ribbon is redraped to its correct position. He helps her pull the seam of her stockings straight. He returns first to the table. She pretends she has business to transact at the bar. She should realise that it doesn't matter. A nod towards etiquette is hardly even required. No one gives a fuck who you fuck.

On the stage the cast and musicians are taking bows, and now the authors—Daniel's hated Stash, his lips slightly apart as if he is asthmatic or as if his tongue is too big for his mouth, too much language she supposes, spilling out; and alongside him, sternly holding his hand, the patrician-looking composer, who had been at the piano throughout.

Take a bow, everyone, and another and another. Whistles and shouts and demands for an encore. Vera curtsies, exits, the dancers skip off behind her.

Then the pianist returns to his stool, smooths down his trouser legs, takes a sip from his water glass, checks his watch, shoots his cuffs, looks to the wings, and spotlit Vera with arms wide, accepting and, we may believe, returning our love, comes back to the stage. This time it's just piano and voice, a reprise of the tango.

> *Let me see Morocco*
> *And the Orinoco*
> *It feels so good to be alive*
> *See the world go slowly by*
> *Drinking bitter sweetness in the tropical night.*

The singer slowly lifts a champagne glass to her mouth. No one presumes to clap until the first sip has been taken. Then enormous applause fills the place burying Gloria inside it. The singer leaves the stage. Rappaport sticks his head out from his hiding place behind the backdrop curtain.

Have they gone yet?

9

Gloria works out that she has to push aside a stranger's arm in order to stand. Its owner grumbles in his sleep, rolls over to crush somebody else. The Arts Club has turned itself into a curfew dormitory for the night. The air is heavy with the stench of night-time odours and extinguished carbide lamps. She totters over sleepers and overturned chairs to the bathroom, peers into the early-morning awfulness of a mirror.

No water in the taps. No way to get rid of the taste in her mouth, which maybe is the authentic taste of her mouth, finally undisguised, dead grapes and dust.

She walks back over sleepers, some of whom stir. Gloria pushes through, chooses her own coat and not a better one in the cloakroom, inadvertently knocks over a stool in the entrance corridor, which falls on a sleeping couple who remain entwined. She fights with the doors, finally manages to heave the doors open, and emerges, blinking in puce sunlight.

The wind assaults her, pushes her back into the thin protection of the Arts Club doorway. Newspaper pages flap around bodies in the street. Someone should come and tidy all that away. It is still curfew. Outdoor life is not yet permitted. She wonders if the ethnographic squad has found its twelve.

She sits down in the doorway, lifts the collar of her overcoat, huddles into herself, and falls relievedly asleep. She dreams. She dreams of flying, of open windows, hot places, of herself quite majestic and wise.

And she is jostled awake into cacophony. Voices. Shrieks. Prayers. Shouts. A beggar man is pulling at her sleeve. Behind him, pushing along, is the interminable crowd, renewed. The beggar keeps pulling. His face is hawklike angry. He wears, she notices, one of Daniel's belts.

Excuse me. Excuse me! Red-haired lady!

I don't have any money for you, I'm sorry.

Save your apology for someone who knows what to do with it. You're sitting in my place.

She makes room for him but that doesn't appease.

This is my patch. Clear off.

When she has conceded the doorway to him, he relaxes, he becomes expansive, his hostility departs.

Thank you. You might be interested in this.

A photograph is shown to her, of an unattractive family group in front of a studio sky.

That was me. In happier times. My wife Betty and our two children, see how attractive and well dressed we all were? Once upon a time I lived very well, probably, I imagine, no disrespect, better than you.

I don't doubt it.

I was an architect. I designed buildings. All this was unthinkable. I used to ask my little boy, in all seriousness, what his ambitions were.

She considers enquiring why the former architect never asked the same question of his little girl who, judging from the evidence of the photograph, is (or was?) the more intelligent child of the two: the boy has the slack jaw and vacant eyes of an imbecile; the girl has hair pulled back in difficult braids from a high broad forehead, clever watchful eyes slightly crossed.

Instead Gloria gives the beggar her final gold coin and moves on before he has time to show her his gratitude or contempt.

It's all a bad dream, a lurid tragic melodrama movie. Say no. Reject it. Wake up. Stop jousting for the armrest. Leave your seat, *Excuse me, excuse me, sorry, excuse me*, knocking the legs and handbags and treading on the feet of the victims who don't have the energy to break the spell and leave. *Excuse me, I'm sorry, excuse me, fuck you.* And out. Breathe the air. Deep soul gulps.

So hard to resist the temptation to change it all, to remake history because, with words, for a moment, we can. Pick a day, maybe at random or else choose a particular day of unfulfilled prophecy. A pietist had predicted that on this day something marvellous was going to happen and that all of us were going to be saved.

Igo Sym is dead and somehow that connects with their demagogue falling from power and dying too. Let him die. Have him dead on that day. Gloria sniffs the air. Steps outside on the cacophonous street. The heatwave is over and the day is chilly but there's more than cold in the air. Something marvellous has happened. The news is announced on loudspeakers in the street. Their newspapers are rimmed with black. The crowd can barely keep from sniggering.

The tortoises are already here. The westerners must be close behind. Without their demagogue they lose their appetite for war. (Gloria is reunited with Heller and Sarah at the Beach Bar, place a black-haired Uri-esque boy on the tycoon's lap, an avuncular smile on his dented face.) They suffer reversals. Heller's wall goes down under a western tank, under sledgehammers and breath.

War is over. The wooden V is dismantled and set alight in Saxon Square. The city smells of lilac. Our parts of town still have chestnut trees. In a fur coat Gloria sits with Mr Mouse and the 'Prince' in an unruined coffee house, and brandy glasses clink and victory is toasted. Laugh at the discredited panicmongers among us, the ones who had taken the idiotic trouble to read their propaganda books and broadcast the logical conclusions to anyone with the time or the indulgence to listen. The ones who had believed that words of ranting obsession can actually come true. (Their leaders died isolated, wild-eyed, foam-flecked mouths, defeated, their mad monologues finally ended by the guns they hold in their shaking left hands . . .) This is the real world, not some madman's dream carved in bone and soaked with blood. Refugees don't get marched naked through the countryside. There are no forbidden zones. Those sorts of things can't happen. This is the modern moment.

The angel of death flapped his wings, we felt the ensuing breeze as he passed over. Life, as it always does, goes on.

The world is the expected, rationally ordered place. It is still possible to believe in justice and God, in hope.

The way into the Beach Bar is denied her. She doesn't have the money to hire a bathing costume. The buck-toothed woman closes the door against her. The ruined walls are too high to peer over, too intact to find a gap through to the tropical beach. The crowd jostles her along unwilling past another doorway.

If this were a movie, as some analogisers suggest, her route would now be revealed, a map superimposed on the screen: a black arrow appears in the city where Gloria stands and it grows, a lengthening black tail, the arrow head takes flight, arcing across frontiers, over mountain ranges. But the screen is filling with wrong ways, with false lines, it's no longer possible to see the original route; one ends at the bottom of an ocean, another in the back street of a dangerous port; some ways end in tremors of broken lines—a city too full of wolves, her own heart is too weak— that way dies at a town on the border, she can't see the line that confidently flies her to Morocco or the Orinoco.

This isn't a movie. Neither is it a dream. Nor is it a boat at night on turbulent seas. If it were, even a leaking one, she could find a blanket and wrap it over her legs and sit on the deck, tasting salt water spray on her face.

10

Gloria returns to Valour Street. It is her most heroic journey, through the obliterating crowd noise of psyches disintegrating further into hers. She goes up the first flight of stairs, she's nearly at the second landing when a pile of green clothing crumpled across two steps shifts its position; startled, she almost slips, the pile is shaking, she loses her footing, finds it again by stopping her weight on the wall, a person is in there somewhere, recognisable, shivering, that's her brother's face emerging, making a gruesome attempt at a smile meant to signify charm.

You're back already. Is the show over?

Is this as far as you got?

I was a little more tired than I thought, I admit that.

Let me help you.

The inevitable flash of annoyance.

No! Go away! I'll be there in a moment.

She reaches down to touch him. He retracts, tortoiselike, but if only he could, if he only had a shell to withdraw further into. His mouth is very wet and red.

Go on up. Let yourself in. The key is hidden above the door lintel. Put it back after you use it. Don't let anyone see.

What happened to you? Did someone beat you?

Yes. No. It doesn't matter. That's not why. There was a misunderstanding. But look. I bet you can't do this.

He reaches into his mouth, three fingers enter, twist, his lips flinch, and he pulls out something that's red which he shows to her in some triumph.

Look.

She last saw that expression on his face in childhood, on those rare occasions when he required a witness and only she was available, to applaud, to admire his trophies— a mutilated animal, a rare postage stamp, a butterfly toothpicked to a tree.

My teeth are falling out.

Did he hit you in—

No no. Coincidence only. It's this.

He pulls uselessly at the canvas belt he wears, which hangs very loosely around his waist.

Your miracle cure.

It does work, it does. Ask my doctor if I have any symptoms of typhus. Ask any one of my dozens of satisfied customers. But I think the solution is too strong. I might have contracted mercury poisoning. I'll be all right. I'll be up in a moment. I'm fine here. I mean it.

She tries sitting down beside him, acting on the thought that maybe he might like it if she cradled his head, but there isn't much room for her on the step and he keeps trying to shake her off so the attempt concludes with Gloria pulling at him to keep her balance, and some of his hair comes wetly off into her hands. She tries to wipe it surreptitiously away but she can't and what she's doing is only irritating him further.

Go away! You're not helping here!

I'm sorry.

Remember. You're on to a good thing with me. Don't worry. It's not just the telephone and the belts. I've got a lot of irons in the fire. Play your cards right and you'll be on to something quite tidy.

He makes a second, even more gruesome attempt at a smile. His mouth is dark and throbbing and broken teeth bob about on his tongue.

Stay. Make the most of it. My loss is your gain. I was going to cut you in anyway. Hey. Stop! Where are you going?

She's going down, and out. Out. Going out.

She's in the street again and heads are turning slowly her way, the crowd is denser than before, there's no space for her down here, she doesn't feel so good, and suddenly people are interested in her. She puts a hand to her throat, it's wet, nothing of Daniel's; that's her own sweat pouring down even though the day has turned very cold. She wavers, staggers, regathers her strength, stands. And nearly falls, when the mass of the crowd pushes her along again.

Gloria!

She tries to become a part of it. Be like Zygelbojm. But she hasn't got his training or inclinations and she can't catch the rhythm. She keeps changing step but she keeps missing it. It's not just her walk that's different. Even on charity food her cheeks are plump. Dozens of eyes examine her, bruise her, evaluate, *That coat, worth something, the shoes, nice shoes . . .* The other side was eyes; here it's eyes and hands. Hands move towards her, advance upon her.

Gloria!

Must move on. Gang of wild boys, lively spinning, tapping every passer-by for money or cigarettes, one grabs hold of her, pretends to be wooing her, he can walk backwards faster than she could imagine running forwards— *Hey Red I'm in love with you Red don't turn your back, I'm in love with you Red . . .*

Keep walking. Keep on. Now that's better, the boy spins away, there's a space to fill, and another; if she keeps her wits, concentrates on the particular, there's another, she steps into it, there are just enough spaces for her to travel from one to the next.

Gloria!

And now she's getting more confident, she can even attempt running. It takes some effort at first to get going, so many people in her way, but she keeps on, she even learns to deflect people out of her path.

Gloria. It's me, Mickey.

She is so pleased with herself, she's doing well, and her mind is rewarded with immediate lucidity, easy to think clearly now. (Mr Mouse? Heart? Mickey!)

Here, he's saying. *Stop.*

She would love to. Release, surrender, voluptuous. Stop. Fall. (Mr Mouse, you look so much better than remembered, you're looking very handsome, nice softness in your shrewd little eyes, even your skin smells sweeter than before, but I'm sorry, I can't stop.) Keep going.

Push through, run, keep running, force a path through the soft pulp of the crowd, keep going, and remember just to breathe, two paces to every breath (already Mr Mouse falls away, his breathing isn't as good as hers), three paces now, gather speed, it doesn't matter if she knows where she's going, go south if you can but just keep going, it is better to trust in momentum than kindness.

Author's note

Igo Sym, actor, manager, collaborator, virtuoso of the musical saw, was executed for treason on 7 March 1941 by a three-person underground assassination squad at his apartment in Warsaw.

The song lyrics on pages 298 to 302 are from *Her First Ball*, words by the poet Władysław Szlengel to music by Władysław Szpilman. The piece was performed at the Sztuka ('Arts') Club in the Warsaw Ghetto in 1941.

Among the books consulted for details of the city, personalities and events, I relied most of all on *Notes From the Warsaw Ghetto*, the journal of Emmanuel Ringelblum.

For Gloria's psychological practice I have drawn on the *Clinical Diary* of Sandor Ferenczi.

Few settings in the book are invented. Names of Warsaw streets and places have been translated, or adapted. The Beach Bar for example was actually called the Bajka ('Fairy Tale'). An inexplicable quantity of tortoises did appear in the city, on both sides of the wall, in the spring of 1941.

My father was born in Warsaw. This book is co-dedicated to his parents and brother, Szlama Flusfeder (1894–1942), Helena Flusfeder (1895–1942) and David Flusfeder (1919–1941).

I would like to thank the Authors' Foundation for money given to assist work on this book.

All Fourth Estate books are available from
your local bookshop

Or visit the Fourth Estate website at:

www.4thestate.co.uk